THE SQUARE EGG

AND OTHER SKETCHES
WITH THREE PLAYS

by

"SAKI" (H. H. MUNRO)

WITH A BIOGRAPHY BY
HIS SISTER

and an Introduction by

J. C. SQUIRE

British Library Cataloguing-in-Publication Data
A catalogue record for this book is available from the
British Library

Hector Hugh Munro

Hector Hugh Munro was born in Akyab, Burma in 1870. He was raised by aunts in North Devon, England, before returning to Burma in his early twenties to join the Colonial Burmese Military Police. Later, Munro returned once more to England, where he embarked on his career as a journalist, becoming well-known for his satirical 'Alice in Westminster' political sketches, which appeared in the *Westminster Gazette*. Munro's first longer work, a historical treatise entitled *The Rise of the Russian Empire* appeared in 1900. His first collection of short stories, *Not-so-Stories*, was published two years later. After a stint as a foreign correspondent in the Balkans and Russia, Munro published *The Chronicles of Clovis* (1911), another collection of short stories which featured his most famous hero, Clovis. During World War I, he reached the rank of Lance Sergeant, and penned a number of short stories from the trenches. However, he was killed by a German sniper in November of 1916, aged 45. Arguably better-remembered by his pen name,

'Saki', Munro is now considered a master of the short story, with tales such as 'The Open Window' regarded as examples of the form at its finest.

BIBLIOGRAPHICAL NOTE

First issued 1924
Reprinted 1924
Collected Edition 1926

The Works of
"Saki"
(H. H. Munro)

Reginald and *Reginald in Russia*
The Chronicles of Clovis
The Unbearable Bassington
When William Came
Beasts and Super-Beasts
The Toys of Peace
The Square Egg

NOTE

THANKS are due to the Editors of the *Morning Post*, the *Westminster Gazette*, and the *Bystander* for their courtesy in allowing tales that appeared in these journals to be reproduced in this volume.

Thanks are also due to the Editor of the *Outlook*.

Saki's drawings, scattered through the biography, have, many of them, no connection with the text. They are given as samples of his whimsical humour.

E. M. M.

CONTENTS

		PAGE
INTRODUCTION	. . . .	xi
BIOGRAPHY OF SAKI	. . . . . .	3
THE SQUARE EGG	. . . . . .	104
BIRDS ON THE WESTERN FRONT	. . .	113
THE GALA PROGRAMME	. . . . .	118
THE INFERNAL PARLIAMENT	. . . .	123
THE ACHIEVEMENT OF THE CAT	. . .	128
THE OLD TOWN OF PSKOFF	. . . .	131
CLOVIS ON THE ALLEGED ROMANCE OF BUSINESS .	.	135
THE COMMENTS OF MOUNG KA	. . .	137
THE DEATH-TRAP	. . . . . .	142
KARL-LUDWIG'S WINDOW	. . . .	150
THE WATCHED POT	. . . . .	161

CONTENTS

INTRODUCTION

THERE are vagrant authors who, with sudden odd zigzags, always elude the butterfly nets of criticism. Nothing much to the point, save in the way of mere unanalytical praise, has ever been said about Peacock's novels or the *Importance of Being Earnest*; and the precise flavour of "Saki" is as easy to recognize and as impossible to define as that of a good Claret or Hock. Those who write about him are always tempted to discuss the latent qualities of the man whom they knew or whom they can deduce : to show that he satirized things that he hated, that he concealed profound affections, and that in spite of his jokes about all manner of catastrophes he was a sensitive and humane man to whom cruelty was repugnant. This no doubt is all true : and occasionally his loves and even his fears peep out in his writing. It is, characteristically, in an appreciative essay on cats that he ends with :

> voicing in its death-yell that agony of bitter remonstrance which human animals, too, have flung at the powers that may be ; the last protest against a destiny that might have made them happy—and has not.

But generally he was reserved in speech as in writing : it is enough, for those who were not his friends, to know that the jester died, over-age and a lance-sergeant, in the trenches, and that his last words were " Put that bloody cigarette out." To the commentator on his books what most matters is not the man Munro who concealed himself behind them but the artist " Saki " who wrote them. And " Saki " was a unique example of the man who tells lies with a grave face.

Defoe told lies with a grave face ; but they were grave lies. Swift told lies with a grave face, but the gravity was often interrupted either by guffaws or by the rasp of indignation. " The Jumping Frog " and " The Stolen White Elephant " were inventions as admirable as " Saki's, " and as seriously recounted ; but the telling was all to Mark Twain and the phraseology nothing. Saki's themes were akin to Mark Twain's, though more extravagant, but his manner was more Max Beerbohm's. He related a fantastic fable with the most matter-of-fact air ; but, not content with that, he polished his sentences with a spinsterish passion for neatness and chose his words as the last of the dandies might choose his ties. Writing brief stories and sketches for evening newspapers he was as careful with the shaping of his paragraphs as the most anchorite of aesthetes writing for an elect few with glass-fronted bookcases. He expended the pains of a poet upon modern fairy-tales, in which wizardry was exercised by or upon cats and dogs, house parties, duchesses and men-about-town, instead of giants, dragons, trolls and princesses, and the logic of magic operated with trim perfection against a background in which villas took the place of castles, and tennis-lawns were substituted for unfathomable forests. And in telling these fairy-tales, it must be admitted that his object was purely to amuse, and his incidental achievement to make the human race ridiculous.

" One half of the world believes what the other half invents." Mendacity and credulity were the spectacles in which he chiefly delighted, and when he was not almost persuading us to swallow his own prodigious lies, he regaled us with the sight of our kindred swallowing the lies of his favourite heroes and heroines, the remorseless children and cynical young idlers. To Clovis the world was a forest of legs, all waiting to be pulled unobtrusively and with gentlemanly grace. In the end the reader of " Saki " is pleased in proportion to the magnitude of the lie. *The Wolf*, in which everybody believes that the lady has been turned into a female Siberian wolf, is delightful ; but even better is *Tobermory*, in which a cat not only is believed to speak, and (without question) accepted as speaking, but actually does speak, and to devastating purpose, the whole theme being perfectly worked out until the grand culmination when the bold discoverer is killed because he tries to teach an elephant German verbs. In this present book the confirmed admirer of " Saki " is almost sorry that the Square Egg is not actually produced, but is represented as an ingenious myth ; the lie is good, but " Saki " could have pushed it farther.

His people have to fit his plots. They are consistent not with life, but with themselves and the queer world of his conception ; and he contrives, even if he be realistic only in this limited way, to throw certain truths into a high light and to express some (for to tell the unexpected truth is as much one of the conventions of his world as to tell the mountainously obvious lie—it is a more charming form of lying, to make people tell truths they would not tell) which are seldom expressed. *The Watched Pot*, most consider-

able of his promising dramatic efforts, may lack
"action" and be unduly strewn with elaborate
witticisms, but there is a great deal of unaccustomed
candour in it. Where it differs from the Slavonic
plays in which people naïvely bare their souls is not in
any extra remoteness from daily life but in an occasional
surprising contact with it. We can conceive of
Tchekov, in his gloomier moments, as writing a play
like *The Watched Pot* in which a household of women
should all be trying to marry a placid young man with
a gorgon of a mother, and all continually confessing
to each other, egging each other on, scratching each
other, or impudently maligning each other. Is
"Saki" any more lacking in reality because he makes
his dialogue witty, or because he shows cook, butler,
and housemaids as having a sweepstake on the event
in the servants' hall? And half his jokes depend for
their force upon their exaggeration of truth. Réné
remarks: "This suit I've got on was paid for last
month, so you may judge how old it is." Here the
truth is not important, except to tailors: with no more
elaboration or afterthought "Saki" would summarize
aspects of "world-problems" as they appeared to him,
as in:

> Government by democracy means government of the
> mentally unfit by the mentally mediocre tempered by the
> saving grace of snobbery.

The form of this reminds one of Wilde. Wilde
also might have written:

> For all I know to the contrary, he may by this time have
> joined the majority who are powerless to resent these in-
> trusions

although it took "Saki" to put it into the mouth of
an almost agreeable lady talking about her sick husband.

We think of Wilde's plays again when, speaking of harvest festivals and the growth of imports, Clare says :

> It shows such a nice spirit for a Somersetshire farmer to be duly thankful for the ripening of the Carlsbad plum

and in

> So many people who are described as rough diamonds turn out to be merely rough paste

and in

> There are heaps of chorus girls who are willing to marry commoners if you set the right way about it

and in the repartee about Mrs. Vulpy's make-up and the sentence about the father who lived at West Kensington but was "sane on most other subjects," and the comparison of the accessibility of Heaven with that of the House of Commons. "Saki" had all Wilde's cleverness at the substitution of a word in a stock saying or the inversion of a familiar proverb, and was an adept at contradicting our favourite clichés of word or thought, or strangely adapting them to unsuitable contexts. Yet though many of his sentences might be mistaken for Wilde's none of his pages could be attributed to another man. They are all pervaded by a personal manner and attitude. The manner is the grave manner of the humorist who opened a story thus :

> In an age when it has become increasingly difficult to accomplish anything new or original, Barton Bidderdale interested his generation by dying of a new disease. "We always knew he would do something remarkable one of these days," observed his aunts ; "he has justified our belief in him." But there is a section of humanity ever ready to refuse recognition to meritorious achievement, and a

large and influential school of doctors asserted their belief that Bidderdale was not really dead. The funeral arrangements had to be held over until the matter was settled one way or the other, and the aunts went provisionally into half-mourning.

As for the attitude, after our initial disclaimer, no more need be said than that it was the attitude of the man who wrote :

Whenever I feel in the least tempted to be business-like or methodical or even decently industrious I go to Kensal Green and look at the graves of those who died in business.

He had seen half the world and had no doubt about his tastes, which he preferred to state by indirection.

J. C. SQUIRE.

THE SQUARE EGG

THE SQUARE EGG

BIOGRAPHY OF SAKI

MY earliest recollection of Hector, my younger brother, was in the nursery at home, where, with my elder brother, Charlie, we had been left alone. Hector seized the long-handled hearth brush, plunged it into the fire, and chased Charlie and me round the table, shouting, " I'm God ! I'm going to destroy the world ! "

The " world " tore round and round the all-too-inadequate table, not daring to leave it to dash for the door, while Hector, his face lit with impish glee and the flare from the brush, enjoyed to the full his self-imposed divinity. Our yells brought Aunt Augusta on the scene, and we all got a dressing down.

The nursery looked on to a field, where appeared various farm animals that served as models for Hector's sketches—models that he kept in his head, for I never saw him drawing from life until years later.

Broadgate Villa, in the village of Pilton, near Barnstaple, North Devon, was the house my father took for us, after our mother's death, before leaving for India. Here his mother, and his two sisters, Charlotte and Augusta, were installed to look after us.

I think Hector must have been about two when we arrived there. He was born in Akyab, Burma, where my father was stationed, on December 18, 1870, and christened Hector Hugh. He was a delicate child, in fact the family doctor at Barnstaple, whom the grown-ups looked upon as an oracle, declared that the three of us would never live to grow up. Probably children not so highly-strung and excitable *would* have succumbed, because, judged by modern methods, our bringing up was quite wrong. The house was too dark, verandas kept much of the sunlight out, the flower and vegetable gardens were surrounded by high walls and a hedge, and on rainy days we were kept indoors.

Also fresh air was feared, especially in winter ; we slept in rooms with windows shut and shuttered, with only the door open on to the landing to admit stale air. All hygienic ideas were to Aunt Augusta, the Autocrat, " choc rot," a word of her own invention.

Then we should have had more country walks than we ever got, there were lovely fields and woods quite handy, but Aunt Augusta wanted shops and gossip—also she was afraid of cows.

Fortunately, there were the three of us, and we lived a life of our own, in which the grown-ups had no part, and to which we admitted only animals and a favourite uncle, Wellesley, who stayed with us about once a year.

Our pleasures were of the very simplest—other children hardly came into our lives—once a year, at Christmas, we went to a children's party, where we were not allowed to eat any attractive, exciting-looking food, " for fear of consequences," and in *case* the party might have done us harm, Granny gave us hot brandy and water on our return.

Also, once a year, in the summer, the child of some

friend visiting the neighbourhood would come to
play with us. "So good a boy," we would be told,
" he always does what he is bid."

From that moment a look of deep purpose settled on
Hector's face, and on the day when the good Claud
arrived an entirely busy and happy time for Hector
was the result.

He saw to it that Claud did all the things we must
never do, the easier to accomplish since his mother
would be indoors tongue-wagging with Granny and
the aunts. Poor Claud really was a good child, with
no inclination to be anything else, but under Hector's
ruthless tuition, backed up by Charlie, he put in a
breathless day of bad deeds.

And when Aunt Tom (Charlotte she was never
called), after the visitors' departure, remarked, " Claud
is not the good child I imagined him to be," Hector
felt it was the end of a perfect day.

But by ourselves we had not the scope for naughty
deeds—it was, " Don't play on the grass," from one
aunt, and " Children, you're not to play on the gravel,"
from the other.

The front garden, with its grass slopes under the
elm-trees where the rooks lived, was the only outdoor
place we had to play in, the kitchen garden being
considered too tempting a place, with its fruit trees.
Therefore the boys had to get into it, by hook or by crook.

So much has been said, in reviews of Hector's
books, about the cruelty element in them, an element
which, personally, I cannot see, that an account of
the aunts' characters may perhaps throw some light
on the environment of his early years.

Our grandmother, a gentle, dignified old lady,
was entirely overruled by her turbulent daughters,

5

who hated each other with a ferocity and intensity worthy of a bigger cause. How it was they were not consumed by the strength of their feelings I don't know. I once asked a friend of the family what had started the antagonism.

" Jealousy," she said ; " when your Aunt Tom, who was fifteen years older than Augusta, returned from a long visit to Scotland, where she had been much admired, and spoilt, and found the little sister growing up, also pretty and admired, she became intensely jealous of her—from that time they have always quarrelled."

Aunt Tom was the most extraordinary woman I have ever known—perhaps a reincarnation of Catherine of Russia. What she meant to know or do, that she did. She had no scruples, never saw when she was hurting people's feelings, was possessed of boundless energy and had not a day's real illness until she was seventy-six.

Her religious convictions would fit into any religion ever invented. She took us regularly to Pilton Church on Sunday mornings. For a long time I was struck by her familiarity with the Psalms, which she apparently repeated without looking at her book, but one day I discovered she was merely murmuring, without saying a word at all, and had put on her long-distance glasses in order to take good stock of the congregation and its clothes. A walk back after church with various neighbours provided material for a dramatic account to Granny (not that she was interested) of the doings of the neighbourhood. Whatever Aunt Tom did was dramatic, and whatever story she repeated, she embroidered. No use to try to get to the end before she intended you should. Without

any sense of humour whatever, she was the funniest
story-teller I've ever met.   She was a colossal humbug,
and never knew it.

The other aunt, Augusta, is the one who, more
or less, is depicted in " Sredni Vashtar " (" Chronicles
of Clovis ").   She was the autocrat of Broadgate—a
woman of ungovernable temper, of fierce likes and
dislikes, imperious, a moral coward, possessing no
brains worth speaking of, and a primitive disposition.
Naturally the last person who should have been
in charge of children.

But the character of the aunt in " The Lumber
Room " is Aunt Augusta to the life.   " It was her
habit, whenever one of the children fell from grace,
to improvise something of a festival nature from
which the offender would be rigorously debarred ;
if all the children sinned collectively they were
suddenly informed of a circus in a neighbouring
town, a circus of unrivalled merit and uncounted
elephants, to which, but for their depravity, they
would have been taken that very day. . . . She
was a woman of few ideas, with immense powers o
concentration. . . . Tea that evening was partaken
of in a fearsome silence."

Well do I remember those " fearsome silences ! "
Nothing could be said, because it was certain to
sound silly, in the vast gloom. With Aunt Tom
alone we should have fared much better—she adored
Hector as long as he kept off the flower-beds and
out of the kitchen garden—but as we could not obey
both aunts (I believe each gave us orders which she
knew were contrary to those issued by the other),
we found it better for ourselves, in the end, to obey
Aunt Augusta.

7

Our best time was during some pitched battle in their internecine warfare, " with Aunt calling to Aunt like mastodons bellowing across primeval swamps ; " * we lived our little lives, criticized our " elders and betters " and rejoiced exceedingly when Aunt Augusta went to bed for a whole day with a headache.

This gave us more scope, and we became more venturesome—Hector always the most daring— even exploring the top story because it was forbidden ground, and contained a mysterious room, the original of " The Lumber Room " in " Beasts and Super-Beasts."

Aunt Augusta's religion was not elastic ; it was definite and High Church and took her into Barn-staple on Sunday evenings. Neither aunt permitted her religion to come between her and her ruling passion, which was, to outwit the other. What they squabbled about never seemed to be of much importance. If Aunt Tom came back from Barn-staple market bearing reports of poultry she had bought at 2s. 6d., Aunt Augusta would know no peace until she had seen a far fatter bird at 2s. 4d. and announced it.

Then a row began—more or less intense, according to the length of time that had elapsed since the last one. Fighting probably relieved their tremendous energy. They never swore, so we heard no bad words. One good effect the quarrelling certainly had on us—it looked so ugly, we never copied them— never in our lives have we three had a row.

The aunts' outside interests lay in politics and the gossip of Pilton. Gardening kept Aunt Tom more

* P. G. Wodehouse.

or less sane, and making yards of useless embroidery had a soothing influence on Aunt Augusta. From morning to night, whether the jobbing gardener were there or not, Aunt Tom would be busy and dirty. Both aunts were exceedingly loyal to their friends, who, in their eyes, could do no wrong, and very generous to the poor.

They did not care at all for animals, but luckily did not interfere with our pets, whom we adored— they were the only young things we had to play with.

Hector had a curious dislike of rooks ; I had a pet young one, and used to feed it with bread and milk ; if he took the spoon he dropped it as it opened its beak. This dislike lasted all his life.

We had charming cats, who gave us all the affection the grown-ups did not know how to show. Tortoises, rabbits, doves, guinea-pigs and mice were other pets we had for a time, but cats and cocks and hens were always with us.

There was a most intelligent Houdan cock, who was Hector's shadow ; he fed out of his hand and loved being petted. Unhappily he got something wrong with one leg, and had to be destroyed. I believe a " Vet." would have cured him, but this would have been considered a sinful extravagance. No one but myself knew what Hector felt at the loss of the bird. We had early learnt to hide our feelings—to show enthusiasm or emotion were sure to bring an amused smile to Aunt Augusta's face. It was a hateful smile, and I cannot imagine why it hurt, but it did ; among ourselves we called it " the meaning smile."

Of course there were lots of days on which life

went smoothly, but, with an autocrat like herself, the most unexpected little things would upset her.

Both aunts were guilty of mental cruelty : we often longed for revenge with an intensity I suspect we inherited from our Highland ancestry. The following episode has already appeared somewhere, years after it happened. I told it to a friend of Hector's, who said he should make it into a story.

We always had plenty of good food, but, of course, plain, and except on our birthdays we never got roast duck, of which we were very fond. Sometimes a friend coming from a distance would be asked to lunch, and then roast duck would be the chief dish. Before the guest arrived Aunt Augusta would tell the three of us that at lunch she should ask us which we would have—roast duck or cold beef, and we were to answer, " Cold beef, please."

Well, on one occasion there were a couple of ducks, which Aunt Augusta was carving, and cold beef, which Granny had before her. All the grown-ups had had their plates filled, and Aunt Augusta turned to us. Hector and I gave the dutiful replies, but Charlie, on her left, was evidently so overcome by the sight and smell of the birds that he replied, " Roast duck, please."

Aunt Augusta glowered at him.

" What did you say ? " she asked, with furious eyes, and kicked him under the table.

" Oh, cold beef, please," said Charlie, hurriedly.

" What extraordinary children, to prefer cold beef to duck ! " remarked the visitor, and the children did not enlighten her.

Charlie really came off worst—Aunt Augusta never liked him, and positively used to enjoy whipping him. Hector and I escaped whipping, being considered too delicate. Fortunately for Charlie, he went to school when he was eight, and so got away from her malign influence. In her queer way she was fond of Hector and me, but being such an unlovable character, we extended only a lukewarm sort of liking to her.

With the best will in the world we could not be really naughty, for there simply was not the scope. Three children with three grown-ups to manage them are really handicapped from the outset.

Granny we were very fond of ; she was always very gentle with us, but appallingly strict on Sunday. No toys, no books except Sunday books, Dr. Watts's ghastly catechism, a collect and piece of a hymn to be learnt and repeated to her, stories read to us from " Peep of Day," and church, of course, in the morning. But at church we saw people and other children.

In the afternoons we had a church service among ourselves, the grown-ups must have been sleeping the Sabbath sleep. Preaching was the favourite part of the game and was a solemn affair, listened to with deep attention, far deeper than the preacher in church ever got, but there had to be three sermons in rapid succession—we all had something to say.

It also, in summer, was the favourite day for the boys to attempt, generally successfully, to get into the kitchen garden. Not every afternoon did the aunts sleep, so either that or to make a marauding expedition into the store-room via the greenhouse, and equally forbidden ground, was naturally the only thing to be done.

On one occasion they emerged from the latter with a jar of tamarinds, and got it safely into the night nursery, where there was a large trunk in which Aunt Augusta kept spare clothes. They ate what

MISSIONARY SUNDAY

"OH WE whose lives are lighted With Wisdom from on High — "

they wanted and put the jar in the trunk between folds of a black silk dress. The jar contained a lot of juice, very sticky, and in the eating much was smeared over the sides. However, the black silk absorbed a lot.

And then Aunt Augusta had occasion to open that trunk !

Broadgate resounded to her bellowings, and the row was frightful. In a former life she must have been a dragon. No toys allowed for two days, disgrace for all of us, and, of course, nothing to do. But mercifully we had fertile brains, and Hector was never nonplussed for occupation. Aunt Tom sometimes read to us—" Robinson Crusoe," " Masterman Ready," and the two " Alice's," which we loved, " Sandford and Merton " we refused to listen to.

" Johnnykin and the Goblins," a very little-known book, had always fascinated Hector. Being a Celt, I suppose it was natural he should be fond of goblins and nature spirits—he was certainly a Puck himself to the end of his life.

Pilton was a sort of Cranford ; there were about ten families, most of them without children, so we got to know grown-ups well and to be quite at ease in their society. When we did see children, it was in a crowd at a Christmas party. Aunt Augusta always went with us, and sometimes left us with the other children while she departed to gossip with the grown-ups. Hector leapt at the opportunity and the nearest boy, and was soon in the ecstasies of a fight.

Then Aunt Augusta would look in and in a restrained fury drag him off to be tidied. But his blood was up and any threat as to subsequent punishment was ignored. It was not that he was pugnacious —he was a very sweet-tempered child, but his high spirits had to have some outlet, and life at Broadgate

Golf in the Wild West

1. A cautious approach:-

2. Bunkers

was very monotonous. At the same party he had to be restrained from dashing on to the stage to rescue a man who was being threatened by another.

At this time he was an extremely fair child—very pink and white skin, blue-grey eyes with long black lashes, and flaxen hair. In his teens he began to get darker. Those who only knew him in his London days cannot understand that he could ever have been fair.

From about seven years old he was a keen politician. There was a most exciting election in Barnstaple, when Lord Portsmouth's son, a Radical, was elected. We were taken to the town to hear the poll declared, and had seats in a window opposite " The Golden Lion." The sights we saw were far too thrilling, and Hector was in a fever of excitement and furious at the result of the poll. He remained Conservative all his life.

He showed no signs of a writing talent as a boy with the exception of contributions to " The Broadgate Paper " which we ran. Drawing animals was his favourite occupation ; he never copied—just drew things out of his head. One rainy day in the holidays we had nothing to do, so we settled to have a Picture Exhibition that afternoon. Hector would be about eight then. We set to work to paint the pictures, of which many were still wet at the time the show opened. The grown-ups knew what we had planned, yet they never troubled to attend and praise our efforts, so we had to be audience and judges as well. With great solemnity and perfect justice Hector's pictures were awarded the prize, an old copy I had of Æsop's Fables.

Once in four years my father came home on leave (he was then a major in the Bengal Staff Corps, and

3. Lofted.

4. one up and one to follow.

Inspector-General of the Burma Police), and for six weeks we had a glorious time.

He took us for picnics, and to the houses of friends who had farmyards, where Hector rode the pigs, climbed haystacks with Charlie and arrived home rakish and buttonless, but in unquenchable spirits, snapping his fingers (figuratively, of course) at Aunt Augusta.

5.   "Dead"

We did not fear her when Papa was about. The wonder was we did not fear God with every inducement to do so. It was patent that our characters were fatally attractive to Him, and when we went a bit too far we were told that He sent a thunderstorm as a warning that we had better be careful.

I think Aunt Augusta must have mesmerized us —the look in her dark eyes, added to the fury in her voice, and the uncertainty as to the punishment, used to make me shiver. She had the strange charac-

teristic of being unable to be just annoyed at anything, she had to be so angry that she would work
herself into a passion. After all, we fared better
than a splendid retriever she had, who was kept
chained up in an outhouse of the back-yard for years,
with nothing to look at, eating his heart out. He
was taken out for a walk perhaps twice in the year
(until my father came home) and frightened Aunt
Augusta with his obstreperous delight. He died of
tumours when he was about eight.

Uncle Wellesley, our only civilian uncle, was a
great favourite with us. He only came about once
a year, and took Hector on fishing and sketching
expeditions. We never had a dull moment when he
was home; in a letter I found lately, written to
his mother, he said (*à propos* of Aunt Augusta's complaint of our behaviour), "the children are never naughty
with me, because I take the trouble to amuse them."

Hector began lessons with a daily governess we had;
our history lessons were read aloud, each taking a page.
All went well until we reached Cromwell's time.

"You must take the Roundheads' part," he said to me.

"But I would rather be Royalist," I objected.

"We can't both be Royalists, so you must be
Roundhead."

(The odd thing is that, from being forced into it,
I have remained Roundhead ever since.) So we
began the period of the Civil Wars with great delight
—it soon became exciting—Hector would gloat
over a victory of his side, even rising up in his chair
to hurl abuse at the Roundheads, which naturally I
wouldn't stand, so I abused back; the governess,
being a fool, at last stopped the concerted history
lesson, but she couldn't stop us; we only waited

until she was off, got down the histories and took the battles at a gallop, going through all the gamut of emotions from depression to exultation, according to the fortune of war. History then and ever afterwards became his favourite study, and as he had a wonderful memory his knowledge of European history from its beginning was remarkable. He was also very keen on natural history. When he was about nine he had brain-fever : the aunts nursed him most carefully ; we had only to be ill, and everything was changed at Broadgate, scoldings were things of the past. This illness delayed his going to school. We went much too seldom to visit my mother's people in Kent. They were much more our sort than the home aunts. My grandfather, Rear-Admiral Mercer, was full of fun, and his daughters were young and lively, and they let us do lots of things we could never do at home. Grandpapa was very fond of practical jokes, which fondness his grandchildren inherited in full measure.

Two or three London visits, and, very seldom, two weeks by the sea, completed our outings.

Hector was rather a favourite with old ladies, with whom he made himself quite at home. Aunt Tom took us once to see a very charming old lady, whose daughter (not a chicken) was then away on a round of visits. In a pause in the conversation Hector approached our hostess and, in a most courtly manner, proceeded :

" And so I hear, Mrs. Simpson, that Miss Janet is away in Scotland, enjoying all kinds of debauchery."

There was an astonished pause, every one laughed, and Aunt Tom exclaimed :

" That dreadful Roman history ! That's where he picks up these extraordinary expressions ! "

19

It was quite true—we had a remarkable, unexpurgated history with novel and lengthy words which needed airing, and this seemed to be a good occasion to have one out.

My father chose a resident governess for me before his last departure for Burma ; she was to teach Hector as well until he was strong enough for school (he was then twelve). It would be a great change for us to have a new-comer in the house, and we gravely discussed the situation.

"After all," said Hector, "we have only the grown-ups' word for it that she is a *real* governess, but how are we to know ? We must put a pea under her mattress, and see how she sleeps."

In one of Hans Andersen's tales, an unknown Princess was admitted on a wild night into a royal castle and given a bed consisting of twenty mattresses and twenty feather beds, after the Queen had thoughtfully put a pea under the lot. If she slept well, she was an impostor ; if badly, that proved her royalty. She slept atrociously.

So before the pseudo-governess arrived we put a dried pea under her mattress, and next morning asked her anxiously how she had slept.

"Very well indeed, thank you," she replied, with a pleased surprise at our solicitude.

"Ah, then, you can't be a *real* governess," said Hector, greatly disappointed, and told her what we had done.

She was, however, a real companion, and took us for the walks we loved and explored the whole countryside. She, like Uncle Wellesley, never found us naughty, because she took the trouble to amuse us. However, Aunt Augusta was afraid of her ; we did

not know it at the time, but she thought Miss J.'s
dark eyes were trying to mesmerize her, so, on the

The was a young girl called O'Brien
Who sang Sunday-school hymns to a lion;
Of this lady there's some
In the lion's tum-tum,
And the rest is an angel in Zion.

day she left for the holidays, after only one term with us, Aunt Augusta, who had not the nerve to do it herself, got Granny, who was then dying, to dismiss her. The following term we had no governess; Granny died, and we had a very sad time.

Another governess arrived for the next term, chosen by Aunt Augusta, and Hector soon after that was considered strong enough to go to school.

He went to Exmouth, where Charlie had preceded him, and was very happy there.

It was on returning to school after the holidays that Aunt Augusta gave a sample of mental cruelty. Some petty naughtiness had angered her the day before his return to school, so she sent him back without any pocket-money. As each boy had to bank his allowance for the whole term with one of the masters, Hector's ordeal may be imagined when he had to confess he had none.

Charlie, who had not yet returned to Charter-house, and I planned what we could do to help Hector. We settled to sell our books—Christmas and birthday presents from friends of the family. So we did, secretly, to a second-hand bookseller for quite a nice sum, and sent a postal order to Hector. Charlie then wrote to Papa, telling him what we had done, and the latter's letter to Aunt Augusta, blaming her for her action, was the first news she had of the affair. There was a row.

At fifteen Hector went to Bedford Grammar School and was there for two years. His school reports used to be, " Plenty of ability, but little application." In his Easter holidays he went bird-nesting with some of our neighbours, and made the beginning of a collection which he added to in our

Heanton days.   This collection is now in the Bideford
Museum.

ELISHA AND THE MOCKING CHILDREN

Two bears came forth from their cubless den—
Their cubless den, for their cubs were robbed—
And hunted about in search of men
Till they came to the spot where the Prophet was mobbed.
For men must hunt, tho' bears will fret,
And a cub will command a good price as a pet
And money is always consoling.

Thirty-two corpses lay stretched on the sward,
Thirty-two corpses, or possibly more,
For the bears were too busy their bag to record
And the Saint didn't stay to attend to the score.

23

My father, who had now retired, took us both to Normandy, our first trip abroad. We had some amusing young playmates, French and Russian, and enjoyed to the hilt the novelty and fascination of life at Etretat, with no aunts to mar our delight : the bathing would certainly have shocked them.

Our second trip abroad was a more educational one, to Germany. We had a lengthy stay in Dresden, Charlie joining us, and my father first began to feel what it was like to look after strictly brought up children ! Although Hector was then eighteen, he was still a boy, with no intention of growing up. One effect of the strict Broadgate *régime* was that he developed late—he remained and looked a boy long after he was in the twenties. We stayed in a Dresden pension run by a German lady, where the other guests were Americans.

On the flat beneath us was a girls' school, all of them ugly. One day, when my father was out, the boys made a weird figure of his bathing costume, stuffed out with paper and clothes, with a sponge for a face, and a rakish-looking hat. This they lowered into the balcony below. The schoolmistress happened to be giving dinner to a pastor, and to them, instead of to the girls, was vouchsafed this appalling vision.

When the boys thought enough time had elapsed, they swiftly drew up the figure. Swiftly, also, a note of complaint arrived for our landlady, who, being a German, saw no fun in the affair, not even with the figure sprawling at her feet. It was the convulsive laughter of a hitherto rather unbending American woman (in fact, the only time we ever knew her to laugh) that thawed her, and a note of apology was sent—insincere, as the school ma'am must have guessed, from the shouts of laughter above.

A " Lohengrin " night at the opera resulted in a sketch in which Hector depicted Lohengrin suffering from sea-sickness, while the swan turns round and gazes at him in astonishment. A German who saw it begged him to send it to the " Fliegende Blätter," but he never bothered to do it. He took long walks by himself in the parks to observe bird-life, and would stop Germans and draw in the gravel path the sort of bird he wanted, and ask if it were to be found. They would then write the bird's name in the gravel, and tell him where to get further information.

He routed out, in some obscure corner, an old man who sold birds' eggs, and from him bought a model of the Great Auk's egg, and insisted on coming home in a cab, for the greater safety of the egg.

Charlie left us to go to a crammer's (he was trying for the Army), and we then began a strenuous tour, beginning with Berlin. At the Palace of Sans Souci at Potsdam we searched for the graves of Frederick the Great's chargers and favourite dogs, and refused to go over the Palace until a park-keeper could be found who knew where they were buried.

We saw an immense number of picture galleries in Berlin, Munich, etc., and were impressed by the love of German artists for St. Sebastian (the arrow-stuck saint), so we started bets on the gallery which would have the most : Berlin won.

Nuremberg delighted Hector—then and always he loved old towns ; in later days Pskoff more than fulfilled his dream of what a mediæval town should be. Prague was another delight, particularly Wallenstein's castle, where I had to engage our guide in

BIOGRAPHY

talk while Hector cut a hair from the tail of Wallenstein's charger. In one room high up, formerly a
council chamber, we were shown the window from
which obstreperous councillors were thrown ; we
leant out while my father hung on to us, to see the
depth they had to fall. This is the one described in
" Karl-Ludwig's Window," in this book.

It was on our way to Prague that we saw snow-
capped mountains for the first time, a never-to-be-
forgotten experience. Any Celt will know the sort
of awesome thrill one gets.

Fortunately, Innsbruck was the last place on our
tour, for we were fagged out, and on arriving at
Davos, where we were to spend several months, we
lay low for a week, drank much milk and took stock
of our fellow-guests at the Hôtel Belvedere.

And then we let ourselves go !

My father was soon nicknamed " the Hen that
hatched out ducklings," and some middle-aged,
self-sacrificing men tried to be extra fathers to us,
but it was no use. Swiss air and freedom went to
our heads—nothing but an avalanche would have
stopped us.

Tennis, paper-chases, riding, dancing, climbing,
searching for marmots on the high reaches, occupied
our bodies, and lectures on all manner of learned
subjects and painting lessons kept our brains busy.
Professor Meyer, a painter of birds of prey, was
a teacher after our own hearts. He understood
that we *had* to play some wild game before settling
down to work. Usually we got to his flat before
he was ready for us, and crept into his bedroom ;
presently a search began, and before he knew where
he was he found himself in the midst of a pillow-

fight—that or a wild scrimmage round the studio, and then we settled down, first eating some excellent cakes he fetched hot from the kitchen.

Hector learnt pastel from him, and did a very good picture of an eagle, life-size, bringing a seagull to her young ones.

John Addington Symonds had a house at Davos ; he and Hector played chess together, and found they had a taste for heraldry in common.

The winter was even more fascinating than the summer—we were tobogganing all day, sometimes at night as well, and " tailed " behind sleighs to far-off runs, picnicking in the sun and snow. Charlie and Uncle Wellesley came out, and the bigger in-door entertainments began, fancy dress and domino balls, sheet and pillow-case dances, theatricals, etc. No better " coming-out " could any young thing desire, it was certainly the happiest winter we three had ever spent. Davos in those days was a friendly, jolly place, not at all fashionable.

We left it in April and went to stay at Schloss Salenstein, on the Swiss side of Lake Constance, the home of some very charming people whom we met at Davos.

Then to England, where we took a house, absurdly large for us, at Heanton, four miles from Barnstaple, also four miles from the aunts. Occasionally they came to visit us, one at a time, but were not encouraged to stay long. On the whole we were far too kind to them—so much water had flowed under the bridge since Broadgate days, and we were now topdogs and they knew it. Moreover, they had mellowed a bit, and Aunt Tom especially was devoted to Hector. She was such an original character we had to forgive her much, simply because of her unusualness. We were certainly blessed in our near relatives in one respect, we had not one who could be called dull !

" GILLIE "

Charlie, having failed, unfortunately, for the Army, being the only one of us with bad sight, left for the Burma Police. At Heanton we had for the first time a dog of our own, a fox-terrier, who accompanied Hector on all his explorings. Toby, our cat, we brought from Broadgate ; she was delighted to have us back, also to find so many hares in the field at the bottom of the garden, but unhappily through them she met her death from some beast of a keeper ; her kitten had the same fate, and we were too sad to have another cat.

It was while roaming the country-side that Hector got to know the Devon character so well. The incidents in "The Blood-Feud of Toad-Water" really happened ; our rector knew the people. There was also a witch in our neighbourhood who had uncanny powers, but we never met her.

For two years we lived at Heanton, studying under my father's direction, then left it for a season in town. Then back to Davos for the winter.

We had no more painting lessons there ; our old friend had died the year before. We soon got together a "Push," of which Hector was the leading spirit, and on one or two occasions we literally painted the place red and blue with Aspinall's enamel. There was a very pious hotel, the Hôtel des Iles, which received Hector's most artistic efforts. Six of us one night kept guard while he painted devils in every stage of intoxication on its pure walls.

The theatricals were on a more ambitious scale than two years previously. Hector took the part of the old lawyer in "Two Roses" ; I heard an old colonel say he had created the part.

We had curling for the first time that winter, a game my father and Hector played a great deal, and some exciting toboggan races. But the event that set the seal on our activities was the gorgeous hoax we played on the Hôtel des Iles. It had committed the unforgivable crime in Hector's eyes of being mean.

The four English hotels at Davos (the Hôtel des Iles was one) at the beginning of the winter season

elected each an Amusement Committee, which
provided the various entertainments, dances, etc.,
for the season, sending round the hat for the funds,
and it was the custom for each hotel to invite the
guests of the others to the weekly dances, concerts,
etc.

The Hôtel des Iles was the only one that invited
no one to anything—the fault, of course, of the guests,
not of the proprietor. They collected the money
and—spent it on a dinner to themselves !

This, naturally, we could not stand, so the " Push,"
at the end of the winter season, decided they should
give an entertainment that would be talked about.
Hector, whose writing was not known there, wrote
the invitations.

" The Hôtel des Iles requests the pleasure of the
company of the Hôtel Belvedere's visitors on 20th
March.

" ' Box and Cox.'

" LE PETIT HOTEL."

This last, we heard, was an improper play, and
was chosen to attract the foreigners.

These invitations were sent to the English hotels
and to some of the visitors at the Kurhaus. We
picked out Russian princes, German barons, Italian
counts, etc., and we left out the distant chalets, so
that no one should be put to any expense in hiring
sleighs. I wanted to stay and see the fun, but Hector
said he had not the nerve to look innocent. The
replies, we stated on the invitations, should be sent
to two men who, we knew, had left the Hôtel des Iles,
and naturally were forwarded on to them.

As the Hôtel des Iles people were so unco' guid
and kept so much to themselves, they did not mix in

the life of Davos and so knew nothing of the excitement their invitation caused.

A Scottish girl, one of our " Push," sent us a thrilling account of the evening. The English hotels were warned in time, not so the people at the Kurhaus, who arrived in strength.

Then there was pandemonium, and a babel of imprecations assailed the chaste ears of the innocent inmates. " I know who did it," shouted an irascible man, and rushing home for a horsewhip he hurled himself into the room of a guiltless American. I mean he was not one of the " Push." Fortunately explanations were satisfactory, and no one was whipped. I believe the authorship of the hoax was never guessed. We heard long afterwards a rumour that early next winter the Hôtel des Iles gave a concert to which everybody was invited and no one turned up !

We went to stay with Aunt Tom at Pilton, that spring of 1893, and in June Hector left for a post my father had got for him in Burma, in the Military Police.

Charlie met him on arrival and they both stopped in Rangoon with the Deputy Inspector-General of Police.

Hector was in Burma only thirteen months and had seven fevers in the time. He got a lot of enjoyment from the animal life surrounding him—to be on a horse was one great delight, and to be at close quarters with wild animals was another.

He also, as his letters show, appreciated the good qualities and resourcefulness of the Burmese servants ; whether other masters have found them so all-round useful I do not know, but Hector had the gift of attracting willing service wherever he was. The

Burman is fond of animals, particularly little animals, and saw nothing extraordinary in a tiger-cat as a pet. I have quoted, in the following letters, almost exclusively the bits dealing with animals, because they are the most characteristic of him.

SINGU, *June 5th,* —93.

MY DEAR E.

The heat during the last few days has been scorching, and I have been quite knocked off my legs in consequence. . . . This is a dreadfully noisy place when one is not feeling well ; there are the children : the little brats have a remarkably good time of it, they are never whacked or scolded, and they take a deliberate pleasure in howling at the slightest opportunity ; you never heard such yells, they throw all their little heathen souls—if they have any—into the performance. I should like to spank them for ever, stopping, of course, for meal times. . . . Then during the night, the frogs and owls and lizards have necessarily lots to say to each other, and whenever my pony hears another neigh she whinnies back, and being a mare always insists on having the last word. As to the dogs they go on at intervals during the twenty-four hours, like the Cherubim which rest not day or night. Have you ever seen a dog bark and yawn at the same time ? I did the other day and nearly had a fit ; it reminded me of a person saying the responses in church. The most welcome noise of all is the whistle of the steam-boat, especially when it brings the English mail. . . . I am agreeably surprised with my servants, they are quick, resourceful, seem honest, and are genuinely attached to their master's interests ; of course they

32

are more or less stupid, they are human beings. . . .
I had quite a nursery establishment last week ; I found
a little house-squirrel which had just left its nest, on
my verandah ; it is like a large dormouse, silver grey
with a mauve grey tail, and orange buff underneath ;
it lives upon milk, and is very tame and snoomified.
. . Then there was a duckling ; I thought of putting
it with the squirrel, but the latter looks upon everything as meant to be eaten and the duck had broad
views on the same subject, so I thought they had
better live in single blessedness. As the squirrel
occupied the only empty biscuit tin the duck had to
go into the waste-paper basket where it was quite
happy.

SINGU, 17.6.93.

I am rather excité over a pony I have unearthed
with zebra markings on its legs ; Darwin believed
that the horse, ass, zebra, quagga and hemonius
were all evolved from an equine animal striped like
the zebra but differently constructed, and in his
book on the descent of domestic animals he attached
great importance to some zebra-like markings which
he observed on an Exmoor pony ; so my discovery
may be of some interest. . . . This is a disappoint-
ing place as far as the flora is concerned ; I have
not seen any decent flowers or shrubs, except a kind
of magnolia which is common here. . . .
Aunt Tom's first letter was full of her grievances—
so interesting to read ; really if Providence perse-
cuted me in the way it does her, I should be too
proud to go to Heaven. Her complaint of loneliness amused me. If she is lonely in a place with
13,000 inhabitants it's her own fault. My boy

continues to give satisfaction in regard to cooking, the way he serves chicken up as beefsteak borders on the supernatural.

I amuse myself by painting, when the midges are not too troublesome. I am doing a picture of the coronation of Albert II, Archduke of Austria, in 1437 ; not a proper picture but a sort of heraldic procession like you would see in old tapestries. The arch-bishop of Trèves looks very smart on a fiery bay ; I shall never forget the trouble I had to find his arms at the Brit. Museum.

MWÉHINTHA OUTPOST, 26.7.93.

I meant to have written to you last mail, but Mr. Carey arrived by the boat and paid me a long visit —it was a relief to have someone human to talk to —and I had to get ready for going out in the district ; you see I have taken to district visiting in my old age. The place is so inundated that no pony can get out so I had to go by boat. . . . The Maid of Sker is charmed with her new quarters, she sees so much more life than formerly, and instead of having to thump on the earth floor when she wants anything, she can now rap her fore hoofs against the wooden partitions, which makes fifty times as much noise and ensures a prompt attendance. . . . There are most charming birds here now the rains are on, egrets, bitterns, pelicans, storks, pond-herons, etc. Shwepyi (the 1st guard on my route) is a great stronghold of these birds, as in the dry weather there are 2 large lakes there and in the rains it is all one big swamp ; so when I arrived there last night I determined to make a hurried excursion next morning before leaving for this place. Accordingly I went forth this morning in a small sort of canoe with my boy and two men to row. We saw lots of pelicans and other birds but no nests, as most of them don't breed till August. As we were getting back, a Malay spotted dove flew up from a nest in a tree, which hung just over us. I sent one man up to get the eggs but he could not get at it, so I gave it a prod with an oar. There was a yell from the men and as I stood back I saw an enormous snake rise "long and slowly" from the nest and glide into the branches. The man in the tree came down with the agility of three apes. · It was a monster snake and looked very venomous. ... As we were coming here in the big boat we passed a tree on which were several nests with darters sitting on them (the darter is a sort of cross between a gannet and a cormorant), a frightful tree to climb, but one of the natives ran up it like a cat and brought me down a lot of eggs and some young birds for them (the natives) to eat; fancy eating unfledged cormorants—oo-ah ! When I got here I found the stockade was ankle deep in water ; I had to be dragged up to the guard house in a small boat, which had to be carefully led round various shallows ; it was like the swan scene in Lohengrin.

Owl and oaf thou art, not to see "Woman of no importance" and "Second Mrs. T." *The* plays of the season ; what would I not give to be able to see them !

25 *Aug.,* 93.

For the last three days I have been at this place (can't remember the name, but it's six miles from Mandalay) where a high festival is being held in honour of two local deities of great repute, called the Nats. Their history is briefly this : they were two brothers who were ordered by the king to build a temple here, which they did, but omitted two bricks, for which reason the king killed them, in the impulsive way these Eastern monarchs have. After they were dead they seemed to think they had gone rather cheap and they made themselves so unpleasant about it that the king gave them permission to become deities, and built them a temple, and here they are, don't you know. Just that. The original temple with the vacant places for the missing bricks is still here ; this is not an orthodox Buddhist belief but the Nats are held in great esteem in Upper Burma and parts of China, and this show is held here every year in their honour. The whole thing is so new to me that I will describe it at some length. Of course I had to come here as the presence of a European officer is necessary to keep order, and twenty-five police had to be drafted here. No martyr ever suffered so much on account of religion as I have. When I arrived the Nats were being escorted to the river to bathe, accompanied by unearthly music which sent the pony I was riding spinning round like a weather-cock in a whirlwind. Then I came to where the chief show is held and to my horror I found a solitary chair had been placed on an elevated platform for my especial use, to which I was conducted with great ceremony ; I am not sure the orchestra did not try to strike up the National Anthem. I inquired wildly for Carey, but was told he was with his wife somewhere. I was in terror lest they might expect a speech, and how could I get up and tell this people, replete with the learning of centuries of Eastern civilization, " this animal will eat rice " ? Fortunately the sparring commenced at once and was very absorbing to watch ; two men fight with hands and legs and go for each other like cats, the one who draws blood first wins. I was quite disappointed to see them stop as soon as one was scratched. I had hoped (such is our fallen nature) that they would fight to the death and was trying hurriedly to remember whether you turned your thumbs up or down for mercy. Some of the encounters were very exciting, but I had to preserve a calm dignity befitting the representative of Great Britain and Ireland, besides which my chair was in rather a risky position and required careful sitting. Noblesse oblige. Then Carey came and told me that he had got quarters in the monastery grounds . . . and had got me a house adjoining the show-place. Not only does it adjoin the building, but it forms part of it and opens on to the arena ! The hours of performance are from 10 a.m. to 3 p.m., and from 8 p.m. to 6 a.m. There are two bands. During performances my dining-room is a sort of dress-circle, so I have to get my meals when I can. As to sleep, it's not kept on the premises, while the heat is so great that you could boil an egg on an iceberg. There are also smells. The acting is not up to much but the audience are evidently charmed with it. I go to bed at ten, finding two hours quite enough, but when I get up at 5.30 the audience are applauding as vigorously as ever. Then I am worried to death by princesses ; some of the native magistrates' wives are relatives of the ex-king and fancy themselves accordingly. One old lady, who carries enough jewels for twenty ordinary princesses, takes an annoying interest in me and is always pressing me to partake of various fruits at all hours of the day. She asked me, through Mrs. Carey, how old I was, and then told me I was too tall for my age, obligingly showing me the height I ought to be. It reminded me of another royal lady's dictum " All persons above a mile high to leave the Court." I told her that in this damp climate one must allow something for shrinkage, and she did not press the matter.

It is no sinecure to keep order with this huge mob of mixed nationalities, and I shall be glad when it is all over.

Singu,
6 Sept., 93.

. . . I found the tiger-kitten quite wild ; pretended it had never seen me before, so I had to go through the ceremony of introduction again. I soon made it tame again, and we have great games together. It has not learnt how to drink properly yet and immerses its nose in the milk, then it gets mad with the saucer and shakes it, which sends the milk all over its paws, upon which it swears horribly. I have another queer creature in the shape of a young darter (same species of bird as the self-hatching one) which I saw sitting on the river bank en route for here ; the men rowed to shore and just picked it up and put it in the boat where it sat as if it didn't care a twopenny damn. What blasé birds those darters are. Then there is the crow-brought chicken which was carried here by a crow and rescued by the syce ; crows often run off with one's chickens but it is not often they add to your poultry. I feel quite like the prophet Elijah (or was it Elisha ?) who was

38

boarded by ravens. Milk is scarce now, but the kitten has to have some of my scanty store, while the ponies feel very annoyed if they don't get a bit of bread now and then ; I believe I am rather expected to share my sardines with the darter, but I draw the line there ! The Burmans have not collected any eggs for me yet ; my boy says the birds are " too much upstairs living." Frightfully thrilling ! . . .

The kitten throws off the cat and assumes the

Problem : To seat two inside.

tiger when it is fed ; I have to throw it its food (gener-ally the head of a chicken) and then bolt ; it is making the day hideous with its growling now, as I gave it the head and wing, and it is trying to eat both at once.

MADAYA, 15.9.93.

A day or two before I left (headquarters) I was enjoying my midday tub, when my boy came and announced that a big bear had been caught and was being brought up to me ; I implored him not to do anything so rash but he went away saying "Master bringing, yes." The bathroom is comparatively small and I knew that if a large bear were introduced there would be unpleasantness. I hastily forgave my enemies and tried to say my prayers, but the only one I could remember was the prayer for fine weather. As it happened my boy meant bird when he said bear, having caught a large sort of buzzard which naturalists have dignified with the name of hawk-eagle; so I left off praying for fine weather and un-forgave my enemies forthwith. The bird has fine plumage but a very sinister expression; when I go near it, it opens its mouth, elevates its crest and glares at me with baleful eyes.

OHNMIN, 17.9.93.

I left Madaya yesterday. . . . My new pony I have called "Microbe" on account of his diminutive size. Poor little neglected beast, he looked on so modestly and wistfully when the mare was being given her corn and he was so charmed and thankful when he found he was going to have some too: and when he had a plantain brought him for dessert he began to think with "Mrs. Erlynne" that the world was "an intensely amusing place." . . . At Yenetha my bullock cart had to be stopped, as two bears were walking along the path in front; I was on ahead, so missed seeing them. It is ever thus. . . . The "Mandalay Herald" had an article on the Toung-bein Pwé, in which it said, "Many Europeans graced the proceedings with their presence, but the one who was most generally noticed and admired was a police-officer in full khaki uniform." This is rather rough on me, as I was the only European in uniform there.

HÔTEL DE FRANCE,
MANDALAY,
24 *Oct.*, 93.

. . . The tiger-kitten has had a nice cage made for it, with an upstair apartment to sleep in, but every afternoon it comes out into my room for an hour or two and has fine romps. It would make a nice pet for you but it would be an awful trouble sending it—it might die—and it won't be safe when it grows up. It goes into lovely tiger attitudes, when it thinks I'm looking.

. . . Tell Mrs. Byrne there is no immediate danger of my marrying a Burmese wife ; there was a woman at Singu—ugly as a Fury—who, I think, had great hopes, but my boy, always ready to save me trouble, married her himself ; he had one wife already, but that was a trifle. I impress upon him that he may have as many as he likes, within reasonable limits, but no babies. To this rule there is no exception. When I was out in the district if a child howled in any neighbouring hut men were sent at once to stop it ; if it wouldn't stop it was conducted out of ear-shot ; wouldn't you like to do that with English brats ! How rabid the mothers would get !

HÔTEL DE FRANCE,
MANDALAY,
30 *Oct.*, 93.

. . . An old lady came to the hotel last week, one of those people with a tongue and a settled conviction that they can manage everybody's affairs. She had the room next to mine—connected by a door—and I was rather astonished when the proprietor came that evening, and with great nervousness, said that there

was an old lady in the next room and er—she was
rather er—fidgety old lady and er—er—er—there
was a door connecting our rooms. I was quite
mystified as to what he was driving at but I answered
languidly that the door was locked on my side and
there was a box against it, so she could not possibly
break in. The proprietor collapsed and retired in
confusion ; I afterwards remembered that the " cub "
had spent a large portion of the afternoon pretending
that this door was a besieged city, and it was a battering
ram. And it does throw such vigour into its play.
I met the old lady at dinner and was greeted with
an icy stare which was refreshing in such a climate.
That night the kitten broke out in a new direction ;
as soon as I went up to bed it began to roar ; " and
still the wonder grew, so small a throat could give
so large a mew." The more I tried to comfort it
the more inconsolable it grew. The situation was
awful—in my room a noise like the lion-house at
4 p.m., while on the other side of the door rose the
beautiful Litany of the Church of England. Then
I heard the rapid turning of leaves, she was evidently
searching for Daniel to gain strength from the perusal
of the lion's den story ; only she couldn't find Daniel
so fell back upon the Psalms of David. As for me,
I fled, and sent my boy to take the cage down to the
stable. When I came back I heard words in the
next room that never came out of the Psalms ; words
such as no old lady ought to use ; but then it is annoying to be woken out of your first sleep by a rendering
of " Jamrach's Evening Hymn." She left. The
beast has behaved fairly well since, except that it eat
up a handkerchief. . . . It also insisted on taking
tea with me yesterday and sent my cup flying into

my plate, trying meanwhile to hide itself in the milk
jug to prove an alibi. I am getting as bad as Aunt
Charlotte with her perpetual cats, but I have seen
very few human beings as yet, every one being away,
as this is a sort of holiday time. . . .

MANDALAY,
1 Feb., 94.

. . . I had a delightful petition brought me by a
native in my guard who had got a Burman clerk to
write it for him ; he wanted to resign the police and
his reasons were that his father and mother had died
after him and that his uncle was generously ill. I
hear you have a Persian kitten ; of course I, who
have the untameable carnivora of the jungle roaming in savage freedom through my rooms, cannot
feel any interest in mere domestic cats, but I am
not intolerant and I have no objection to your keeping
one or two. My beast does not show any signs of
getting morose ; it sleeps on a shelf in its cage all day
but comes out after dinner and plays the giddy goat
all over the place. I should like to get another
wild cat to chum with it, there are several species in
Burma : the jungle-cat, the bay-cat, the lesser leopard-
cat, the tiger-cat, marbled cat, spotted wild-cat, and
rusty-spotted cat ; the latter, I have read, make
delightful pets.

I hope you have no more bother with servants ;
my boy gives me notice about once a month but I
never think of accepting it ; if he doesn't know a
good master I know a good servant, to paraphrase
an old remark. He has a great idea of my consequence and of his own reflected importance ; I sent
him to a village with a message, and Beale A.S.P.,

who was expecting some fowls from that place, asked if they had been sent by him ; he told me he should never forget the tone in which he said " I am Mr. Munro's boy ! "   Civis Romanus sum.

MANDALAY,
7 *Feb.*, 94.

. . . The men who bring grass carry it in two bundles thus :

the other day just as my grass man was bringing the fodder into the stable the mare came up from

behind and catching hold of the hind bundle gave it a violent jerk, which brought the whole bag of tricks to the ground.   I luckily had no stays on or they would certainly have burst.

MANDALAY, 11.2.94.

I went to watch a game of polo last week ; I long to play, and I am told that Gordon, of the military police, would mount anyone who cared to play, but at present I can scarcely find time to go and look on, much less go in for it regularly. . . .

I am very interested in watching the vultures which congregate in great numbers just here ; there are three kinds, 2 brown and 1 black ; the latter is a fine bird and very much cock of the walk ; whenever one comes to a carcase the brown birds have to leave off eating and wait till he's finished, trying to look as if they weren't in the least hungry. Usually only one eats at a time at a small carcase, but this morning there was a regular Rugby scrimmage over a particularly " ripe " pariah puppy, about 14 birds struggling for the choice morsel. Among the vultures I was astonished to see a lovely black eagle (Neopus Malayensis) but just as I got my field-glasses to bear on him, off he flew.

MANDALAY,
30 *March*, 94.

. . . My boy has just got me some crows' eggs ; the Burmans don't quite approve of my taking them as they have an idea that the spirits of their grandmothers turn into crows, but I cannot be expected to respect the eggs of other people's grandmothers. Some absurd owls built themselves a nest inside my roof, which was a rash thing to do ; of course I promptly took care of their eggs for them. Where would one find English servants who, besides cooking one's food and bottle-washing generally, hunted for birds' eggs and routed out police cases (my boy is of more use to me that way than any of my police men, and is invaluable in the witness box, as he will swear not only to what he saw, but to what he thinks I should like him to have seen) ? Fancy saying to an English cook " Dinner at 7 sharp, and I've three guests coming ; and, by the way, just see if the buzzard's nest in the high elm has any eggs in it ; and while you're about it find out if there is any gambling going on in the Red Lion, etc., etc." Pedrica would have wept scalding tears at such requests.

MAYMYO,
23.4.94.

I am still delighted with this place, it is delightfully cool and we have whist every night and dine and breakfast in each other's houses rather more frequently than in our own ; not much work to do, and a fair amount of sport to be had. . . . I heard a good story of some police officer to whom one of the Petty Burman princelings wrote an official letter, styling himself as usual " Lord of a 100 elephants," etc., etc. The police officer in reply called himself Lord of 1 pony, a half-bred terrier, 3 puppies, 13 fowls, and 1 duck. The princeling kicked up no end of a row.

My goose has hatched out a brood of goslings in spite of 40 miles' transit in a jolting bullock cart.

MAYMYO,
26.5.94.

Don't count your chickens after they're hatched ; it's quite as fatal as it was to number one's subjects in David's time. I was writing to Mr. Lamb out in the jungle last week and telling him what gentlemanly geese and ducks I had and how they multiplied exceedingly and waxed fat, etc., when a con-founded messenger rode up with the following letter from the Head Constable :

"Your syce report that 2 goose and 2 gooseling, duck 3, hen 1, died yesterday with deceased. Syce weeping tears,

Your obedient servant, etc.

P.S. I saw them lying dead and ordered them to dry in the sun."

English's poultry are dying too ; he has just built a swagger fowl house so I wrote and told him that he was like the Rich Fool who built bigger barns, not that I wished to suggest for a moment that he was rich.

In the summer months Hector got malaria very badly, and in August had to resign and come home, to my great delight. He told me that while lying in bed, feeling wretchedly ill, in some hotel, he heard footsteps passing in the corridor and called out. A German, a visitor like himself, and a stranger to Hector, came in and asked what was the matter ? Hector told him he wanted a servant to bring him something to drink ; the German stood and argued that it was not his business and he could not attend to sick people, neither should he give a message to anyone, and then departed. Of course he may have been mad, or madder than usual. It was some time after that Hector attracted the attention of a servant passing by and got what he wanted.

My father went to meet him in London and found he was too ill to travel down to Devon at once, so they stopped in town for a time, a nurse was engaged, and he gradually got better.

47

When he did arrive home, although looking ghastly ill, he lost no time in getting well, and soon bought a horse for the hunting season. But the fevers had weakened him so much that he could not last out a whole day's hunting until quite the end of the season.

However, we had some lovely times out together, in the hilly country between Devon and Cornwall, and these were priceless opportunities for Hector to study Devon types.

We had settled down at Westward Ho, in those days a gay and jolly place, and separated by eleven miles from the aunts.

A fox terrier, some Persian cats, and Agag, a jackdaw, with a passion for bathing, were our pets at that time. Hector shared that passion—not that they bathed together, but, wherever water was, he was not happy unless he was in it. We thought of keeping bears, but there were difficulties in the way, how to get them, chiefly. If a merchant travelling in wild animals had come our way, he would not have passed our gates in vain.

In the summer, in addition to sea-bathing and riding, there was tennis, a game Hector loved more than any other, and we had lots of fun on our sporting " putting " green, but apart from putting he never played golf.

Not more than three miles from Westward Ho there lived another witch, known personally to our housemaid, whose brother had been uncivil to her one day, and who was punished by a plague of creeping things all over him, which only left him next morning ; but she is not the original of the witch in Hector's stories.

In 1896, Hector left for London, to earn his living

by writing. Some Devon friends introduced him to Sir Francis Gould (then Carruthers Gould), who launched him in the literary world. He wrote for the *Westminster Gazette* political satires, called "Alice in Westminster," illustrated by Carruthers Gould, and afterwards published in book form, as "The Westminster Alice."

In these sketches all the characters are public men, chiefly Cabinet Ministers, portrayed as the animals, etc., in "Alice in Wonderland."

These were followed in 1902 by the "Not So Stories," also political satires.

The Munro clan has always been composed of fighters and writers. Our grandfather, a colonel in the Indian Army, had a great compliment paid him by the Marquis Wellesley of his day, who said tha he wrote purely classical language. His writing was entirely, I believe, on Indian politics. Aunt Tom told us this—she always said Hector had inherited his grandfather's gift. At any rate, he wrote naturally and never went through a literary correspondence course. My mother's mother was a very clever woman, and she, through her mother, belonged to the Macnab clan. So Hector was Celtic on both sides of his family.

To me, his strongest characteristics were—whimsicality, keen sense of humour, love of animals, and pride in being Highland. There are people who think that to be fond of animals means domestic animals only ; to include wild ones shows madness. Well— Hector must have been raving ! It is possible to get a good deal more out of madness than sane people have any conception of !

Another characteristic was his indifference to money.

His attitude to business is shown in " Clovis on the Romance of Business," in this volume.

I have kept, unfortunately, very few of his letters written from town. Some, in fact, I destroyed as soon as read, because my father insisted on reading any letters his sons ever wrote, and Hector and I sometimes had plans which we did not divulge to him at once.

Here is an extract from one written when he was chumming with a friend, one Tocke.

" My Dear E.

" The duck was a bird of great parts and as tender as a good man's conscience when confronted with the sins of others. Truly a comfortable bird. Tockling is looking well and is in better health and spirits generally, and everything in the garden's lovely. Except the ' Cambridgeshire ' which we all came a cropper over. We put our underclothing on the wrong horse and are now praying for a mild Winter."

Sometimes when I left Westward Ho for a short visit, he came down to " understudy " me, chiefly in looking after the animals, and to see that Aunt Tom, who made a bee line for our house as soon as she knew I had started, did not have everything at sixes and sevens before I came back. This is one from home.

" Aunt Tom came on a visit the day Ker left, but I am still understudying your place. She is horrified at the rapidity of my marketing (which has been so far successful), but I pointed out to her that it was doubtful economy to spend an hour trying to save a few halfpennies on the price of vegetables when other people spent pounds to snatch a short time by the sea-side—and the quicker I marketed the sooner I got back. Of course she was not converted to my view. . . . On Wednesday we drove to Bucks and met a menagerie, so with two other traps we turned into a field to let it pass. Bertie and I went in on both nights to see the beasts, and made friends with the young trainer, who was quite charming, and had sweet little lion cubs (born in the first coronation week) taken out of their cage and put into our arms, also seductive little wolf-puppies which you would have loved."

He spent much time in the British Museum Reading Room getting material for his book, " The Rise of the Russian Empire." This was published in 1900, his only entirely serious book, tracing the beginnings of Russian history to the time of Peter the Great.

A friend writes that he is sorry the book is so little known, " for it is better written and more interesting than Rambaud's ' History of Russia,' which I fancy is still the most widely read book on this subject."

Hector himself had not a great opinion of the book. He was charmed with the remark of our coachman who asked for the loan of it. I don't know how much of it he read, but one day he said to Hector, " I've read your book, sir, and I must say I shouldn't care to have written it myself."

Hector said it was the biggest compliment he had ever had.

The *Bookman* considered he had provided " an historical outline of no little value."

In August 1901 he had the experience of going to Edinburgh with Aunt Tom. At one time I wished that she had invited me too, but not after reading the following account.

"MY DEAR E.

"Travelling with Aunt Tom is more exciting than motorcarring. We had four changes and on each occasion she expected the railway company to bring our trunks round on a tray to show that they really had them on the train. Every 10 minutes or so she was prophetically certain that her trunk, containing among other things ' poor mother's lace,' would never arrive at Edinburgh. There are times when I almost wish Aunt Tom had never had a mother. Nothing but a merciful sense of humour brought me through that intermittent unstayable outpour of bemoaning. And at Edinburgh, sure enough her trunk was missing !

"It was in vain that the guard assured her that it would come on in the next train, half-an-hour later ; she denounced the vile populace of Bristol and Crewe, who had broken open her box and were even then wearing the maternal lace. I said no one wore lace at 8 o'clock in the morning and persuaded her to get some breakfast in the refreshment-room while we waited for the alleged train. Then a worse thing befel —no baps ! There were lovely French rolls but she demanded of the terrified waiter if he thought we had come to Edinburgh to eat bread !

"In the midst of our bapless breakfast I went out and lit upon her trunk and got a wee bit laddie to carry it in and lay it at her very feet. Aunt Tom received it with faint interest and complained of the absence of baps.

"Then we spent a happy hour driving from one hostelry to another in search of rooms, Aunt Tom reiterating the existence of a Writer to the Signet who went away and let his rooms 30 years ago, and ought to be doing it still. 'Anyhow' she said, 'we are seeing Edinburgh,' much as Moses might have informed the companions of his 40 years' wanderings that they were seeing Asia. Then we came here, and she took rooms after scolding the manageress, servants and entire establishment nearly out of their senses because everything was not to her liking. I hurriedly explained to everybody that my aunt was tired and upset after a long journey, and disappointed at not getting the rooms she had expected ; after I had comforted two chambermaids and the boots, who were crying quietly in corners, and coaxed the hotel kitten out of the waste-paper basket, I went to get a shave and a wash—when I came back Aunt Tom was beaming on the whole establishment and saying she should recommend the hotel to all her friends. 'You can easily manage these people,' she remarked at lunch, 'if you only know the way to their hearts.' She told the manageress that I was frightfully particular. I believe we are to be here till Tuesday morning, and then go into rooms ; the hotel people have earnestly recommended a lot to us.

"Aunt Tom really is marvellous ; after 16 hours in the train without a wink of sleep, and an hour spent in hunting for rooms, her only desire is to go out and see the shops. She says it was a remarkably comfortable journey ; personally I have never known such an exhausting experience.

"y. a. b.
"H. H. Munro."

I told Hector once that Aunt Tom's character should be immortalized in some story.

" I shall write about her some day," he said, " but not until after her death."

She died in 1915 when he was learning to be a soldier, and has only appeared sketchily in his stories ; " The Sex that Doesn't Shop," is chiefly about her.

Somewhere before 1902 Hector had a severe attack of double pneumonia in London. After his recovery he seemed to be much stronger than he had ever been before and continued so for the rest of his life.

In 1902 he was in the Balkans as correspondent for the *Morning Post*, a part of the world that had always attracted him.

To find a horse to ride, a river to bathe in and a game of tennis or bridge, were his first considerations after work had been seen to.

Sophia, 7.1.03.

Have been elected a visiting member of the Union Club, which is the social hub of the local universe ; the English vice-consul and I fell into each other's arms when we each discovered that the other played Bridge. I have voluminous discussions in French with some of the leaders in the Bulgarian Parliament ; I don't mean to say the discussions take place there ; mercifully neither can criticize the other's accent.

Don't get humpy with L. B. ; it is part of his nature to do odd things and he will never be otherwise. I can imagine him walking out of Heaven and saying " This place is run by the Jews." And at heart he is friendly.

Wyntour sent me a tiny silver crucifix to keep off vampires, which up to the present it has done.

USKUB, 20.4.03.

This is the most delightfully outlandish and primitive place I have ever dared to hope for. Rustchuk was elegant and up-to-date in comparison. The only hotel in the place is full; I am in the other. A small ragged boy swooped on my things and marched before me like a pillar of dust, while two blind beggars came behind with suggestions of charitable performances on my part. Then I was walked upstairs and offered the alternative of sharing a bedroom with a Turk or a nicer bedroom with two Turks.

I pleaded a lonely and morose disposition and was at last given a room without carpet, stove, or wardrobe, but also without Turks. The only person on the "hotel" staff that I can converse with is a boy who speaks Bulgarian with a stutter. The country round is "apart"; lovely rolling hills and huge snow-capped mountains, and storks nesting in large communities; everything wild and open and full of life. There are two magpies who seem to have some idea of living in this room with me.

SALONIQUE, 9.5.03.

There is a "Young Turk," if you know what that means, staying in this hotel, very interesting and amusing. He has learnt and forgotten a little English, but the other day in the midst of a political discussion in French he took our breath away by starting off at a great rate "Twinkle, twinkle, little star," and went on with more of it than I had ever heard before. It's a funny world.

There is rather a nice Turkish dish one gets here, a cross between a junket and a cream cheese, eaten with sugar.

In the stampede here the other day when the attempt was made on the Telegraph Office I picked up a tiny kitten that was in danger of being trampled on and put it into a place of safety.

There was a highly-coloured account of our adventure with the piquet in the *Neue Freie Presse.*

This refers to his experience when " held up " as a dynamiter—he sent the following account to the *Morning Post* :

SALONICA RAILWAY STATION,
April 30, 1903.
(MIDNIGHT.)

The reports which reached Uskub on Wednesday night and this morning of sinister doings at Salonica, of attempts to dynamite the line to Constantinople, and of the Ottoman Bank having been blown up, tempered by a cheerful official optimism that parts of the bank were still standing, prompted an immediate move towards the scene of disturbance.

In company with an American newspaper representative, whose last act in Uskub was to snapshot almost the entire Consular Body, which had turned out to see our departure, I started south by the train leaving at two o'clock in the afternoon along a line dotted throughout its length by frequent picquets, patrols, and small camps of railway guards. Before the train, slightly overdue, drew into the dark and apparently deserted terminal station the news was passed along by obviously demoralized officials that the town was in a state of siege, and that no one could be allowed to leave the station that night.

The first duty of a correspondent is to correspond, and a town in the throes of a revolutionary outbreak seemed to offer more attractions than a railway station tenanted with herded humans.

In the hope of slipping out by a side exit we therefore picked up our valises and made for an apparent outlet some five hundred yards distant across a waste of inconveniently overgrown grass. As a slight precaution against being mistaken for prowling Komitniki we turned down the collars of our overcoats so as to display the white collar, if not of a blameless life, at least of a business that did not call for concealment.

About four hundred yards of the distance had been covered when a frantic challenge in Turkish brought us to a standstill, and five armed and agitated figures sprang forward in the starlight and began to interrogate us at a distance, which they seemed disinclined to lessen. As five triggers had clicked and five rifles were covering us we dropped our valises and " up-handed," but without reassuring our questioners, who seemed to be possessed of a panic which might more reasonably have been displayed on our part.

Neither of us knew a word of Turkish, and Bulgarian was obviously unsuited to the occasion. Never in my study of that tongue have its words come so readily and persistently to my lips, and every French sentence I began became entangled with the phraseology of the debarred language.

The men had reached a point whence they were unwilling to approach nearer, and for a minute or two they took deliberate aim from a ridiculously easy range in a state of excitement which was unpleasant to witness from our end of the barrels.

At last two lowered their rifles, and after stalking round us with elaborate caution managed to secure our hands with a rope or sash-cord, which was hurriedly produced from somewhere. The operation would have been shorter if they had not tried to hold their rifles at our heads at the same time. When it was safely accomplished the statement that I was " Inglesi effendi " and the demand for our Consuls allayed their suspicions to a certain extent, but nothing would induce them to pick up my valise until the light of day should show its real nature, and it is still lying out on the waste land, where, if it explodes violently, no great harm will be done.

Arrived at the railway waiting-room, where the accumulation of apparently several trainloads was gathered in philosophic discomfort, the horrified officials flocked to release us with a haste which made the untying process almost as long as the binding.

The explanations on both sides had to be accepted for the moment, and two loud explosions in the distance made us feel that we had gained our security none too soon.

According to the information, doubtless panic-coloured, which was given us in nervous scraps by non-Turkish railway officials, the town is in a condition which makes it dangerous to venture into the streets, the Ottoman Bank is in ruins, the Colombo and other hotels have been damaged by bombs, and many persons have been killed and wounded.

The exits of the station are closed until daylight. On my asking the members of the picquet why they had not fired they answered that they had only hesitated on seeing our collars, which made them doubt if we were Bulgarian desperadoes.

In the spring of 1904 he was in Warsaw, corresponding for the *Morning Post*. His experiences with young men in Poland and Russia were always the same —he could not get them to be energetic.

WARSAW, 19.6.04.

The American Consul has a schoolboy nephew staying with him, who goes to swimbath every day with me, and afterwards we play tennis, he, I, Consul and an Irish girl. Poles of my own age are pleasant enough, but it is impossible to get them to do anything ; on the most scorching days nothing will induce them to join my amphibious afternoons in the Vistula ; they agree to come, with every sign of nervous depression, but return presently beaming to say they have remembered they have got a cold and it would be dangerous, etc. . . .

P.S.—A 14 year old Polish kid belonging to the house has constituted himself my valet and carries on my toilet every day with extreme minuteness, besides doing most of my shopping. On a hot day I can thoroughly recommend a syphon of soda-water turned on between the shoulder-blades.

1.8.04.

The amateur valet continues to be amusing. Nearly all the time I have known him he has gone every night to sleep at his aunt's house on the other side of the river, in consequence of a row with his mother. I asked him when matters were going to be smoothed over between him and his hen parent and he said he didn't intend to be reconciled, he only got tea in the morning at home, while at his aunt's house there was always chocolate. After that I realized that the matter was beyond even the healing touch of time ; what is home and a mother where no chocolate is ?

" I have got some more coins, old Russian, Polish, Bohemian, etc., going back to 1300, from a man here who has an immense collection. I fairly took his breath away when he started on mediæval history, as he found I knew rather more about the old lines of east-European princes than he did, and an English-man is expected to be profoundly ignorant of such things.

Have you thought of getting a wolf instead of a hound ? There would be no license to pay and at first it could feed largely on the smaller Inktons, with biscuits sometimes for a change. You would have to train it to distinguish the small Vernon boys from other edible sorts, or else Cook would be coming with trembling lip nigh upon breakfast-time to say there was no milk in the house. Also you and Aunt Tom could do marketing in comfort. Think it over.

The poorer people here have nice feudal ways and kiss your hand on the least provocation. The Russian officers, whatever their private sentiments may be, have not the atrocious manners of the Prussians, which I believe cannot be matched anywhere in Europe. . . . I heard from T— ; I had mentioned to her that I had had enough of bad news this year, which I have in one way and another, and she observes that she didn't know that I had experienced misfortune of any sort lately. I suppose it is impossible for her to realize what the loss of that little dog means to you and me. I keep dreaming that he is found, and then comes the waking disappointment. Of course it's worse for you because he was always with you.

In 1904 "Reginald" was published, having first appeared in the *Westminster Gazette*. The characters in the various stories are all imaginary. Reginald is a type composed of several young men, studied during his years of town life ; Hector told me that more than one of his acquaintances considered himself the original. Some friends wrote him that the identity of the duchess had been established. He wrote me from Petersburg :

Thanks for your letter and the cuttings. The *Athenæum* consoled me for Aunt Tom's remark that it was a pity the book had been published as, after the " Alice," people would expect it to be clever and of course be disappointed. The " of course " was terribly crushing but I am able to sit up now and take a little light nourishment.

He was settled in Petersburg in the autumn and had a delightful two years there. I joined him in the winter : with the exception of Davos it was the most perfect time abroad we had ever had together. He always lunched at the Hôtel de France, which was quite a club for journalists ; the food was good, and there were generally interesting people to be met there ; moreover, being close to the Nevsky Prospekt, it was the hub of Petersburg.

It was to be a very exciting place for us, the day of Father Gapon's attempt, with his legion of followers, to reach the Winter Palace to present his petition to the Tsar. Knowing that there was likely to be trouble, Hector settled that we must go early to the Hôtel de

France that Sunday, which by its close proximity to the Palace was the best centre from which to watch events. We were joined at the hotel by a Polish friend and lunched quickly.

Hector and the Pole then went out to scout, leaving me in the smoking-room to watch the street and the archway leading to the Winter Palace.

They soon returned at a trot with a lot of others, troops being in possession of the Palace Square, allowing no one to enter it. The Nevsky Prospekt at this time (between one and two) was the favourite promenade of Russians, as Church Parade in Hyde Park is with us.

The crowds were curious to see what was going on in the Square, but soon came scampering back, being driven by Cossacks, who were using their whips freely. A second time they tried, and this time the Cossacks charged them with drawn swords. Hector and the Pole had gone out by another exit to the Moïka Embankment, and a page presently came to fetch me to them. Here we waited for something to happen. Meanwhile the troops in the Palace Square had fired on the deputation arriving by the bridge, and here there was great slaughter.

Thinking nothing would happen on our side of the hotel, I went in, and immediately soldiers arrived on the scene and fired three volleys. Hector and his friend pressed themselves flat against a doorway ; a bullet whizzed past Hector's head and lodged a foot off in the wall.

By 2.50 the Palace Square was cleared of people and the corpses and wounded were being collected. As Hector had to get all the information he could, he took a sleigh to go to another part of the city where the fighting was reported to be severe. He got his news, wired to the *Post* and returned to take me to another hotel, where we dined with one of Reuter's men, who appeared to think the Revolution had begun.

The next two days were very exciting, the Cossacks were doing some killing on their own account, and murdered some unfortunate students merely because they had called out insults to them. They were an evil-looking lot, pronounced Mongolian type, with criminal faces. Hector scowled so at them as they passed, we being in a sleigh going slowly along rather empty streets, that I hurriedly tried to draw his attention to something on the opposite side of the road, seeing that they were scowling worse at us.

For two nights we had to get back to the flat before dark because the electricians had struck and the lampless streets were not safe. Hector went out to forage and had to run the hardest he knew in one street, an officer shouting that his men would shoot anyone remaining in that street in two minutes' time. (Fact was, all Petersburg had nerves at that time.) He returned with eggs, sweet biscuits, smoked tongue and Bessarabian wine, snatching them up just as the shops, in a panic, were closing. Better dinner have I never tasted, with excitement as a sauce.

Hardly had we finished our meal when excited Russians, friends of Hector's, dashed in and gave us the news of the latest Cossack atrocities, pacing up and down the room all the time. It was more exciting than any play. On the second evening, after telling us harrowing tales of searching hospitals for his friend, whom at last he found dead, one Russian calmly invited us to go to the opera with him that night! It was such a jump from horrors to frivolity that I could hardly keep grave, especially as Hector was making signs to me, behind the man's back, to refuse.

Hector was the only foreign correspondent whom General Trépoff, Governor of Petersburg, did not send for. The others had given to their papers very high figures for the casualties, and Hector, from information supplied by his spies, put the number of dead at about 1500.

When the excitement had simmered down we did a lot of sight-seeing, and tried to " do " the Winter Palace in one afternoon, but it was too vast. The evening generally saw us at the telegraph office where Hector sent off his report and where we met the other journalists doing the same thing. We both noticed the extraordinary slackness and inertia of Russian men and boys of all classes. This is Hector's impression of men in Russian towns :

ST. PETERSBURG,
August 29, 1905.

The inquiry which has been going on in the columns of the *Morning Post* into the existence and causes of physical deterioration might be extended if Russia were brought within the scope of the discussion to a study of physical stagnation in the life of a nation. Such a study would open out interesting speculations as to the political consequences which such stagnation is likely to have on the immediate future of the race in question.

One of the most striking discoveries which one makes in the course of a residence in this country is the all-prevailing inertia of the stalwart and seemingly lusty Russian race, an inertia that appears to be common to all classes, and to spring from no particular

64

accident of circumstance, unless the long Russian winter can be held partly responsible. I have before alluded to the impression of convalescents out for an airing produced by the heavily overcoated, aimlessly lounging soldiers and sailors off duty in the streets of the capital ; the officers, in spite of their brilliant and imposing uniforms, do not succeed much better in imparting a tone of dash and vigour to their surroundings.

A young officer stationed in a town drives from his quarters to his club, from his club to his restaurant, back to his club and so forth, and that represents about the sum of his non-professional exertions ; by driving it must not be supposed that he climbs into a high dogcart and steers a spirited pony through the streets. If he possesses a private carriage it takes the form of a roomy, well-cushioned brougham or victoria drawn by a pair of heavy, long-maned, flowing-tailed horses and driven by a fat, bearded coachman swathed in thick quilted garments into the semblance of a huge human sack. In this conveyance he takes the air if the weather should be sufficiently tempting. The daily routine of an old lady at Bath with a taste for cards would not be very widely different, except that she would perhaps go less often to church and never to parade or café chantant.

Brave, charming, and good-natured as the Russian officer is universally acknowledged to be by those who know him, he has certainly no compelling impulse towards the recreations of saddle and greensward, and one contrasts wonderingly the unceasing outdoor programme of an Indian military station under the enervating influence of a tropical atmosphere. One senior officer, probably not of Russian stock, may be seen at times taking horse exercise in the streets of St.

Petersburg, and I believe that a letter addressed to this city, "to the General who rides," would find him without difficulty.

With the younger generation of the military caste it is the same story. In the spacious grounds attached to one of the cadet headquarters in St. Petersburg one may find on a late summer evening the youths of the British and German colonies vigorously engaged in football practice or in the milder activities of lawn tennis, while the cadets walk sedately along the gravel paths or find an outlet for their superfluous energies in the game of gorodki, somewhat resembling ninepins.

In civilian walks of life the same stagnation has universal sway ; among peasant agriculturists in the country districts and among certain classes of townsfolk there are of course seasons and occasions when energy is a matter of necessity, but when that compulsion of circumstance is removed or non-existent the Russian relapses naturally into an atmosphere of congenial torpidity.

In every Russian town of any size there are thousands or hundreds of well-built, healthy-looking men, ranging from eighteen years upwards, but mostly in the prime of early manhood, who occupy the posts of door-keepers and yard-keepers, and whose most laborious functions consist of a little sweeping and wood-chopping, an occasional errand, and sometimes escorting an over-drunken wayfarer to his destination. For the rest of their time they sleep, or gossip by the hour over sweetened concoctions of weak tea, or play mild baby games with their children or any friendly dog or kitten that comes their way. And in their peaked caps, gay shirts, and high Blücher boots, they convey the impression of a sort of Prætorian Guard in undress.

Probably the custom of dressing nearly every male civilian, from small errand-boys to postmen and such minor officials, in high military boots is responsible for many of our earliest notions of the Russians as a stern, truculent warrior breed. An army, it has been said, marches on its stomach ; the Russians for several generations have lived on their boots. If an average British boy were put at an early age into such boots he would become a swashbuckling terror to his family and neighbourhood, and in due course would rove abroad and found an Empire, or at any rate die of a tropical disease. A Russian would not feel impelled by the same influence further than the nearest summer garden.

Hector had a very good little servant at his rooms, but after I left there was a change, and a girl arrived who helped herself to food. Hector and a friend who was chumming with him then noticed that mince-pies were irresistible to her, so one day they opened those that were left over and put mustard underneath the mince-meat. After that nothing was touched, and everything was understood !

From Petersburg Hector went to Paris, in 1906, found himself an *appartement*, and sought for an original servant. One after another he inspected at a Registry Office—all were correct and probably excellent, but not original. At last one offered who gave the desired impression, one Marcellin, and an invaluable valet he proved, with a taste for cooking and an imperturbable temper. Hector attended the French Chamber a good deal and suffered from the closeness of the atmosphere ; this probably gave him an attack of " intermittent something, which people insist is influenza, all the symptoms being absent; it might as well be snake-bite."

In addition to writing for the *Morning Post* he wrote some articles in French for a French paper, but not regularly, I think. He had an amusing time in Paris, made many friends (he had a gift for friendship), and having an intelligent interest in food, the only one of our family so gifted, appreciated the restaurants there. But not all the American tourists whom he met had the same appreciation. I think they were chiefly people from *very* country parts. " I seem fated," he wrote once, " to learn the inmost yearnings of American stomachs ; was dining at Constan's one night when an elderly American lady was leaving the restaurant after her dinner, and informing the busy manager in a high scream which grew higher and higher as she neared the door : ' I like *roast lamb*. My sister likes *roast lamb*. At the Grand hô-tel Godknowswhere we had some roast lamb that was *real good*. Yes, we both like *roast lamb*.' Then the Roumanian orchestra struck up, so I never knew what her little son's feelings were towards roast lamb."

My father became very ill in May, 1907, and we wired for Hector. The incident in " The Unbearable Bassington " of the little black dog happened to himself. He was playing bridge at a friend's flat and saw the dog, which only appeared to people when bad news was on the way to them. So far he had only heard that my father was ill, the next morning he got the wire to come home, and arrived two days before he died.

A very close friendship existed between the two. Hector told me afterwards that writing for the papers had lost much of its incentive since he had lost his most appreciative reader (my father).

Later in the summer he invited me to stay with him in Normandy. We lit upon Pourville because it was small and unfashionable (I don't know what it is like now) and picturesque.

We settled ourselves at a newly-opened little hotel whose landlady possessed a temperament. Hector chose the hotel; he had an unerring instinct for a place a little out of the ordinary. Next door to our caravanserai was a post-office which sold odds and ends as well as stamps. Choosing some picture post-cards one day I asked how much they were and was answered from behind the counter by Hector, who sold them to me, and some stamps to another customer, suggesting further outlay on his part on various goods, the owner looking on and beaming.

We bathed in the mornings, explored the country-side in the afternoons and sometimes watched the play at the Casino in the evenings, studying types all the time. The place, Pourville, was thick with types; one of them was the original of " The Soul of Laploshka," in " Reginald in Russia." We found he had a reputation for meanness, and in the fullness of time Hector played a hoax on him; if there were a crime on which he had no pity it was meanness, and this man had apparently plenty of money, so there was no shadow of excuse for him.

In September Hector returned to Paris, and next year, 1908, was settled in London. He bought a charming cottage on the Surrey Hills, where I was his tenant; as it was only twenty-three miles from London he could come down whenever he liked. With Logie, my Dandy, and Ho, the black Persian, and a garden that we planned and made ourselves, we had the most delightful home.

In this garden was a bed planted with May-flowering tulips ; we were both of us tulip mad. One night at supper I set fire to the lamp by swinging it to release the oil.

We stood gazing at the flames, wondering what to do.

" Earth is the best thing," said Hector, and dashed into the garden.

A friend, supping with us, who had more sense than either of us, seized the hearth-rug and extinguished the lamp under it. When Hector at last appeared I said to him, " You've been a long time fetching that earth."

" Well," he said, " the tulip bed came first, and of course I couldn't disturb *that*, so I had to go farther on to the cabbage plot."

One summer we had rather a sunless period and I was deploring the effect on the garden. " We will invoke Apollo's aid to-night, round a bonfire," said Hector.

So, with a guest who was with us, we draped sheets round us to look more Grecian and therefore more pleasing to Apollo, while we craved the boon of sunshine. The next day there was a brilliant sun and every day after for three weeks.

In London Hector lived at 97 Mortimer Street, where he did all his writing, and spent his evenings chiefly at his club, the " Cocoa Tree," playing Bridge.

In the summer of 1909, I think it was, the Russian dancers, Nijinsky Karsarvina, and the others, first came to London. Hector and his friend of Petersburg days, Mr. Reynolds, gave an " At Home " at a friend's studio, " to meet the dancers." No one to be invited who could not speak French, that being the only foreign language the Russians understood.

It was a *succès fou*, sixty people turned up eager to meet the novelties. The Russians up to that time had been nowhere and were delighted at their first glimpse of English social life and also at being greeted in Russian by their hosts.

I found Nijinsky and another man peering eagerly under a table.

" What is it ? " I asked.

" C'est le diable," cried Nijinsky, and out walked an Aberdeen terrier.

He had never seen the breed before from the way he gazed at it. He told me he was surprised not to see bulldogs about. " In Russia we heard that every Englishman walks out accompanied by a bulldog."

We finished that day, a few of us, by dining at the " Gourmets," beloved of Hector and myself. We always dined at some Italian restaurant, because I liked the food, but the " Gourmets " was our favourite. An air of gaiety met us at the door and an air of gaiety we took in with us. It is haunted ground for me now and I never go there. The Café Royal was another favourite place—generally we wound up there. And one New Year's Eve we had hilarious revels with some friends at Gambrinus, dancing afterwards. Hector had thoughtfully provided himself with one of those toys, new at that time, which imitate a dog growling. I think ours *must* have been the liveliest table !

" Foreigners must be puzzled by all this," said he ; " I'm sure they never make as much noise themselves."

It was on another New Year's Eve that, meeting a party of strangers, he insisted on seizing hands and dancing " Here we go round the mulberry bush " in

Oxford Circus. He could throw himself into whatever he was doing at the moment as though no other kind of life existed ; this characteristic he certainly inherited from his mother's family, whose vitality and youngness were uncommon.

Tapestry painting he was very keen on ; he painted a large canvas when staying with me, " A Boar-hunt in the Middle Ages " ; the background looked exactly as though it were faded needlework. But he did a much better one, which when I saw it for the first time I took for an old French tapestry he had bought in Paris which I had never seen. I wish I knew where it is now ; he lent it to a friend who died, and of course his people did not know the ownership of the tapestry and probably gave it away.

In going over Hector's papers I came across a pencilled fragment on " the Garden of Eden." Eve is depicted as a very stubborn, even mule-like character. The serpent simply cannot get her to eat the forbidden fruit. She does not see that any good will come of it, and she is placidly happy in her limited knowledge.

" The Serpent elaborated all the arguments and inducements that he had already brought forward, and improvised some new ones, but Eve's reply was unfailingly the same. Her mind was made up. The Serpent gave a final petulant wriggle of its coils and slid out of the landscape with an unmistakable air of displeasure.

" ' You haven't tasted the Forbidden Fruit. I suppose ? ' said a pleasant but rather anxious voice at Eve's shoulder a few minutes later. It was one of the Archangels who was speaking.

" ' No,' said Eve placidly, ' Adam and I went into

the matter very thoroughly last night and we came to the conclusion that we should be rather ill-advised in eating the fruit of that tree ; after all, there are heaps of other trees and vegetables for us to feed on.'

" ' Of course it does great credit to your sense of obedience,' said the Archangel, with an entire lack of enthusiasm in his voice, ' but it will cause considerable disappointment in some quarters. There was an idea going about that you might be persuaded by specious arguments into tasting the Forbidden Fruit.'

" ' There *was* a Serpent here speaking about it the last few days,' said Eve ; ' he seemed rather huffed that we didn't follow his advice, but Adam and I went into the whole matter last night and we came to t——'

" ' Yes, yes,' said the Archangel in an embarrassed voice, ' a very praiseworthy decision, of course. At the same time, well, it's not exactly what every one anticipated. You see Sin has got to come into the world, somehow.'

" ' Yes ? ' said Eve, without any marked show of interest.

" ' And you are practically the only people who *can* introduce it.'

" ' I don't know anything about that,' said Eve placidly ; ' Adam and I have got to think of our own interests. We went very thoroughly——'

" ' You see,' said the Archangel, ' the most elaborate arrangements have been foreordained on the assumption that you *would* yield to temptation. No end of pictures of the Fall of Man are destined to be painted and a poet is going one day to write an immortal poem called " Paradise L——" ' '

73

" ' Called what ? ' asked Eve as the Archangel suddenly pulled himself up.

" ' " Paradise Life." It's all about you and Adam eating the Forbidden Fruit. If you don't eat it I don't see how the poem can possibly be written."

Eve is still dogged—says she has no appetite for more fruit.

" ' I had some figs and plantains and half a dozen medlars early this morning, and mulberries and a few mangosteens in the middle of to-day, and last night Adam and I feasted to repletion on young asparagus and parsley-tops with a sauce of pomegranate juice ; and yesterday norning——'

" ' I must be going,' said the Archangel, adding rather sulkily, ' if I should see the Serpent would it be any use telling him to look round again——? '

" ' Not in the least,' said Eve. Her mind was made up.

.   .   .   .

" ' The trouble is,' said the Archangel as he folded his wings in a serener atmosphere and recounted his Eden experiences, ' there is too great a profusion of fruit in that garden ; there isn't enough temptation to hunger after one special kind. Now if there was a partial crop failure——' The idea was acted on. Blight, mildew and caterpillars and untimely frosts worked havoc among trees and bushes and herbs ; the plantains withered, the asparagus never sprouted, the pineapples never ripened, radishes were worm-eaten before they were big enough to pick. The Tree of Knowledge alone flaunted itself in undiminished luxuriance.

" ' We shall have to eat it after all,' said Adam,

74

who had breakfasted sparsely on some mouldy tamarinds
and the rind of yesterday's melon.

" ' We were told not to, and we're not going to,'
said Eve stubbornly. Her mind was made up on the
point——"

How she eventually succumbed I don't know.
Hector had a special detestation for this type of character, stubborn, placid, unimaginative, like the awful,
good child in " The Story Teller," who is from life,
though we never knew her as a child. We tried to
change her by playing a few hoaxes off on her——but she
had been in the mould too long.

In the summers Hector and I tried various out-of-
the-way seaside places, and in one very hot spell we
bathed in what he considered an ideal way——we spent
the day in the sea with intervals on land, Logie guarding
our clothes and food-basket.

Charlie was at this time with his wife and child
in Dublin, where he was Governor of Mountjoy
Prison, having left the Burma Police service ; though
stronger than Hector, the climate rather told on him.
Hector and I spent Christmas with them one year
and next summer we were all together again on the
Donegal coast at Innishowen, where, the house
being just on the sea, he had as much bathing as he
wanted. In London, swimming-baths helped to keep
him fit.

All this time he was writing sketches for the *Morning
Post*, the *Bystander* and the *Westminster Gazette*, and
some political sketches, illustrated by " Pat," for the
Daily Express.

In 1910 " Reginald in Russia " was published, a
further collection of Reginald's doings ; " Judkin of the

Parcels " and " The Soul of Laploshka " are from characters he knew.

In 1912 " The Chronicles of Clovis " appeared, Clovis being an irrepressible young man, something after the style of " Reginald," and this year he wrote his first novel, " The Unbearable Bassington." The chief character is taken from life, but the original, so far, has not had a tragic ending ; many of the other characters are also real people, in fact some of the reviews kindly gave clues as to the originals.

There is, as Mr. Reynolds said in his Memoir to " The Toys of Peace," a little bit of autobiography in the account of the loneliness Comus felt when exiled to Africa. Opinion varied very much about the book—one friend, whom Hector asked for a candid opinion, said it was unbalanced, this Hector rather thought himself. The Press was pretty unanimously enthusiastic, the *Observer* calling it " one of the wittiest books, not only of the year but of the decade," and another paper pronounced it " clever to distraction."

" Beasts and Super-Beasts," another collection of short stories, was published in 1914, and late in 1913, " When William Came." Hector wrote part of it while staying with me near Rye, and in order to get absolute quiet spent hours writing in a wood near, while Logie hunted rabbits.

Many of the characters in that too are from life— one of them, the most sympathetic, the lady of Torywood, being that of a well-known London Conservative hostess, for whom Hector had a great admiration. Lord Roberts wrote him a most appreciative note, which pleased him tremendously.

The story is an account of the conditions of English

life after a successful invasion by the Germans. Two
women friends, to whom I lent it during the war,
got as far as the middle and dared not finish it, they
were more than half afraid that William might come.

Hector chose the name " Saki " from the cup-
bearer in the " Rubáiyát " of Omar Khayyám.

> " Yon rising Moon that looks for us again—
> How oft hereafter will she wax and wane ;
> How oft hereafter rising look for us
> Through this same Garden—and for *one* in vain !
> And when like her, oh Sákí, you shall pass
> Among the Guests Star-scatter'd on the Grass,
> And in your joyous errand reach the spot
> Where I made One—turn down an empty Glass ! "

He loved Persian poetry and Eastern stories ;
Flecker's " The Golden Journey to Samarkand " was
an especial favourite.

For one who knew him only through his books
Mr. S. P. B. Mais has an uncanny insight into his
character. He wrote of him : " Munro's under-
standing of children can only be explained by the fact
that he was in many ways a child himself : his sketches
betray a harshness, a love of practical jokes, a craze for
animals of the most exotic breeds, a lack of mellow
geniality that hint very strongly at the child in the
man. Manhood has but placed in his hands a perfect
sense of irony and withheld all other adult traits.

" In ' The Mappined Life ' we get for the first
time near to the secret of a genius who did not unlock
his heart. Here at last, behind the child, the buffoon,
the satirist, the eclectic, the aristocrat, the elegant man
of the world, we can trace the features of one who
discovered that the only way to make life bearable was
to laugh at it.

" Meredith would have acclaimed him as a true master of the Comic : posterity will acknowledge him as one of our great writers."

But a friend of Hector's, a man who knew him well, summed him up best of all, I think, in the following words : " The elusive charm of the man-in-himself—this charm, being the perfume of personality, was even more subtly, strongly felt in his conversation than in anything he ever wrote. We who loved him as the kindliest of companions who was utterly incapable of boring a fellow-creature—man or dog or woman or cat or child of any age you like—always felt the keen sense of honour and strength of purpose and stark simplicity which were his essential qualities. As a companion he was an unfailing antidote to boredom. He loved to make an impracticable jest practical in action. On the way to a mixed dinner we rehearsed an elaborate quarrel which was to lead, by nice gradations of invective, to threats of personal violence. Saki worked out the idea with a sure sense of the theatre, and the crisis came (just before the arrival of the port) when another Scot—the kind who develops a " mither " in moments of exaltation—had his hand on my shoulder, and was imploring me not to mind what Saki said, for he didn't mean it. He didn't."

In the spring of 1914 he was writing " Potted Parliament " for the *Outlook*, and attended the House regularly for his data. These are some of his characteristic remarks :

" An army moves at the rate of its slowest unit, it is the fate of a Coalition to move at the rate of its most headlong section."

" Mr. Lloyd George expressed unstinted approval of his various taxation schemes ; the spectacle of the

Chancellor of the Exchequer approving of all his works is almost as familiar as the companion picture of the Chancellor of the Exchequer finding words to express his loathing of the private lives and family histories of his opponents."

" The member for North Carnarvonshire always gives me the impression of one who in his long-ago youth heard the question-half of a very good riddle, and has spent the remainder of his life in the earnest expectation of hearing some one disclose the answer. Even when such politely wearisome speakers as Reginald McKenna are in possession of the House one can see Mr. William Jones, with a happy smile of strained expectancy on his face, listening intently to every syllable that falls from the orator's lips ; one of these days, one feels sure, he will give a wild scream of joy and rush away to apply for the Chiltern Hundreds, with his life's desire at last achieved."

" The Scotsman is sometimes accused of being ' slow in the uptake ' ; he likes to enjoy the full flavour of a joke before he chuckles at it ; the ' bubble-and-squeak ' brigade on the Ministerial benches like to giggle before they have heard the point—and with regard to some of their own humour there is a good deal to be said for the arrangement."

" Conversations and suggestions with regard to the Amending Bill are supposed to be welcome in Ministerial circles at the present moment. There is one suggestion that has occurred to me that seems so eminently practical that I know it will have no chance of being considered. The Protestants of the North of Ireland regard the prospect of being governed by a Nationalist Parliament with a horror and alarm that is admitted to be genuine ; on the other hand, the members representing Protestant Wales have again and again, by an overwhelming vote, recorded their opinion that a Nationalist Parliament would be a tolerant, fair-minded, pleasant, peaceful, and sweetly reasonable body, from which no safeguards need be exacted, and from which no oppression need be apprehended. The Welsh members and their constituents seem as firmly rooted in their championship of a Dublin Parliament as the Ulster Protestants are resolute in their opposition to it. Therefore why not exclude Ulster and include Wales in a Hiberno-Cambrian Parliament. . . . The Nationalists have not been able to win Ulster, but they have always been able to win Wales."

" The political situation has lost none of its gravity, but the House of Commons has lost touch with the political situation. In the House of Lords, which is not at present sitting, a measure is to be introduced on which the hopes and fears of the peacemakers are centred. Lord Haldane announces that he knows the details of this measure, and that therefore his lips are sealed ; everybody else's lips are sealed for a precisely opposite reason. . . ."

" The Home Rule Amending Bill passed its third reading in the Upper House. Crewe was dignified, correct, and dispassionate, suggesting to one's mind an archangel who regarded the Creation of the World as a risky and unnecessary experiment but had no intention of saying so. . . ."

" One of the most exasperating features of the House of Commons is its resemblance to an over-crowded kitchen-range. Pots that are at boiling-point have to be set aside to simmer while others take their place."

The next " Potted Parliament " is the last he wrote.

Monday, *August* 3, 1914.

For one memorable and uncomfortable hour the House of Commons had the attention of the nation and most of the world concentrated on it. Grey's speech, when one looked back at it, was a statesman-like utterance, delivered in excellent manner, dignified and convincing. To sit listening to it, in uncertainty for a long time as to what line of policy it was going to announce, with all the accumulated doubts and suspicions of the previous forty-eight hours heavy on one's mind, was an experience that one would not care to repeat often in a lifetime. Men who read it as it was spelled out jerkily on the tape-machines, letter by letter, told me that the strain of uncertainty was even more cruel ; and I can well believe it. When the actual tenor of the speech became clear, and one knew beyond a doubt where we stood, there was only room for one feeling ; the miserable tension of the past two days had been removed, and one discovered that one was slowly recapturing the lost sensation of being in a good temper. Redmond's speech was the dramatic success of the occasion ; it obviously isolated the action of the Labour members and the few, but insistent, Radicals who were clamorous against the war, but one hardly realized at the moment with what feelings of dismay and discouragement it would be read in Berlin.

Of the men who rose in melancholy succession to counsel a standing aloof from the war, a desertion of France, a humble submission to the will of Potsdam in the matter of Belgium's neutrality, one wishes to speak fairly. Many of them are men who have gloatingly threatened us with class warfare in this country —warfare in which rifles and machine-guns should be used to settle industrial disputes ; they have seemed to take a ghoulish pleasure in predicting a not-far-distant moment when Britons shall range themselves in organized combat, not against an aggressive foreign enemy, but against their own kith and kin. Never have they been more fluent with these hints and incitements than during the present Session ; if a crop of violent armed outbreaks does not spring up one of these days in this country it will not be for lack of sowing of seed. Now these men read us moral lectures on the wickedness of war. One is sometimes assured that every man has at least two sides to his character ; so one may charitably assume that an honest Quaker-like detestation of war and bloodshed is really the motive which influences at the present moment some of these men who have harped so assiduously on the idea—one might almost say the ideal—of armed collision between the classes. There are other men in the anti-war party who seem to be obsessed with the idea of snatching commercial advantages out of the situation, regardless of other considerations which usually influence men of honour. The Triple Entente, after all, is no new thing ; even if the nature of its obligations was not clearly defined or well understood, at least it was perfectly well known that there were obligations ; it was perfectly well known that the people of the other countries involved in its scope believed that there were obligations—at the very least a sentimental sympathy. And this is how the *Daily News* writes of our possible and desirable action at this crisis :

" If we remained neutral we should be, from the

commercial point of view, in precisely the same
position as the United States. We should be able
to trade with all the belligerents (so far as the
war allows of trade with them); we should be
able to capture the bulk of their trade in neutral
markets."

There seems to be some confusion of mind in these
circles of political thought between a nation of shop-
keepers and a nation of shoplifters.

If these men are on the side of the angels, may I
always have a smell of brimstone about me.

Hector wired to me when war was declared;
his next wire, " Enrolled," is the most exciting and
delightful I have ever received. The account of
his early days as a Tommy at Shepherd's Bush is
given by a comrade of his, at the end of this biography. Hector told a friend that, having written
" When William Came," he ought to go half-way
to meet him.

Once in training he had very little time for writing :
the following is from Horsham.

29th Nov., 14.

MY DEAR ETHEL,
   The Board of Education is now taking over
the teaching arrangements for the troops, and from
next week onwards I shall have to teach 4 hours a
week. Of course the Board wanted us to *begin* by
teaching German grammar, but the other fellows
and myself flatly refused, pointing out that a class of
tired men simply wouldn't listen to a lot of dry rules
about an unknown language. . . . Lady C. sent me
two dictionaries and her mother has sent me a lovely

lot of chocolates and acid drops which I am distribut-
ing among the men, especially some of the poorer
ones who can't afford much.   It makes an enormous
difference when one is marching to have something
in one's mouth to suck.   We did about 23 miles on
Thursday, most of it at a very quick rate and a lot of
it over difficult ground, and I was glad to find I was
not stiff or tired next day. . . .   Do you remember
Capt. C. of B.T. ?   He has written to ask me if I
would like a commission in the Argyll and Sutherland
Highlanders ; he is Major in the —th Battalion. . . .
I would not accept it, as I should have so much to
learn that it would be a case of beginning all over
again and I might never see service at all.   The
3½ months' training that I have had will fit me to
be a useful infantry soldier and I should be a very
indifferent officer.   Still it is nice to have had the
offer."

In January 1915 Hector and I had to hurry down
to Barnstaple : Aunt Tom had died suddenly of a
stroke.
    It was a frightfully sad time, especially for
Hector. Although exasperating, she had a tremendous love for him and he felt the loss of so virile a
character.
    He only had a few days' leave and had to hurry
back to Horsham.

A. COMPANY,
22nd BATTALION, ROYAL FUSILIERS,

Mar. 5th, 15.   HORSHAM, SUSSEX.

MY DEAR ETHEL,
    We have been here for eight days and most of us

84

find the life very jolly, though of course there are a lot of extra fatigues to be done. Yesterday I was hut orderly (there are 30 of us in a hut) and I found that drawing rations, cleaning the hut, washing plates, cups, etc., kept me busy from a quarter to 6 a.m. till 5.30 p.m. with hasty intervals for meals. We have a good deal of fun, with skirmishing raids at night with neighbouring huts, and friendly games of footer ; it is like being boy and man at the same time. All the same I wish we could count on going away soon ; it is a poor game to be waiting when others are bearing the brunt and tasting the excitement of real war-fare. . . . I have done 3 days digging in water-logged trenches ; it sounds a formidable job, but I am a good digger and like the work of draining off the water. . . . A youth I know, about 22, in the pink of health as far as I know, wrote asking if I would use my influence with the papers I wrote for to get him an engagement at Daly's or some other London theatre (I don't know how he imagined it was to be done !) as he wanted to study voice-production in Town and it was really rather important. You may imagine the perfectly horrible reply he got.

April 2nd, 15.

. . . We have a lot of fun in our hut and never seem too tired to indulge in sport or ragging ; the work is hard some days but it is not incessant like it was in the K.E.H. I was O.C.'s orderly on a field-day on Wednesday and was jumping brooks and scrambling up slippery banks and through thickets with a pack on my back that I should scarcely have thought myself capable of carrying at all a few months ago, and I came home quite fit.

The following pages contain an account that Hector sent to *The Bystander*, in June, 1915, describing his life as a corporal. It was accompanied by a snapshot of himself in his shirt-sleeves, carrying a bucket, but his expression is so severe and unlike him that I have not included it.

A leading French newspaper a few years ago published an imaginary account of the difficulties experienced by Noah in mobilizing birds and beasts and creeping things for embarkation in the Ark. The arctic animals were the chief embarrassment ; the polar bears persistently ate the seals long before the consignment had reached the rendezvous, and while a fresh supply was being sent for certain South American insects, which only live for a few hours, had to be kept alive by artificial respiration. When everything seemed at length to have been got ready, and the last bale of hay and the last hundredweight of bird-seed had been taken on board, some one asked, with cold reproach, " I suppose you know you've forgotten the Australian animals ? "

The job of Company Orderly Corporal resembles in some respects the labours of Noah ; one can never safely flatter oneself at any given moment that one has got to a temporary end of it. When one has drawn the milk and doled out the margarine, and distributed the letters and parcels, and seen to the whereabouts of migratory tea-pails and flat-pans and paraded defaulters and off-duty men under the cold scrutiny of the canteen sergeant—and disentangled recruits from messes to which they do not belong —and induced unwilling hut-orderlies to saddle themselves with buckets full of unpeeled potatoes which they neither desire nor deserve—and has begun to think that the moment has arrived in which one may indulge in a cigarette and read a letter—then some detestably thoughtful friend will sidle up to one and say, " I suppose you know there's the watercress waiting at the cook-house ? "

There are at least two distinct styles in use by those who hold the office of Company Orderly Corporal. One is to stalk at the head of one's hut-orderlies like a masterful rainproof hen on a wet day, followed by a melancholy string of wish-they-had-never-been-hatched chickens ; the other is to rush about in a demented fashion, as though one had invented the science of modern camp organization and had forgotten most of the details.

There are certain golden rules to be observed by the C.O.C. who wishes to make a success of his job.

Cultivate an indifference to human suffering ; if Heaven intended hut-orderlies to be happy you have received no instructions on the point.

Develop your imagination ; if the officer of the day remarks on the paleness of a joint of meat, hazard the probable explanation that the beast it was cut from was fed on Sicilian clover, which fattens quickly, but gives a pale appearance ; there may be no such thing as Sicilian clover, but one-half of the world believes what the other half invents. At any rate, you will get credit for unusual intelligence.

Be kind to those who live in cook-houses.

It has been said that " great men are lovable for their mistakes " ; do not imagine for a moment that this applies, even in a minor degree, to Company Orderly Corporals. If you make the mistake of forgetting to draw the Company's butter till the Company's tea is over, no one will love you or pretend to love you.

A gifted woman writer has observed "it is an extravagance to do anything that some one else can do better." Be extravagant.

Of all the labours that fall to the lot of C.O.C. the most formidable is the distribution of the post-bag. There are about seven men in every hut who are expecting important letters that never seem to reach them, and there are always individuals who glower at you and tell you that they invariably get a letter from home on Tuesday; by Thursday they are firmly convinced that you have set all their relations against them. There was one young man in Hut 3 whose reproachful looks got on my nerves to such an extent that at last I wrote him a letter from his Aunt Agatha, a letter full of womanly counsel and patient reproof, such as any aunt might have been proud to write. Possibly he hasn't got an Aunt Agatha; anyhow, the reproachful look has been replaced by a puzzled frown.

TIDWORTH CAMP, HANTS.
10.10.15.

MY DEAR E.,

. . . We have been doing field operations this last week, sleeping out under the stars, and luckily having fine weather. The villages we moved through, particularly Amport and Abbot's Ann, are about the most beautiful I have seen anywhere, and the villagers the most friendly, running out to give us basketfuls of apples. There is some prospect of us going to Serbia, which I should like; I told one rather timorous youth that the forests there swarmed with wolves, which came and pounced on men on outpost duty. I do hope it won't be Gallipoli.

TIDWORTH. *Nov. 7th, 15.*

After the long months of preparation and waiting we are at last on the eve of departure and there is a good prospect of our getting away this week. It seems almost too good to be true that I am going to take an active part in a big European war. I fear it will be France, not the Balkans, but there is no knowing where one may find oneself before the war is over; anyhow, I shall keep up my study of the Servian language. I expect at first we shall be billeted in some French town.

It was France, and France all the time of his service. He again was offered a commission, and again refused. One day, so one of his comrades told me, Hector was washing potatoes when a General came along who had last met him in his own house at Bridge.

"What on earth are you doing here, Munro?" he asked, and tried to persuade him to accept another job, a softer one, but also farther from the fighting line. But he was genuinely attached to his comrades, and quite determined to get to close quarters with the Boche.

His letters from the front were chiefly descriptions of things he wanted sent out to him, but he managed to write some sketches for the *Morning Post* and the *Westminster Gazette*, two being in this volume, and " For the Duration of the War" in " The Toys of Peace."

The following are extracts from letters he wrote to me, and one to Charlie (who was trying to get temporarily released from his job of governing Mountjoy Prison, and having a go at the fighting himself; but he did not succeed).

Dec. 19*th*, 15.

MY DEAR ETHEL,

... I came away yesterday to the nearest town for 2 weeks' attendance at a mixed officers' and n.c.o.s' instruction class ; 2 officers, a sergeant and myself, are the only ones from my battalion ; it seems likely to be interesting and I don't suppose I should miss any lively fighting. I had a longish way to march, with all my possessions on my back, my overcoat in addition being twice its normal weight through soaked-in mud, so I was glad enough to get to my billet, especially as I had had very little sleep for the previous 3 or 4 nights. ... At a village where we were quartered for a few days' rest there was a dog in a farmyard, chained always to a kennel without any floor, and only sharp cobble-stones to lie on. I gave it a lot of straw from my own bed allowance, much to the astonishment of the farm-folk.

25.12.15.

Am spending a quaint Christmas in a quaint town. The battalion is in the trenches.

" While Shepherds watched their flocks by night
   All seated on the ground
A high-explosive shell came down
   And mutton rained around."

The above is my adaptation of a Christmas carol. Most things here are at semi-famine prices : the French have been saying all their lives *la vie coûte chère* and now it really does.

Feb. 8, 16.

. . . We are holding a rather hot part of the line and I must say I have enjoyed it better than any we have been in. There is not much dug-out accommodation so I made my bed (consisting of overcoat and waterproof sheet) on the fire-step of the parapet ; on Sunday night, while I was on my round looking up the sentries, a bomb came into the trench, riddled the overcoat and sheet and slightly wounded a man sleeping on the other side of the trench. I assumed that no 2 bombs would fall exactly in the same spot, so remade the bed and had a good sleep. . . . Got some chocolates from Reynolds and his book * with a very charming dedication to myself. . . . A lot of owls come to the trenches ; they must have a good time as there is a large selection of ruined buildings to accommodate them and hordes of mice to prey on.

March 11, 16.

. . . For the moment, in a spasm between trenches, we are in a small village where I have found excellent Burgundy, but we leave this oasis in a few hours. . . . We are having plenty of snow, but my blood must be in very good condition as I go out on night watches without any wrapping up and don't

* " My Slav Friends."

91

feel cold. . . . Our line is so close to the Germans in some places that one can talk to them : one of them called out to me that the war would soon be over, so I said "in about 3 years' time," whereat there was a groan from him and his comrades.

20 May, 16.

. . . We are for the moment in a very picturesque hill-top village, where we have been twice before ; I had a boisterous welcome from elderly farm-wives, yard dogs and other friends. . . . I am in very good health and spirits ; the fun and adventure of the whole thing and the good comradeship of some of one's companions make it jolly, and one attaches an enormous importance to little comforts such as a cup of hot tea at the right moment.

In June 1916 Hector came back on short leave : Charlie and I hurried to London and all three put up at the Richelieu (now Dean) Hotel. It was a breathless time, with friends and relatives coming to see him, theatres, the Academy and shopping. He showed signs of wear and tear, but was in great spirits and was discussing his project of going out to Siberia when the war was over, with a friend and having a little farm there.

"I could never settle down again to the tameness of London life," he told me. This idea appealed strongly to me—I saw myself bringing up the rear with all the things he would find on arrival he ought to have brought and had not. It would have been a remarkable life, wild animals beyond the dreams

92

of avarice, at our very doors, and, before long, inside them.

This delightful time in town passed with lightning swiftness, and the day came for us to see him off at Victoria, Charlie and I and a friend, never thinking it was the last time we should see him. Such an appalling idea never entered my head, nor even that he might be wounded. So we were quite gay ; in any case we should have sent him off in good spirits.

Not being allowed to stand nearer the troop train than the outside edge of the platform, what we had to say had to be shouted. And the last words I called out to him were, " Kill a good few for me ! " I believe he did——he was never, though, to have the satisfaction of a bayonet charge, which was his ambition.

A letter I had from him in July was full of depression because of a " most melancholy post-bag," telling of the death of a friend. " Equally sad was a letter from Lady L——, sending me a pathetic message of greeting from S—— Macnaughtan (the author), who is slowly dying, the doctors giving no hope. Her journey to Russia seems to have overtaxed her strength and she never would spare herself. . . . Three men of my section were hit by a shell yesterday, and one, a dear, faithful, illiterate old sort, who used to make tea for me and do other little services, was killed outright, so I am not feeling at my gayest, but luckily there is a good deal to take the mind off unhappy things."

In September he was promoted to Lance-Sergeant, and late in the month was down with malaria. He wrote to Charlie from hospital, full of impatience at being laid up, and feeling very lonely among strangers.

" I keep thinking of the boys all the time : when one is sharing dangers they don't seem big, but when one is in safety and the others in the front line all sorts of catastrophes seem possible and probable."

The following account is from a comrade in the 22nd Royal Fusiliers who was with him through all his training, and service in France, Mr. W. R. Spikesman :

Saki's humour, wit and gift of satire, never malicious, are well known to his readers of " Reginald," " Bassington " and " When William Came," etc., but the generosity and sincerity of purpose only probably imagined by a few outside those who knew him personally.

Of his country and his service to his country there can be no doubt of his sincerity, as he was one of the first to enlist ; despite the age limit ; which recalls August 2nd, 1914, a Saturday night. We had spent the afternoon swimming at baths ; tea, a walk in the Green Park ; these places were often visited by him ; then after dinner a short visit to the Cocoa Tree Club. On leaving his Club we passed the Geographical Society's Club, where a dinner or an address was being given in honour of Sir E. Shackleton, who was then, shortly, after long and extensive preparation, about to start for the South Pole. It recalled to his mind " When William Came " and he was keenly sorry for " S," who was leaving England and civilization, where communication of current events could not reach him. It seemed so tragic to him. Then the excitement watching the changing posters of the newsboys and the motley cries and loud opinions of passers-by. We parted early that evening, being unable to settle down to anything definite.

It was not until early September of 1914 that I saw him again. I had been rejected four times previously, but by luck I managed to enlist, and from that time until the end we were always, if possible, together or knew where to find each other.

Knowing Hector as I did in peace time, many thoughts crossed my mind, how would he like the discipline, the early rising, etc., but I never knew him to be late for any parade of any description or at any time. He quickly settled down to a life so entirely different from that which he had left, like so many others, but to me there was a difference. He saw the beginning of a titanic struggle, he had visited the Continent and other parts of the globe and knew the French, Germans, Austrians, and Russians well, as will be seen from previous chapters of this book, and he intended to play his part, and that part was to be as big a part as he could attain. It is remembered that he repeatedly refused the offers of a commission, as he wanted to know a soldier's duties before he felt justified in expecting a soldier to obey a command given by a superior officer, so he determined to be a soldier first. I remember in this connection that he was one of the first to volunteer, and was chosen, to form the first "wiring party" of A Company in our maiden trench visit in November 1915 at Vermelles.

From the White City to Horsham and Roffey, where a very thorough and sound training began, he was just like a fine, healthy boy, full of life, fun, and devilment, but with the main purpose always in view ; and here I must digress as an amusing incident is recalled.

Out of a hut of thirty fellows, two only were known to have returned to camp, during our occupation of about four months, perfectly sober. To even things up Hector decided that it was up to us two to be like the rest. At the time of this decision Cyril Winterscale, then Captain, who was home from the Front, convalescent, promised to visit him at Roffey ; the result was a good dinner and talk and farewells about 11.30 p.m., leaving just time to get back to camp without having to " wake the guard." We were perfectly sober and in our right minds, but two " drunks " were expected in No. 2 Hut, ours, and the fellows got what they expected. We explained the next morning that it was a " rag " and cited the sergt.-major, whom we had passed on our way back to camp, as a witness, but the story was discredited. I think the fellows could not understand what the sergt.-major was doing out just before midnight, and sober too.

Time passed and we left Horsham for Clipstone, and after a short time went to Tidworth for " firing " and the final touches. Up till this time there was a certain straining of nerves and anxiety, wondering if the war would cease before the battalion got out, but eventually, on 15th November, 1915, we left England for France, arriving the same night. It was a fine crossing, but St. Martin's Camp, Boulogne, was a good example of what was to come, a long, dreary march, fully equipped and tired, up steep hills to reach a snow-covered plateau, and into tents which were wet both sides.

At the beginning Hector showed great fortitude, for then, as afterwards, it did not matter what the circumstances were, he thought first of those who were under him, he was a corporal at this time, before ministering to his own needs. I got the biggest " slating " from him on this subject at a later date. Briefly the circumstances were these : I was attached to Coy. H.Q. as well as having charge of a section of No. 1 Platoon, Hector's, to wit, and thought that after a heavy march and arriving at " billets " Coy. H.Q. had first call on me, my section second call, but in the middle of a street of a small mining town, Hersin Coupigny, he soon gave me to understand that I was wrong. Again his splendid character was shown, he would with justification lose his temper, but after having said his say with no little heat perhaps there was an end to it. There was not the slightest trace of " littleness " in anything he did or thought, if one can judge by his spoken thoughts, which were many, as numerous times we spent discussing people and things in general.

His consideration for others was most marked in his actions, especially in the trenches. To those who know the life, this point will be appreciated, but to the uninitiated a little explanation is necessary.

An N.C.O. has numerous duties to perform, tours or patrols with or without an officer, and a two-, three-, or even perhaps four-hour patrol of this particular duty properly performed is a heavy task, especially in such parts of the line as Givenchy, and one was ready for his relief. It was so often necessary to spend five or ten minutes rousing one's relief and a further five minutes in handing over reports, and the situation is excusable perhaps, especially if the day had been a " jumpy " one and the only rest you had got was disturbed by a rough hand or foot which belonged to a person who demanded " What in the name, etc." did one mean by keeping a fellow waiting ? Hector realized that if " resters " were kept they must be like time-tables, I mean artillery, not railway time-tables, absolutely adhered to, so in consequence he was always waiting to meet or going to meet his prior relief. On one occasion his punctuality saved his life, at Givenchy—the home of grenades and " Minnies." Awaking a quarter of an hour before his tour, he immediately aroused himself by taking a short prowl and a stretch, and within two minutes of leaving the firing step a grenade fell into the bay on to his ground sheet, on which he had been lying. One knows of many narrow escapes, but few happening because of that fixed idea of being just.

As the war seemed to be one of " duration," it was necessary to think of something besides war, so Hector hit upon the brilliant idea of forming a Club. The battalion was at Ham-en-Artois about April 1916, and I think it was seeing a pig killed and fancying something different from " bully " that suggested it. It was at this place that the Back Kitchen Club was formed. Pork was purchased and a search was made throughout the village to find some one who would prepare a meal for the evening's enjoyment. We soon found a dear old French-woman who kept a small epicerie, and after listening patiently to her long story of the vicissitudes of the war and how she had suffered, she took us into her kitchen and showed us a most elaborate " kitchen stove or kitchener," most beautifully polished and in the finest condition, with the exception of a crack in one of the top plates, which, with tears in her eyes, she explained was caused by a piece of shell, German. She was retreating from " Mons," where she had lived for a few years till war broke up her home ; the stove was one of the things she managed to get away. Here, of course, was a splendid opportunity, and Hector explained his mission. The pork was left and we were told to call at 7.30 p.m. sharp. On our arrival we were told to go to the back kitchen, and found the dear lady there to receive us with the words " Messieurs, bon appétit," and a splendidly cooked dinner of pork, roast potatoes, green peas ("packet peas") and the usual dressing that goes with pork laid on the table. She then told us that as long as we remained at Ham or were ever on a visit, the back kitchen was at our disposal. There and then I took down a card advertising " Chocolat Ménier " and reversing it wrote the words " The Back Kitchen Club " and four signatures followed, Hector, the founder, coming first. This card was seen about a year later by some one we knew, and it is my hope that it still hangs there. Hector, after we had dined, then enumerated a few rules which were never departed from. Because of the spirit of this Club, the Rules as given out on that night are worthy of note :

Membership not to exceed nine, and to re-place members " passing on " the unanimous approval of all existing members of a name chosen.

On all days, when possible, without departing

from military discipline, the members to meet to partake of an evening meal, however frugal.

When free, "out of the line," all members to take dinner, which consisted of "omelettes, salad, meat and wine, together at some house or estaminet," duty being accepted only as an excuse for non-attendance.

All parcels received from home by members to be common property of the Club.

In the event of any member or members being "broke," their share of expenses to be paid by the member with the most ready money available, or by two or more jointly.

The conduct of all members to be beyond reproach.

Needless to say, these rules were never broken during Hector's time. It was hoped to continue the Club in London after the war, but the moving spirit having "passed on" there is little likelihood of this happening.

The battalion moved on from one field of battle to another, and many more heavy marches were experienced, and although fatigued at times to breaking point, Hector always showed that same dogged spirit, and on a fifteen-mile march in the heat of a very hot July day, full pack and ammunition, I remember him finishing up plus another rifle, that of a much younger man of his platoon.

Delville Wood in August 1916 is vivid in my memory because of the terrible "gunfire" experienced, and the undaunted bravery and courage of "Saki." Just imagine a wood, the trees battered to splintered stumps, trenches about two feet deep, no definite trench line, troops from many battalions in isolated knots having during the attack become disintegrated, looking for "leaders," ready to attach themselves to any officer as long as they had some one to command them, a terrific fire from enemy heavy batteries (I remember one shell which fell to my right killing 16 men) and so many dead.

Hector on this occasion even surprised me, who had always tried to emulate some one worth while ; he stood and gave commands to frightened men, in such a cool, fine manner that I saw many backs stiffen, and he was responsible for the organization of a strong section, giving them a definite "front" to face, and a reassuring word of advice.

Still another move, and a winter to face, but about October 1916 malaria, a fever that had attacked him in India when a boy, sent Hector to the M.O., who asked no question but immediately sent him to the Base. It was a big miss, and I felt just lonely and I know was severely "told off" by my friends for being such a misery, but if I had seen the results of the next "do," I would have borne a longer miss. Unfortunately, it has been known for men to go sick for the purpose of missing something, many did not go sick who should have done, especially if it was a question of "over the top." News travelled, and although the attack on Beaumont Hamel was a sure thing, the date was uncertain, but Hector heard it at the Base and I saw him again about the 11th November. He looked a very sick man and should have been in bed, but I knew his thoughts and the reason for his being fit. We were in position by 3 a.m. on 13th November, 1916, left of Beaumont

Hamel in front of " Pendant Copse " and the Quadrilateral, and remained till the early morning of the 14th November, when we left our front line to " flank out " on the left of our advanced line, the troops on the left, through the marsh-like conditions of the ground (men had sunk in mud to their stomachs), being unable to come up.

It was a very dark winter morning, but after much excitement we were hailed by voices and a figure rose to the top of the trenches in front of us and shouting greetings to the Company Commander (one Capt. Roscoe, one of the finest of fellows, who was killed in February 1917) engaged him in conversation. A number of the fellows sank down on the ground to rest, and Hector sought a shallow crater, with the lip as a back-rest. I heard him shout, " Put that bloody cigarette out," and heard the snip of a rifle-shot. Then an immediate command to get into the trenches. It was some time later, about an hour, when a fellow came to me and said, " So they got your friend." My feelings then I cannot describe, but I knew I had lost something inestimable, the friendship of a man whose ideas and thoughts I tried to emulate, some one whom I loved for his being just " Saki."

In writing all I have cared to tell of Hector's life, it has been impossible not to have a good deal of my own life in the picture. We were such chums. I have not touched upon his social life, visits to country-house parties, etc., because they would not be of interest to the general reader.

The softer, sympathetic side of him never, I think, appeared in his writings, except, perhaps, in " The

Image of the Lost Soul." He had a tremendous sympathy for young men struggling to get on, and in practical ways helped many a lame dog.

ETHEL M. MUNRO.

THE SQUARE EGG

(A BADGER'S-EYE VIEW OF THE WAR
MUD IN THE TRENCHES)

ASSUREDLY a badger is the animal that one most resembles in this trench warfare, that drab-coated creature of the twilight and darkness, digging, burrowing, listening ; keeping itself as clean as possible under unfavourable circumstances, fighting tooth and nail on occasion for possession of a few yards of honeycombed earth.

What the badger thinks about life we shall never know, which is a pity, but cannot be helped ; it is difficult enough to know what one thinks about, oneself, in the trenches. Parliament, taxes, social gatherings, economies, and expenditure, and all the thousand and one horrors of civilization seem immeasurably remote, and the war itself seems almost as distant and unreal. A couple of hundred yards away, separated from you by a stretch of dismal untidy-looking ground and some strips of rusty wire-entanglement, lies a vigilant, bullet-spitting enemy ; lurking and watching in those opposing trenches are foemen who might stir the imagination of the most sluggish brain, descendants of the men who went to battle under Moltke, Blücher, Frederick the Great, and the Great Elector, Wallenstein, Maurice of Saxony, Barbarossa, Albert the Bear, Henry the

Lion, Witekind the Saxon. They are matched against you there, man for man and gun for gun, in what is perhaps the most stupendous struggle that modern history has known, and yet one thinks remarkably little about them. It would not be advisable to forget for the fraction of a second that they are there, but one's mind does not dwell on their existence ; one speculates little as to whether they are drinking warm soup and eating sausage, or going cold and hungry, whether they are well supplied with copies of the *Meggendorfer Blätter* and other light literature or bored with unutterable weariness.

Much more to be thought about than the enemy over yonder or the war all over Europe is the mud of the moment, the mud that at times engulfs you as cheese engulfs a cheesemite. In Zoological Gardens one has gazed at an elk or bison loitering at its pleasure more than knee-deep in a quagmire of greasy mud, and one has wondered what it would feel like to be soused and plastered, hour-long, in such a muck-bath. One knows now. In narrow-dug support-trenches, when thaw and heavy rain have come suddenly atop of a frost, when everything is pitch-dark around you, and you can only stumble about and feel your way against streaming mud walls, when you have to go down on hands and knees in several inches of soup-like mud to creep into a dug-out, when you stand deep in mud, lean against mud, grasp mud-slimed objects with mud-caked fingers, wink mud away from your eyes, and shake it out of your ears, bite muddy biscuits with muddy teeth, then at least you are in a position to understand thoroughly what it feels like to wallow—on the other hand the bison's idea of pleasure becomes more and more incomprehensible.

When one is not thinking about mud one is probably thinking about *estaminets*. An *estaminet* is a
haven that one finds in agreeable plenty in most
of the surrounding townships and villages, flourishing
still amid roofless and deserted houses, patched up
where necessary in rough-and-ready fashion, and
finding a new and profitable tide of customers from
among the soldiers who have replaced the bulk of
the civil population. An *estaminet* is a sort of com-
pound between a wine-shop and a coffee-house,
having a tiny bar in one corner, a few long tables
and benches, a prominent cooking stove, generally
a small grocery store tucked away in the back premises,
and always two or three children running and bump-
ing about at inconvenient angles to one's feet. It
seems to be a fixed rule that *estaminet* children should
be big enough to run about and small enough to get
between one's legs. There must, by the way, be one
considerable advantage in being a child in a war-zone
village ; no one can attempt to teach it tidiness. The
wearisome maxim, " A place for everything and
everything in its proper place," can never be insisted
on when a considerable part of the roof is lying in the
backyard, when a bedstead from a neighbour's demo-
lished bedroom is half buried in the beetroot pile,
and the chickens are roosting in a derelict meat-safe
because a shell has removed the top and sides and front
of the chicken-house.

Perhaps there is nothing in the foregoing description to suggest that a village wine-shop, frequently
a shell-nibbled building in a shell-gnawed street,
is a paradise to dream about, but when one has lived
in a dripping wilderness of unrelieved mud and sodden
sandbags for any length of time one's mind dwells

on the plain-furnished parlour with its hot coffee and *vin ordinaire* as something warm and snug and comforting in a wet and slushy world. To the soldier on his trench-to-billets migration the wine-shop is what the tavern rest-house is to the caravan nomad of the East. One comes and goes in a crowd of chance-foregathered men, noticed or unnoticed as one wishes, amid the khaki-clad, be-putteed throng of one's own kind one can be as unobtrusive as a green caterpillar on a green cabbage leaf ; one can sit undisturbed, alone or with one's own friends, or if one wishes to be talkative and talked to one can readily find a place in a circle where men of divers variety of cap badges are exchanging experiences, real or improvised.

Besides the changing throng of mud-stained khaki there is a drifting leaven of local civilians, uniformed interpreters, and men in varying types of foreign military garb, from privates in the Regular Army to Heaven-knows-what in some intermediate corps that only an expert in such matters could put a name to, and, of course, here and there are representatives of that great army of adventurer purse-sappers, that carries on its operations uninterruptedly in time of peace or war alike, over the greater part of the earth's surface. You meet them in England and France, in Russia and Constantinople ; probably they are to be met with also in Iceland, though on that point I have no direct evidence.

In the *estaminet* of the Fortunate Rabbit I found myself sitting next to an individual of indefinite age and nondescript uniform, who was obviously deter-mined to make the borrowing of a match serve as a formal introduction and a banker's reference. He had the air of jaded jauntiness, the equipment of temporary amiability, the aspect of a foraging crow, taught by experience to be wary and prompted by necessity to be bold; he had the contemplative downward droop of nose and moustache and the furtive sidelong range of eye—he had all those things that are the ordinary outfit of the purse-sapper the world over.

"I am a victim of the war," he exclaimed after a little preliminary conversation.

"One cannot make an omelette without breaking eggs," I answered, with the appropriate callousness of a man who had seen some dozens of square miles of devastated country-side and roofless homes.

"Eggs!" he vociferated, "but it is precisely of eggs that I am about to speak. Have you ever considered what is the great drawback in the excellent and most useful egg—the ordinary, everyday egg of commerce and cookery?"

"Its tendency to age rapidly is sometimes against it," I hazarded; "unlike the United States of North America, which grow more respectable and self-respecting the longer they last, an egg gains nothing by persistence; it resembles your Louis the Fifteenth, who declined in popular favour with every year he lived—unless the historians have entirely misrepresented his record."

"No," replied the Tavern Acquaintance seriously, "it is not a question of age. It is the shape, the roundness. Consider how easily it rolls. On a table, a shelf, a shop counter, perhaps, one little push, and it may roll to the floor and be destroyed. What catastrophe for the poor, the frugal!"

I gave a sympathetic shudder at the idea ; eggs here cost 6 sous apiece.

" Monsieur," he continued, " it is a subject I had often pondered and turned over in my mind, this economical malformation of the household egg. In our little village of Verchey-les-Torteaux, in the Department of the Tarn, my aunt has a small dairy and poultry farm, from which we drew a modest income. We were not poor, but there was always the necessity to labour, to contrive, to be sparing. One day I chanced to notice that one of my aunt's hens, a hen of the mop-headed Houdan breed, had laid an egg that was not altogether so round-shaped as the eggs of other hens ; it could not be called square, but it had well-defined angles. I found out that this particular bird always laid eggs of this particular shape. The discovery gave a new stimulus to my ideas. If one collected all the hens that one could find with a tendency to lay a slightly angular egg and bred chickens only from those hens, and went on selecting and selecting, always choosing those that laid the squarest egg, at last, with patience and enterprise, one would produce a breed of fowls that laid only square eggs."

" In the course of several hundred years one might arrive at such a result," I said ; " it would more probably take several thousands."

" With your cold Northern conservative slow-moving hens that might be the case," said the Acquaintance impatiently and rather angrily ; " with our vivacious Southern poultry it is different. Listen. I searched, I experimented, I explored the poultry-yards of our neighbours, I ransacked the markets of the surrounding towns, wherever I found a hen laying

an angular egg I bought her; I collected in time
a vast concourse of fowls all sharing the same tendency; from their progeny I selected only those
pullets whose eggs showed the most marked devia-
tion from the normal roundness. I continued, I
persevered. Monsieur, I produced a breed of hens
that laid an egg which could not roll, however much
you might push or jostle it. My experiment was
more than a success; it was one of the romances
of modern industry."

Of that I had not the least doubt, but I did not
say so.

"My eggs became known," continued the *soi-
disant* poultry-farmer; "at first they were sought
after as a novelty, something curious, bizarre. Then
merchants and housewives began to see that they
were a utility, an improvement, an advantage over
the ordinary kind. I was able to command a sale
for my wares at a price considerably above market
rates. I began to make money. I had a monopoly.
I refused to sell any of my ' square-layers,' and the
eggs that went to market were carefully sterilized,
so that no chickens should be hatched from them.
I was in the way to become rich, comfortably rich.
Then this war broke out, which has brought misery
to so many. I was obliged to leave my hens and
my customers and go to the Front. My aunt carried
on the business as usual, sold the square eggs, the
eggs that I had devised and created and perfected,
and received the profits; can you imagine it, she
refuses to send me one centime of the takings! She
says that she looks after the hens, and pays for their
corn, and sends the eggs to market, and that the
money is hers. Legally, of course, it is mine; if I

could afford to bring a process in the Courts I could recover all the money that the eggs have brought in since the war commenced, many thousands of francs. To bring a process would only need a small sum; I have a lawyer friend who would arrange matters cheaply for me. Unfortunately I have not sufficient funds in hand; I need still about eighty francs. In war-time, alas! it is difficult to borrow."

I had always imagined that it was a habit that was especially indulged in during war-time, and said so.

"On a big scale, yes, but I am talking of a very small matter. It is easier to arrange a loan of millions than of a trifle of eighty or ninety francs."

The would-be financier paused for a few tense moments. Then he recommenced in a more confidential strain.

"Some of you English soldiers, I have heard, are men with private means : is it not so ? It is perhaps possible that among your comrades there might be some one willing to advance a small sum—you yourself, perhaps—it would be a secure and profitable investment, quickly repaid——"

"If I get a few days' leave I will go down to Verchey-les-Torteaux and inspect the square-egg hen-farm," I said gravely, "and question the local egg-merchants as to the position and prospects of the business."

The Tavern Acquaintance gave an almost imperceptible shrug to his shoulders, shifted in his seat, and began moodily to roll a cigarette. His interest in me had suddenly died out, but for the sake of appearances he was bound to make a perfunctory show of winding up the conversation he had so laboriously started.

" Ah, you will go to Verchey-les-Torteaux and make inquiries about our farm. And if you find that what I have told you about the square eggs is true, Monsieur, what then ? "

" I shall marry your aunt."

CONSIDERING the enormous economic dislocation which the war operations have caused in the regions where the campaign is raging, there seems to be very little corresponding disturbance in the bird life of the same districts. Rats and mice have mobilized and swarmed into the fighting line, and there has been a partial mobilization of owls, particularly barn owls, following in the wake of the mice, and making laudable efforts to thin out their numbers. What success attends their hunting one cannot estimate; there are always sufficient mice left over to populate one's dug-out and make a parade-ground and race-course of one's face at night. In the matter of nesting accommodation the barn owls are well provided for; most of the still intact barns in the war zone are requisitioned for billeting purposes, but there is a wealth of ruined houses, whole streets and clusters of them, such as can hardly have been available at any previous moment of the world's history since Nineveh and Babylon became humanly desolate. Without human occupation and cultivation there can have been no corn, no refuse, and consequently very few mice, and the owls of Nineveh cannot have enjoyed very good hunting; here in Northern France the owls have desolation and mice at their disposal in unlimited quantities, and as these birds breed in winter as well as in summer, there should be a goodly output of war owlets to cope with the swarming generations of war mice.

Apart from the owls one cannot notice that the campaign is making any marked difference in the bird life of the country-side. The vast flocks of crows and ravens that one expected to find in the neighbourhood of the fighting line are non-existent, which is perhaps rather a pity. The obvious explanation is that the roar and crash and fumes of high explosives have driven the crow tribe in panic from the fighting area ; like many obvious explanations, it is not a correct one. The crows of the locality are not attracted to the battlefield, but they certainly are not scared away from it. The rook is normally so gun-shy and nervous where noise is concerned that the sharp banging of a barn door or the report of a toy pistol will sometimes set an entire rookery in commotion ; out here I have seen him sedately busy among the refuse heaps of a battered village, with shells bursting at no great distance, and the impatient-sounding, snapping rattle of machine-guns going on all round him ; for all the notice that he took he might have been in some peaceful English meadow on a sleepy Sunday afternoon. Whatever else German frightfulness may have done it has not frightened the rook of North-Eastern France ; it has made his nerves steadier than they have ever been before, and future generations of small boys, employed in scaring rooks away from the sown crops in this region, will have to invent something in the way of super-frightfulness to achieve their purpose. Crows and magpies are nesting well within the shell-swept area, and over a small beech-copse I once saw a pair of crows engaged in hot combat with a pair of sparrow-hawks, while considerably higher in the sky, but almost directly above them, two Allied battle-planes were engaging an equal number of enemy aircraft.

Unlike the barn owls, the magpies have had their choice of building sites considerably restricted by the ravages of war; the whole avenues of poplars, where they were accustomed to construct their nests, have been blown to bits, leaving nothing but dreary-looking rows of shattered and splintered trunks to show where once they stood. Affection for a particular tree has in one case induced a pair of magpies to build their bulky, domed nest in the battered remnants of a poplar of which so little remained standing that the nest looked almost bigger than the tree; the effect rather suggested an archiepiscopal enthronement taking place in the ruined remains of Melrose Abbey. The magpie, wary and suspicious in his wild state, must be rather intrigued at the change that has come over the erstwhile fearsome not-to-be-avoided human, stalking everywhere over the earth as its possessor, who now creeps about in screened and sheltered ways, as chary of showing himself in the open as the shyest of wild creatures.

The buzzard, that earnest seeker after mice, does not seem to be taking any war risks, at least I have never seen one out here, but kestrels hover about all day in the hottest parts of the line, not in the least disconcerted, apparently, when a promising mouse-area suddenly rises in the air in a cascade of black or yellow earth. Sparrow-hawks are fairly numerous, and a mile or two back from the firing line I saw a pair of hawks that I took to be red-legged falcons, circling over the top of an oak-copse. According to investigations made by Russian naturalists, the effect of the war on bird life on the Eastern front has been more marked than it has been over here. " During the first year of the war rooks disappeared, larks no longer sang in the fields, the wild pigeon disappeared also." The skylark in this region has stuck tenaciously to the meadows and crop-lands that have been seamed and bisected with trenches and honeycombed with shell-holes. In the chill, misty hour of gloom that precedes a rainy dawn, when nothing seemed alive except a few wary waterlogged sentries and many scuttling rats, the lark would suddenly dash skyward and pour forth a song of ecstatic jubilation that sounded horribly forced and insincere. It seemed scarcely possible that the bird could carry its insouciance to the length of attempting to rear a brood in that desolate wreckage of shattered clods and gaping shell-holes, but once, having occasion to throw myself down with some abruptness on my face, I found myself nearly on the top of a brood of young larks. Two of them had already been hit by something, and were in rather a battered condition, but the survivors seemed as tranquil and comfortable as the average nestling.

At the corner of a stricken wood (which has had a name made for it in history, but shall be nameless here), at a moment when lyddite and shrapnel and machine-gun fire swept and raked and bespattered that devoted spot as though the artillery of an entire Division had suddenly concentrated on it, a wee hen-chaffinch flitted wistfully to and fro, amid splintered and falling branches that had never a green bough left on them. The wounded lying there, if any of them noticed the small bird, may well have wondered why anything having wings and no pressing reason for remaining should have chosen to stay in such a place. There was a battered orchard alongside the stricken wood, and the probable explanation of the bird's presence was that it had a nest of young ones whom it was too scared to feed, too loyal to desert. Later on, a small flock of chaffinches blundered into the wood, which they were doubtless in the habit of using as a highway to their feeding-grounds ; unlike the solitary hen-bird, they made no secret of their desire to get away as fast as their dazed wits would let them. The only other bird I ever saw there was a magpie, flying low over the wreckage of fallen tree-limbs ; " one for sorrow," says the old superstition. There was sorrow enough in that wood.

The English gamekeeper, whose knowledge of wild life usually runs on limited and perverted lines, has evolved a sort of religion as to the nervous debility of even the hardiest game birds ; according to his beliefs a terrier trotting across a field in which a partridge is nesting, or a mouse-hawking kestrel hovering over the hedge, is sufficient cause to drive the distracted bird off its eggs and send it whirring into the next county.

The partridge of the war zone shows no signs of such sensitive nerves. The rattle and rumble of transport, the constant coming and going of bodies of troops, the incessant rattle of musketry and deafening explosions of artillery, the night-long flare and flicker of star-shells, have not sufficed to scare the local birds away from their chosen feeding grounds, and to all appearances they have not been deterred from raising their broods. Gamekeepers who are serving with the colours might seize the opportunity to indulge in a little useful nature study.

THE GALA PROGRAMME

AN UNRECORDED EPISODE IN ROMAN HISTORY

IT was an auspicious day in the Roman Calendar, the birthday of the popular and gifted young Emperor Placidus Superbus. Every one in Rome was bent on keeping high festival, the weather was at its best, and naturally the Imperial Circus was crowded to its fullest capacity. A few minutes before the hour fixed for the commencement of the spectacle a loud fanfare of trumpets proclaimed the arrival of Cæsar, and amid the vociferous acclamations of the multitude the Emperor took his seat in the Imperial Box. As the shouting of the crowd died away an even more thrilling salutation could be heard in the near distance, the angry, impatient roaring and howling of the beasts caged in the Imperial menagerie.

"Explain the programme to me," commanded the Emperor, having beckoned the Master of the Ceremonies to his side.

That eminent official wore a troubled look.

"Gracious Cæsar," he announced, "a most promising and entertaining programme has been devised and prepared for your august approval. In the first place there is to be a chariot contest of unusual brilliancy and interest ; three teams that have never hitherto suffered defeat are to contend for the Herculaneum Trophy, together with the purse which your Imperial generosity has been pleased to add. The chances of the competing teams are accounted to be as nearly as possible equal, and there is much wagering among the populace. The black Thracians are perhaps the favourites——"

"I know, I know," interrupted Cæsar, who had listened to exhaustive talk on the same subject all the morning ; "what else is there on the programme ? "

"The second part of the programme," said the Imperial Official, "consists of a grand combat of wild beasts, specially selected for their strength, ferocity, and fighting qualities. There will appear simultaneously in the arena fourteen Nubian lions and lionesses, five tigers, six Syrian bears, eight Persian panthers, and three North African ditto, a number of wolves and lynxes from the Teutonic forests, and seven gigantic wild bulls from the same region. There will also be wild swine of unexampled savageness, a rhinoceros from the Barbary coast, some ferocious man-apes, and a hyæna, reputed to be mad."

"It promises well," said the Emperor.

"It *promised* well, O Cæsar," said the official dolorously, "it promised marvellously well ; but between the promise and the performance a cloud has arisen."

"A cloud ? What cloud ? " queried Cæsar, with a frown.

"The Suffragetæ," explained the official ; "they threaten to interfere with the chariot race."

"I'd like to see them do it ! " exclaimed the Emperor indignantly.

"I fear your Imperial wish may be unpleasantly gratified," said the Master of the Ceremonies ; "we are taking, of course, every possible precaution, and guarding all the entrances to the arena and the stables with a triple guard ; but it is rumoured that at the signal for the entry of the chariots five hundred women will let themselves down with ropes from the public seats and swarm all over the course. Naturally no race could be run under such circumstances ; the programme will be ruined."

"On my birthday," said Placidus Superbus, "they would not dare to do such an outrageous thing."

"The more august the occasion, the more desirous they will be to advertise themselves and their cause," said the harassed official ; "they do not scruple to make riotous interference even with the ceremonies in the temples."

"Who *are* these Suffragetæ ? " asked the Emperor. "Since I came back from my Pannonian expedition I have heard of nothing else but their excesses and demonstrations."

"They are a political sect of very recent origin, and their aim seems to be to get a big share of political authority into their hands. The means they are taking to convince us of their fitness to help in making and administering the laws consist of wild indulgence in tumult, destruction, and defiance of all authority. They have already damaged some of the most historic-ally valuable of our public treasures, which can never be replaced."

"Is it possible that the sex which we hold in such honour and for which we feel such admiration can produce such hordes of Furies ? " asked the Emperor.

"It takes all sorts to make a sex," observed the Master of the Ceremonies, who possessed a certain amount of worldly wisdom ; "also," he continued anxiously, "it takes very little to upset a gala pro-gramme."

"Perhaps the disturbance that you anticipate will turn out to be an idle threat," said the Emperor consolingly.

"But if they should carry out their intention," said the official, "the programme will be utterly ruined."

The Emperor said nothing.

Five minutes later the trumpets rang out for the commencement of the entertainment. A hum of excited anticipation ran through the ranks of the spectators, and final bets on the issue of the great race were hurriedly shouted. The gates leading from the stables were slowly swung open, and a troop of mounted attendants rode round the track to ascertain that everything was clear for the momentous contest. Again the trumpets rang out, and then, before the foremost chariot had appeared, there arose a wild tumult of shouting, laughing, angry protests, and shrill screams of defiance. Hundreds of women were being lowered by their accomplices into the arena. A moment later they were running and dancing in frenzied troops across the track where the chariots were supposed to compete. No team of arena-trained horses would have faced such a frantic mob ; the race was clearly an impossibility. Howls of disappointment and rage rose from the spectators, howls of triumph echoed back from the women in possession. The vain efforts of the circus attendants to drive out the invading horde merely added to the uproar and confusion ; as fast as the Suffragetæ were thrust away from one portion of the track they swarmed on to another.

The Master of the Ceremonies was nearly delirious from rage and mortification. Placidus Superbus, who remained calm and unruffled as ever, beckoned to him and spoke a word or two in his ear. For the first time that afternoon the sorely-tried official was seen to smile.

A trumpet rang out from the Imperial Box ; an instant hush fell over the excited throng. Perhaps the Emperor, as a last resort, was going to announce some concession to the Suffragetæ.

" Close the stable gates," commanded the Master of the Ceremonies, " and open all the menagerie dens. It is the Imperial pleasure that the second portion of the programme be taken first."

It turned out that the Master of the Ceremonies had in no wise exaggerated the probable brilliancy of this portion of the spectacle. The wild bulls were really wild, and the hyæna reputed to be mad thoroughly lived up to its reputation.

THE INFERNAL PARLIAMENT

IN an age when it has become increasingly difficult
to accomplish anything new or original, Bavton
Bidderdale interested his generation by dying of a
new disease. "We always knew he would do something remarkable one of these days," observed his
aunts; "he has justified our belief in him." But
there is a section of humanity ever ready to refuse
recognition to meritorious achievement, and a large
and influential school of doctors asserted their belief
that Bidderdale was not really dead. The funeral
arrangements had to be held over until the matter was
settled one way or the other, and the aunts went
provisionally into half-mourning.

Meanwhile, Bidderdale remained in Hell as a guest
pending his reception on a more regular footing. "If
you are not really supposed to be dead," said the
authorities of that region, "we don't want to seem in
an indecent hurry to grab you. The theory that Hell
is in serious need of population is a thing of the past.
Why, to take your family alone, there are any number
of Bidderdales on our books, as you may discover later.
It is part of our system that relations should be encouraged to live together down here. From observations made in another world we have abundant evidence
that it promotes the ends we have in view. However,
while you are a guest we should like you to be treated
with every consideration and be shown anything that

specially interests you. Of course, you would like to see our Parliament ? "

" Have you a Parliament in Hell ? " asked Bidderdale in some surprise.

" Only quite recently. Of course we've always had chaos, but not under Parliamentary rules. Now, however, that Parliaments are becoming the fashion, in Turkey and Persia, and I suppose before long in Afghanistan and China, it seemed rather ostentatious to stand outside the movement. That young Fiend just going by is the Member for East Brimstone ; he'll be delighted to show you over the institution."

" You will just be in time to hear the opening of a debate," said the Member, as he led Bidderdale through a spacious outer lobby, decorated with frescoes representing the fall of man, the discovery of gold, the invention of playing cards, and other traditionally appropriate subjects. " The Member for Nether Furnace is proposing a motion ' that this House do arrogantly protest to the legislatures of earthly countries against the wrongful and injurious misuse of the word " fiendish," in application to purely human misdemeanours, a misuse tending to create a false and detrimental impression concerning the Infernal Regions.' "

A feature of the Parliament Chamber itself was its enormous size. The space allotted to Members was small and very sparsely occupied, but the public galleries stretched away tier on tier as far as the eye could reach, and were packed to their utmost capacity.

" There seems to be a very great public interest in the debate," exclaimed Bidderdale.

" Members are excused from attending the debates

if they so desire," the Fiend proceeded to explain; " it is one of their most highly valued privileges. On the other hand, constituents are compelled to listen throughout to all the speeches. After all, you must remember, we are in Hell."

Bidderdale repressed a shudder and turned his attention to the debate.

" Nothing," the Fiend-Orator was observing, " is more deplorable among the cultured races of the present day than the tendency to identify fiendhood, in the most sweeping fashion, with all manner of disreputable excesses, excesses which can only be alleged against us on the merest legendary evidence. Vices which are exclusively or predominatingly human are unblushingly described as inhuman, and, what is even more contemptible and ungenerous, as fiendish. If one investigates such statements as ' inhuman treatment of pit ponies ' or ' fiendish cruelties in the Congo,' so frequently to be heard in our brother Parliaments on earth, one finds accumulative and indisputable evidence that it is the human treatment of pit ponies and Congo natives that is really in question, and that no authenticated case of fiendish agency in these atrocities can be substantiated. It is, perhaps, a minor matter for complaint," continued the orator, " that the human race frequently pays us the doubtful compliment of describing as ' devilish funny ' jokes which are neither funny nor devilish."

The orator paused, and an oppressive silence reigned over the vast chamber.

" What is happening ? " whispered Bidderdale.

" Five minutes Hush," explained his guide; " it is a sign that the speaker was listened to in silent approval, which is the highest mark of appreciation that can be bestowed in Pandemonium. Let's come into the smoking-room."

"Will the motion be carried?" asked Bidderdale, wondering inwardly how Sir Edward Grey would treat the protest if it reached the British Parliament; an *entente* with the Infernal Regions opened up a fascinating vista, in which the Foreign Secretary's imagination might hopelessly lose itself.

"Carried? Of course not," said the Fiend; "in the Infernal Parliament all motions are necessarily lost."

"In earthly Parliaments nowadays nearly everything is found," said Bidderdale, "including salaries and travelling expenses."

He felt that at any rate he was probably the first member of his family to make a joke in Hell.

"By the way," he added, "talking of earthly Parliaments, have you got the Party system down here?"

"In Hell? Impossible. You see we have no system of rewards. We have specialized so thoroughly on punishments that the other branch has been entirely neglected. And besides, Government by delusion, as you practise it in your Parliament, would be unworkable here. I should be the last person to say anything against temptation, naturally, but we have a proverb down here 'in baiting a mouse-trap with cheese, always leave room for the mouse.' Such a party-cry, for instance, as your 'ninepence for fourpence' would be absolutely inoperative; it not only leaves no room for the mouse, it leaves no room for the imagination. You have a saying in your country, I believe, 'there's no fool like a damned fool'; all the fools down here are, necessarily, damned, but—you wouldn't get them to nibble at ninepence for fourpence."

" Couldn't they be scolded and lectured into believing it, as a sort of moral and intellectual duty ? " asked Bidderdale.

"We haven't all your facilities," said the Fiend ; "we've nothing down here that exactly corresponds to the Master of Elibank."

At this moment Bidderdale's attention was caught by an item on a loose sheet of agenda paper : " Vote on account of special Hells."

" Ah," he said, " I've often heard the expression ' there is a special Hell reserved for such-and-such a type of person.' Do tell me about them."

" I'll show you one in course of preparation," said the Fiend, leading him down the corridor. " This one is designed to accommodate one of the leading playwrights of your nation. You may observe scores of imps engaged in pasting notices of modern British plays into a huge press-cutting book, each under the name of the author, alphabetically arranged. The book will contain nearly half a million notices, I suppose, and it will form the sole literature supplied to this specially doomed individual."

Bidderdale was not altogether impressed.

"Some dramatic authors wouldn't so much very mind spending eternity poring over a book of contemporary press-cuttings," he observed.

The Fiend, laughing unpleasantly, lowered his voice.

" The letter ' S ' is missing."

For the first time Bidderdale realized that he was in Hell.

THE ACHIEVEMENT OF THE CAT

IN the political history of nations it is no uncommon experience to find States and peoples which but a short time since were in bitter conflict and animosity with each other, settled down comfortably on terms of mutual goodwill and even alliance. The natural history of the social developments of species affords a similar instance in the coming-together of two once warring elements, now represented by civilized man and the domestic cat. The fiercely waged struggle which went on between humans and felines in those far-off days when sabre-toothed tiger and cave lion contended with primeval man, has long ago been decided in favour of the most fitly equipped combatant —the Thing with a Thumb—and the descendants of the dispossessed family are relegated to-day, for the most part, to the waste lands of jungle and veld, where an existence of self-effacement is the only alternative to extermination. But the *felis catus*, or whatever species was the ancestor of the modern domestic cat (a vexed question at present), by a master-stroke of adaptation avoided the ruin of its race, and " captured " a place in the very keystone of the conqueror's organiza- tion. For not as a bond-servant or dependent has this proudest of mammals entered the human fraternity ; not as a slave like the beasts of burden, or a humble camp-follower like the dog. The cat is domestic only

128

as far as suits its own ends ; it will not be kennelled or harnessed nor suffer any dictation as to its goings out or comings in.   Long contact with the human race has developed in it the art of diplomacy, and no Roman Cardinal of mediæval days knew better how to ingratiate himself with his surroundings than a cat with a saucer of cream on its mental horizon.   But the social smoothness, the purring innocence, the softness of the velvet paw may be laid aside at a moment's notice, and the sinuous feline may disappear, in deliberate aloofness, to a world of roofs and chimney-stacks, where the human element is distanced and disregarded.   Or the innate savage spirit that helped its survival in the bygone days of tooth and claw may be summoned forth from beneath the sleek exterior, and the torture-instinct (common alone to human and feline) may find free play in the death-throes of some luckless bird or rodent. It is, indeed, no small triumph to have combined the untrammelled liberty of primeval savagery with the luxury which only a highly developed civilization can command ; to be lapped in the soft stuffs that commerce has gathered from the far ends of the world ; to bask in the warmth that labour and industry have dragged from the bowels of the earth ; to banquet on the dainties that wealth has bespoken for its table, and withal to be a free son of nature, a mighty hunter, a spiller of life-blood.   This is the victory of the cat. But besides the credit of success the cat has other qualities which compel recognition.   The animal which the Egyptians worshipped as divine, which the Romans venerated as a symbol of liberty, which Europeans in the ignorant Middle Ages anathematized as an agent of demonology, has displayed to all ages two closely-blended characteristics—courage and self-respect. No matter how unfavourable the circumstances, both qualities are always to the fore. Confront a child, a puppy, and a kitten with a sudden danger ; the child will turn instinctively for assistance, the puppy will grovel in abject submission to the impending visitation, the kitten will brace its tiny body for a frantic resistance. And disassociate the luxury-loving cat from the atmosphere of social comfort in which it usually contrives to move, and observe it critically under the adverse conditions of civilization—that civilization which can impel a man to the degradation of clothing himself in tawdry ribald garments and capering mountebank dances in the streets for the earning of the few coins that keep him on the respectable, or non-criminal, side of society. The cat of the slums and alleys, starved, outcast, harried, still keeps amid the prowlings of its adversity the bold, free, panther-tread with which it paced of yore the temple courts of Thebes, still displays the self-reliant watchfulness which man has never taught it to lay aside. And when its shifts and clever managings have not sufficed to stave off inexorable fate, when its enemies have proved too strong or too many for its defensive powers, it dies fighting to the last, quivering with the choking rage of mastered resistance, and voicing in its death-yell that agony of bitter remonstrance which human animals, too, have flung at the powers that may be ; the last protest against a destiny that might have made them happy—and has not.

RUSSIA at the present crisis of its history not unnaturally suggests to the foreign mind a land pervaded with discontent and disorder and weighed down with depression, and it is certainly difficult to point to any quarter of the Imperial dominions from which troubles of one sort or another are not reported. In the *Novoe Vremya* and other papers a column is now devoted to the chronicling of disorders as regularly as a British news-sheet reports sporting events. It is the more agreeable therefore occasionally to make the acquaintance of another phase of Russian life where the sombreness of political mischance can be momentarily lost sight of or disbelieved in. Perhaps there are few spots in European Russia where one so thoroughly feels that one has passed into a new and unfamiliar atmosphere as the old town of Pskoff, once in its day a very important centre of Russian life. To the average modern Russian a desire to visit Pskoff is an inexplicable mental freak on the part of a foreigner who wishes to see something of the country he is living in ; Petersburg, Moscow, Kieff, perhaps, and Nijni-Novgorod, or the Finnish watering-places if you want a country holiday, but why Pskoff ? And thus happily an aversion to beaten tracks and localities where inspection is invited and industriously catered for turns one towards the old Great Russian border town, which probably gives as accurate a picture as can be obtained of a mediæval Russian burgh, untouched by Mongul influence, and only slightly affected by Byzantine-imported culture.

The little town has ample charm of situation and structure, standing astride of a bold scarp of land wedged into the fork of two rivers, and retaining yet much of the long lines of ramparts and towers that served for many a hundred years to keep out Pagan Lithuanians and marauding Teuton knights. The powers of Darkness were as carefully guarded against in those old days as more tangible human enemies, and from out of thick clusters of tree-tops there still arise the white walls and green roofs of many churches, monasteries, and bell-towers, quaint and fantastic in architecture, and delightfully harmonious in colouring. Steep winding streets lead down from the rampart-girt heart of the town to those parts which lie along the shores of the twin rivers, and two bridges, one a low, wide, wooden structure primitively planted on piles, gives access to the further banks, where more towers and monasteries, with other humbler buildings, continue the outstraggling span of the township. On the rivers lie barges with high masts painted in wonderful bands of scarlet, green, white, and blue, topped with gilded wooden pennons figured somewhat like a child's rattle, and fluttering strips of bunting at their ends. Up in the town one sees on all sides quaint old doorways, deep archways, wooden gable-ends, railed staircases, and a crowning touch of pleasing colour in the sage green or dull red of the roofs. But it is strangest of all to find a human population in complete picturesque harmony with its rich old-world setting. The scarlet or blue blouses that are worn by the working men in most Russian towns give way here to a variety of gorgeous-tinted garments, and the women-folk are similarly gay in their apparel, so that streets and wharves and market-place glow with wonderfully effective groupings of colour. Mulberry, orange, dull carmine, faded rose, hyacinth purple, greens, and lilacs and rich blues mingle their hues on shirts and shawls, skirts and breeches and waistbands. Nature competing with Percy Anderson was the frivolous comment that came to one's mind, and certainly a mediæval crowd could scarcely have been more effectively staged. And the business of a town in which it seemed always market day went forward with an air of contented absorption on the part of the inhabitants. Strings of primitively fashioned carts went to and from the riverside, the horses wearing their bits for the most part hung negligently under the chin, a fashion that prevails in many parts of Russia and Poland.

Quaint little booths line the sides of some of the steeper streets, and here wooden toys and earthenware pottery of strange local patterns are set out for sale. On the broad market-place women sit gossiping by the side of large baskets of strawberries, one or two long-legged foals sprawl at full stretch under the shade of their parental market carts, and an extremely contented pig pursues his leisurely way under the guardianship of an elderly dame robed in a scheme of orange, mulberry, and white that would delight the soul of a colourist. A stalwart peasant strides across the uneven cobbles, leading his plough-horse, and carrying on his shoulder a small wooden plough, with iron-tipped shares, that must date back to some stage of agriculture that the West has long left behind. Down in the buoyant waters of the Velikaya, the larger of the two rivers, youths and men are disporting them-

THE OLD TOWN OF PSKOFF

selves and staider washerwomen are rinsing and smack-
ing piles of many-hued garments. It is pleasant to
swim well out into the stream of the river, and, with
one's chin on a level with the wide stretch of water,
take in a " trout's-eye view " of the little town, ascend-
ing in tiers of wharfage, trees, grey ramparts, more
trees, and clustered roofs, with the old cathedral of the
Trinity poised guardian-like above the crumbling walls
of the Kremlin. The cathedral, on closer inspection,
is a charming specimen of genuine old Russian architecture, full of rich carvings and aglow with scarlet
pigment and gilded scroll-work, and stored with yet
older relics or pseudo-relics of local hero-saints and
hero-princes who helped in their day to make the
history of the Pskoff Commonwealth. After an hour
or two spent among these tombs and ikons and
memorials of dead Russia, one feels that some time
must elapse before one cares to enter again the drearily
magnificent holy places of St. Petersburg, with their
depressing *nouveau riche* atmosphere, their price-list
tongued attendants, and general lack of historic interest.

The heart knoweth its own bitterness, and maybe
the Pskoffskie, amid their seeming contentment and
self-absorption, have their own hungerings for a new
and happier era of national life. But the stranger
does not ask to see so far ; he is thankful to have found
a picturesque and apparently well-contented corner of a
weary land, a land " where distress seems like a bird of
passage that has hurt its wing and cannot fly away."

CLOVIS ON THE ALLEGED ROMANCE OF BUSINESS

" IT is the fashion nowadays," said Clovis, " to talk about the romance of Business. There isn't such a thing. The romance has all been the other way, with the idle apprentice, the truant, the run-away, the individual who couldn't be bothered with figures and book-keeping and left business to look after itself. I admit that a grocer's shop is one of the most romantic and thrilling things that I have ever happened on, but the romance and thrill are centred in the groceries, not the grocer. The citron and spices and nuts and dates, the barrelled anchovies and Dutch cheeses, the jars of *caviar* and the chests of tea, they carry the mind away to Levantine coast towns and tropic shores, to the Old World wharfs and quays of the Low Countries, to dusty Astrachan and far Cathay ; if the grocer's apprentice has any romance in him it is not a business education he gets behind the grocer's counter, it is a standing invitation to dream and to wander, and to remain poor. As a child such places as South America and Asia Minor were brought painstakingly under my notice, the names of their principal rivers and the heights of their chief mountain peaks were committed to my memory, and I was earnestly enjoined to consider them as parts of the world that I lived in ; it was only when I visited a large well-stocked grocer's shop that I realized that they certainly existed. Such galleries of romance and fascination are not bequeathed to us by the business man ; he is only the dull custodian, who talks glibly of Spanish olives and Rangoon rice, a Spain that he has never known or wished to know, a Rangoon that he has never imagined or could imagine. It was the unledgered wanderer, the careless-hearted seafarer, the aimless outcast, who opened up new trade routes, tapped new markets, brought home samples or cargoes of new edibles and unknown condiments. It was they who brought the glamour and romance to the threshold of business life, where it was promptly reduced to pounds, shillings, and pence ; invoiced, double-entried, quoted, written-off, and so forth ; most of those terms are probably wrong, but a little inaccuracy sometimes saves tons of explanation.

"On the other side of the account there is the industrious apprentice, who grew up into the business man, married early and worked late, and lived, thousands and thousands of him, in little villas outside big towns. He is buried by the thousand in Kensal Green and other large cemeteries ; any romance that was ever in him was buried prematurely in shop and warehouse and office. Whenever I feel in the least tempted to be business-like or methodical or even decently industrious I go to Kensal Green and look at the graves of those who died in business."

MOUNG KA, cultivator of rice and philosophic virtues, sat on the raised platform of his cane-built house by the banks of the swiftly flowing Irrawaddy. On two sides of the house there was a bright-green swamp, which stretched away to where the uncultivated jungle growth began. In the bright-green swamp, which was really a rice-field when you looked closely at it, bitterns and pond-herons and elegant cattle-egrets stalked and peered with the absorbed air of careful and conscientious reptile-hunters, who could never forget that, while they were undoubtedly useful, they were also distinctly decorative. In the tall reed growth by the river-side grazing buffaloes showed in patches of dark slaty blue, like plums fallen amid long grass, and in the tamarind trees that shaded Moung Ka's house the crows, restless, raucous-throated, and much-too-many, kept up their incessant afternoon din, saying over and over again all the things that crows have said since there were crows to say them.

Moung Ka sat smoking his enormous green-brown cigar, without which no Burmese man, woman, or child seems really complete, dispensing from time to time instalments of worldly information for the benefit and instruction of his two companions. The steamer which came up-river from Mandalay thrice a week brought Moung Ka a Rangoon news-sheet, in which the progress of the world's events was set forth in telegraphic messages and commented on in pithy paragraphs. Moung Ka, who read these things and retailed them as occasion served to his friends and neighbours, with philosophical additions of his own, was held in some esteem locally as a political thinker ; in Burma it is possible to be a politician without ceasing to be a philosopher.

His friend Moung Thwa, dealer in teakwood, had just returned down-river from distant Bhamo, where he had spent many weeks in dignified, unhurried chaffering with Chinese merchants ; the first place to which he had naturally turned his steps, bearing with him his betel-box and fat cigar, had been the raised platform of Moung Ka's cane-built house under the tamarind trees. The youthful Moung Shoogalay, who had studied in the foreign schools at Mandalay and knew many English words, was also of the little group that sat listening to Moung Ka's bulletin of the world's health and ignoring the screeching of the crows.

There had been the usual preliminary talk of timber and the rice market and sundry local matters, and then the wider and remoter things of life came under review.

" And what has been happening away from here ? " asked Moung Thwa of the newspaper reader.

" Away from here " comprised that considerable portion of the world's surface whch lay beyond the village boundaries.

" Many things," said Moung Ka reflectively, " but principally two things of much interest and of an opposite nature. Both, however, concern the action of Governments."

Moung Thwa nodded his head gravely, with the air of one who reverenced and distrusted all Governments.

"The first thing, of which you may have heard on your journeyings," said Moung Ka, "is an act of the Indian Government, which has annulled the not-long-ago accomplished partition of Bengal."

"I heard something of this," said Moung Thwa, "from a Madrassi merchant on the boat journey. But I did not learn the reasons that made the Government take this step. Why was the partition annulled?"

"Because," said Moung Ka, "it was held to be against the wishes of the greater number of the people of Bengal. Therefore the Government made an end of it."

Moung Thwa was silent for a moment. "Is it a wise thing the Government has done?" he asked presently.

"It is a good thing to consider the wishes of a people," said Moung Ka. "The Bengalis may be a people who do not always wish what is best for them. Who can say? But at least their wishes have been taken into consideration, and that is a good thing."

"And the other matter of which you spoke?" questioned Moung Thwa, "the matter of an opposite nature."

"The other matter," said Moung Ka, "is that the British Government has decided on the partition of Britain. Where there has been one Parliament and one Government there are to be two Parliaments and two Governments, and there will be two treasuries and two sets of taxes."

Moung Thwa was greatly interested at this news.

"And is the feeling of the people of Britain in favour of this partition?" he asked. "Will they not dislike it, as the people of Bengal disliked the partition of their Province?"

"The feeling of the people of Britain has not been consulted, and will not be consulted," said Moung Ka; "the Act of Partition will pass through one Chamber where the Government rules supreme, and the other Chamber can only delay it a little while, and then it will be made into the Law of the Land."

"But is it wise not to consult the feeling of the people?" asked Moung Thwa.

"Very wise," answered Moung Ka, "for if the people were consulted they would say 'No,' as they have always said when such a decree was submitted to their opinion, and if the people said 'No' there would be an end of the matter, but also an end of the Government. Therefore, it is wise for the Government to shut its ears to what the people may wish."

"But why must the people of Bengal be listened to and the people of Britain not listened to?" asked Moung Thwa; "surely the partition of their country affects them just as closely. Are their opinions too silly to be of any weight?"

"The people of Britain are what is called a Democracy," said Moung Ka.

"A Democracy?" questioned Moung Thwa. "What is that?"

"A Democracy," broke in Moung Shoogalay eagerly, "is a community that governs itself according to its own wishes and interests by electing accredited representatives who enact its laws and supervise and control their administration. Its aim and object is government of the community in the interests of the community."

" Then," said Moung Thwa, turning to his neighbour, " if the people of Britain are a Democracy——"

" I never said they were a Democracy," interrupted Moung Ka placidly.

" Surely we both heard you ! " exclaimed Moung Thwa.

" Not correctly," said Moung Ka ; " I said they are what is called a Democracy."

THE DEATH-TRAP

Characters.

DIMITRI. *(Reigning Prince of Kedaria.)*
Dr. STRONETZ ⎫
Col. GIRNITZA ⎪ *Officers of the Kranitzki*
Major VONTIEFF ⎬ *Regiment of Guards.*
Captain SHULTZ ⎭

SCENE :—*An Ante-chamber in the Prince's Castle at Tzern.*

TIME :—*The Present Day. The scene opens about ten o'clock in the evening.*

An ante-chamber, rather sparsely furnished. Some rugs of Balkan manufacture on the walls. A narrow table in centre of room, another table set with wine bottles and goblets near window, R. Some high-backed chairs set here and there round room. Tiled stove, L. Door in centre.

GIRNITZA, VONTIEFF and SHULTZ are talking together as curtain rises.

GIRNITZA. The Prince suspects something : I can see it in his manner.

SHULTZ. Let him suspect. He'll know for certain in half an hour's time.

GIR. The moment the Andrieff Regiment has marched out of the town we are ready for him.

SHULTZ *(drawing revolver from case and aiming it at an imaginary person).* And then—short shrift for

142

your Royal Highness !   I don't think many of my bullets will go astray.

GIR.   The revolver was never a favourite weapon of mine.   I shall finish the job with this (*half draws his sword and sends it back into its scabbard with a click*).

VONTIEFF.   Oh, we shall do for him right enough. It's a pity he's such a boy, though.   I would rather we had a grown man to deal with.

GIR.   We must take our chance when we can find it.   Grown men marry and breed heirs and then one has to massacre a whole family.   When we've killed this boy we've killed the last of the dynasty, and laid the way clear for Prince Karl.   As long as there was one of this brood left our good Karl could never win the throne.

VONT.   Oh, I know this is our great chance.   Still I wish the boy could be cleared out of our path by the finger of Heaven rather than by our hands.

SHULTZ.   Hush !   Here he comes.

(*Enter, by door, centre,* PRINCE DIMITRI, *in undress cavalry uniform.   He comes straight into room, begins taking cigarette out of a case, and looks coldly at the three officers.*)

DIMITRI.   You needn't wait.

(*They bow and withdraw,* SHULTZ *going last and staring insolently at the* PRINCE.   *He seats himself at table, centre.   As door shuts he stares for a moment at it, then suddenly bows his head on his arms in attitude of despair. . . .   A knock is heard at the door.* DIMITRI *leaps to his feet. Enter* STRONETZ, *in civilian attire.*)

DIMITRI (*eagerly*).   Stronetz !   My God, how glad I am to see you !

STRONETZ. One wouldn't have thought so, judging by the difficulty I had in gaining admission. I had to invent a special order to see you on a matter of health. And they made me give up my revolver; they said it was some new regulation.

DIM. (*with a short laugh*). They have taken away every weapon I possess, under some pretext or another. My sword has gone to be reset, my revolver is being cleaned, my hunting-knife has been mislaid.

STRON. (*horrified*). My God, Dimitri! You don't mean——?

DIM. Yes, I do. I am trapped. Since I came to the throne three years ago as a boy of fourteen I have been watched and guarded against this moment, but it has caught me unawares.

STRON. But your guards!

DIM. Did you notice the uniforms? The Kranitzki Regiment. They are heart and soul for Prince Karl; the artillery are equally disaffected. The Andrieff Regiment was the only doubtful factor in their plans, and it marches out to camp to-night. The Lonyadi Regiment comes in to relieve it an hour or so later.

STRON. They are loyal surely?

DIM. Yes, but their loyalty will arrive an hour or so too late.

STRON. Dimitri! You mustn't stay here to be killed! You must get out quick!

DIM. My dear good Stronetz, for more than a generation the Karl faction have been trying to stamp our line out of existence. I am the last of the lot; do you suppose that they are going to let me slip out of their claws now? They're not so damned silly.

STRON. But this is awful ! You sit there and talk as if it were a move in a chess game.

DIM. (*rising*). Oh, Stronetz ! if you knew how I hate death ! I'm not a coward, but I do so want to live. Life is so horribly fascinating when one is young, and I've tasted so little of it yet. (*Goes to window.*) Look out of the window at that fairyland of mountains with the forest running up and down all over it. You can just see Grodvitz where I shot all last autumn, up there on the left, and far away beyond it all is Vienna. Were you ever in Vienna, Stronetz ? I've only been there once, and it seemed like a magic city to me. And there are other wonderful cities in the world that I've never seen. Oh, I do so want to live. Think of it, here I am alive and talking to you, as we've talked dozens of times in this grey old room, and to-morrow a fat stupid servant will be washing up a red stain in that corner—I think it will probably be in that corner. (*He points to corner near stove,* L.)

STRON. But you mustn't be butchered in cold blood like this, Dimitri. If they've left you nothing to fight with I can give you a drug from my case that will bring you a speedy death before they can touch you.

DIM. Thanks, no, old chap. You had better leave before it begins ; they won't touch you. But I won't drug myself. I've never seen anyone killed before, and I shan't get another opportunity.

STRON. Then I won't leave you ; you can see two men killed while you are about it.

(*A band is heard in distance playing a march.*)

DIM. The Andrieff Regiment marching out ! Now they won't waste much time ! (*He draws himself up tense in corner by stove.*)   Hush, they are coming !

STRON. (*rushing suddenly towards* DIMITRI). Quick ! An idea !   Tear open your tunic ! (*He unfastens* DIMITRI's *tunic and appears to be testing his heart. The door swings open and the three officers enter.* STRONETZ *waves a hand commanding silence, and continues his testing.   The officers stare at him.*)

GIRN.   Dr. Stronetz, will you have the goodness to leave the room ?   We have some business with His Royal Highness.   Urgent business, Dr. Stronetz.

STRON. (*facing round*).   Gentlemen, I fear my business is more grave.   I have the saddest of duties to perform.   I know you would all gladly lay down you lives for your Prince, but there are some perils which even your courage cannot avert.

GIRN. (*puzzled*).   What are you talking of, sir ?

STRON.   The Prince sent for me to prescribe for some disquieting symptoms that have declared themselves.   I have made my examination.   My duty is a cruel one. . . .   I cannot give him six days to live !

(DIMITRI *sinks into chair near table in pretended collapse.   The officers turn to each other, nonplussed.*)

GIRN.   You are certain ?   It is a grave thing you are saying.   You are not making any mistake ?

STRON. (*laying his hand on* DIMITRI's *shoulder*). Would to God I were !

(*The officers again turn, whispering to each other.*)

GIRN.   It seems our business can wait.

VONT. (*to* DIMITRI).   Sire, this is the finger of Heaven.

DIM. (*brokenly*). Leave me.

(*They salute and slowly withdraw.* DIMITRI *slowly raises his head, then springs to his feet, rushes to door and listens, then turns round jubilantly to* STRONETZ.)

DIM. Spoofed them! Ye gods, that was an idea, Stronetz!

STRON. (*who stands quietly looking at* DIMITRI). It was not altogether an inspiration, Dimitri. A look in your eyes suggested it. I had seen men who were stricken with a mortal disease look like that.

DIM. Never mind what suggested it, you have saved me. The Lonyadi Regiment will be here at any moment and Girnitza's gang daren't risk anything then. You've fooled them, Stronetz, you've fooled them.

STRON. (*sadly*). Boy, I haven't fooled them. . . . (DIMITRI *stares at him for a long moment.*) It was a real examination I made while those brutes were waiting there to kill you. It was a real report I made ; the malady *is* there.

DIM. (*slowly*). Was it *all* true, what you told them?

STRON. It was all true. You have not six days to live.

DIM. (*bitterly*). Death has come twice for me in one evening. I'm afraid he must be in earnest. (*Passionately.*) Why didn't you let them kill me? That would have been better than this " to-be-left-till-called-for " business. (*Paces across to window, R., and looks out. Turns suddenly.*) Stronetz! You offered me a way of escape from a cruel death just now. Let me escape now from a crueller one.

I am a monarch. I won't be kept waiting by death.
Give me that little bottle.

(STRONETZ *hesitates, then draws out a small
case, extracts bottle and gives it to him.*)

STRON. Four or five drops will do what you ask
for.

DIM. Thank you. And now, old friend, good-
bye. Go quickly. You've seen me just a little brave
—I may not keep it up. I want you to remember me
as being brave. Good-bye, best of friends, go.

(STRONETZ *wrings his hand and rushes from
the room with his face hidden in his arm. The
door shuts.* DIMITRI *looks for a moment after his
friend. Then he goes quickly over to side table
and uncorks wine bottle. He is about to pour
some wine into a goblet when he pauses as if
struck by a new idea. He goes to door, throws it
open and listens, then calls, " Girnitz, Vontieff,
Shultz ! " Darting back to the table he pours the
entire phial of poison into the wine bottle, and
thrusts phial into his pocket. Enter the three
officers.*)

DIM. (*pouring the wine into four goblets*). The
Prince is dead—long live the Prince ! (*He seats himself.*) The old feud must be healed now, there is
no one left of my family to keep it on, Prince Karl must
succeed. Long life to Prince Karl ! Gentlemen
of the Kranitzki Guards, drink to your future
sovereign.

(*The three officers drink after glancing at each
other.*)

GIR. Sire, we shall never serve a more gallant
Prince than your Royal Highness.

DIM. That is true, because you will never serve

another Prince. Observe, I drink fair! (*Drains goblet.*)

Gir. What do you mean, never serve another Prince?

Dim. (*rises*). I mean that I am going to march into the next world at the head of my Kranitzki Guards. You came in here to-night to kill me. (*They all start.*) You found that Death had fore-stalled you. I thought it a pity that the evening should be wasted, so I've killed *you*, that's all!

Shultz. The wine! He's poisoned us!

(Vontieff *seizes the bottle, and examines it.* Shultz *smells his empty goblet.*)

Gir. Ah! Poisoned! (*He draws his sword and makes a step towards* Dimitri, *who is sitting on the edge of the centre table.*)

Dim. Oh, certainly, if you wish it. I'm due to die of disease in a few days and of poison in a minute or two, but if you like to take a little extra trouble about my end, please yourself. (Girnitza *reels and drops sword on table and falls back into chair groaning.* Shultz *falls across table and* Vontieff *staggers against wall. At that moment a lively march is heard ap-proaching.* Dimitri *seizes the sword and waves it.*)

Dim. Aha! the Lonyadi Regiment marching in! My good loyal Kranitzki Guards shall keep me company into the next world. God save the Prince! (*Laughs wildly.*) Colonel Girnitza, I never thought death . . could be . . . so amusing.

(*He falls dying to the ground.*)

Curtain.

149

KARL-LUDWIG'S WINDOW

A Drama in One Act

Kurt von Jagdstein.
The Gräfin von Jagdstein (*his mother*).
Isadora (*his betrothed*)
Philip (*Isadora's brother*)   *Guests at*
Viktoria (*niece of the Gräfin*)   *Schloss Jagdstein.*
Baron Rabel (*a parvenu*)
An Officer.

Scene :—" *Karl-Ludwig's Room* " *in the Schloss Jagdstein, on the outskirts of a town in Eastern Europe.*
Time :—*An evening in Carnival Week, the present day.*
A room furnished in mediæval style. In the centre a massive tiled stove of old-German pattern, over which, on a broad shelf, a large clock. Above the clock a painting of a man in sixteenth-century costume. Immediately to Left, *in a deep embrasure, a window with a high window-seat. Immediately on* Right *of stove an old iron-clamped door, approached by two steps. The* Walls *to* Left *and* Right *are hung with faded tapestry. In the foreground a long oak table, with chairs right, left and centre, and a low armchair on* Left *of stage. On the table are high-stemmed goblets*

and wine bottles, and a decanter of cognac with some smaller glasses.

THE GRÄFIN, in an old Court costume, and BARON RABEL, also in some Court attire of a bygone age, are discovered. Both wear little black velvet masks. The BARON bows low to the lady, who makes him a mock curtsey. They remove their masks.

GRÄFIN (*seating herself at left of table*). Of course we old birds are the first to be ready. Light a cigar, Baron, and make yourself at your ease while the young folks are completing their costumes.

BARON (*seating himself at table*). At my ease in this room I could never be. It makes my flesh creep every time I enter it. I am what the world calls a parvenu (*lights cigar*), a man of to-day, or perhaps I should say of this afternoon, while your family is of the day before yesterday and many yesterdays before that. Naturally I envy you your ancestry, your title, your position, but there is one thing I do not envy you.

GRÄF. (*helping herself to wine*). And that is——?

BAR. Your horrible creepy traditions.

GRÄF. You mean Karl-Ludwig, I suppose. Yes, this room is certainly full of his associations. There is his portrait, and there is the window from which he was flung down. Only it is more than a tradition : it really happened.

BAR. That makes it all the more horrible. I am a man who belongs to a milder age, and it sickens me to think of the brutal deed that was carried through in this room. How his enemies stole in upon him and took him unawares, and how they dragged him screaming to that dreadful window.

GRÄF. Not screaming, I hope; cursing and storming, perhaps. I don't think a Von Jagdstein would scream even in a moment like that.

BAR. The bravest man's courage might be turned to water, looking down at death from that horrid window. It makes one's breath go even to look down in safety; one can see the stones of the court-yard fathoms and fathoms below.

GRÄF. Let us hope he hadn't time to think about it. It would be the thinking of it that would be so terrible.

BAR. (*with a shudder*). Ah, indeed! I assure you the glimpse down from that window has haunted me ever since I looked.

GRÄF. The window is not the only thing in the room that is haunted. They say that whenever one of the family is going to die a violent death that door swings open and shuts again of its own accord. It is supposed to be Karl-Ludwig's ghost coming in.

BAR. (*with apprehensive glance behind him*). What an unpleasant room! Let us forget its associations and talk about something more cheerful. How charming Fräulein Isadora is looking to-night. It is a pity her betrothed could not get leave to come to the ball with her. She is going as Elsa, is she not?

GRÄF. Something of the sort, I believe. She's told me so often that I've forgotten.

BAR. You will be fortunate in securing such a daughter-in-law, is it not so?

GRÄF. Yes, Isadora has all the most desirable qualifications : heaps of money, average good looks, and absolutely no brains.

BAR. And are the young people very devoted to each other ?

GRÄF. I am a woman of the world, Baron, and I don't put too high a value on the sentimental side of things, but even I have never seen an engaged couple who made less pretence of caring for one another. Kurt has always been the naughty boy of the family, but he made surprisingly little fuss about being betrothed to Isadora. He said he should never marry anyone he loved, so it didn't matter whom I married him to.

BAR. That was at least accommodating.

GRÄF. Besides the financial advantages of the match the girl's aunt has a very influential position, so for a younger son Kurt is doing rather well.

BAR. He is a clever boy, is he not ?

GRÄF. He has that perverse kind of cleverness that is infinitely more troublesome than any amount of stupidity. I prefer a fool like Isadora. You can tell beforehand exactly what she will say or do under any given circumstances, exactly on what days she will have a headache, and exactly how many garments she will send to the wash on Mondays.

BAR. A most convenient temperament.

GRÄF. With Kurt one never knows where one is. Now, being in the same regiment with the Archduke ought to be of some advantage to him in his career, if he plays his cards well. But of course he'll do nothing of the sort.

BAR. Perhaps the fact of being betrothed will work a change in him.

GRÄF. You are an optimist. Nothing ever changes a perverse disposition. Kurt has always been a jarring element in our family circle, but I don't regard one unsatisfactory son out of three as a bad average. It's usually higher.

> (*Enter* ISADORA, *dressed as Elsa, followed by* PHILIP, *a blond loutish youth, in the costume of a page, Henry III period.*)

ISADORA. I hope we haven't kept you waiting. I've been helping Viktoria ; she'll be here presently.

> (*They sit at table.* PHILIP *helps himself to wine.*)

GRÄF. We mustn't wait much longer ; it's nearly half-past eight now.

BAR. I've just been saying, what a pity the young Kurt could not be here this evening for the ball.

ISA. Yes, it is a pity. He is only a few miles away with his regiment, but he can't get leave till the end of the week. It is a pity, isn't it ?

GRÄF. It is always the way : when one particularly wants people they can never get away.

ISA. It's always the way, isn't it ?

GRÄF. As for Kurt, he has a perfect gift for never being where you want him.

> (*Enter* KURT, *in undress Cavalry uniform. He comes rapidly into the room.*)

GRÄF. (*rising with the others*). Kurt ! How come you to be here ? I thought you couldn't get leave.

> (KURT *kisses his mother's hand, then that of* ISADORA, *and bows to the two men.*)

KURT. I came away in a hurry (*pours out a glass of wine*) to avoid arrest. Your health everybody. (*Drains glass thirstily.*)

GRÄF. To avoid arrest !

BAR. Arrest !

> (KURT *throws himself wearily into armchair, Left of Stage. The others stand staring at him.*)

GRÄF. What *do* you mean ? Arrest for what ?

KURT (*quietly*). I have killed the Archduke.

GRÄF. Killed the Archduke ! Do you mean you have murdered him ?

KURT. Scarcely that : it was a fair duel.

GRÄF. (*wringing her hands*). Killed the Archduke in a duel ! What an unheard-of scandal ! Oh, we are ruined !

BAR. (*throwing his arms about*). It is unbelievable ! What, in Heaven's name, were the seconds about to let such a thing happen ?

KURT (*shortly*). There were no seconds.

GRÄF. No seconds ! An irregular duel ? Worse and worse ! What a scandal ! What an appalling scandal !

BAR. But how do you mean—no seconds ?

KURT. It was in the highest degree desirable that there should be no seconds, so that if the Archduke fell there would be no witnesses to know the why and wherefore of the duel. Of course there will be a scandal, but it will be a sealed scandal.

GRÄF. Our poor family ! We are ruined.

BAR. (*persistently*). But *you* are alive. You will have to give an account of what happened.

KURT. There is only one way in which my account can be rendered.

BAR. (*after staring fixedly at him*). You mean——?

KURT (*quietly*). Yes. I escaped arrest only by giving my *parole* to follow the Archduke into the next world as soon as might be.

GRÄF. A suicide in our family ! What an appalling affair. People will never stop talking about it.

ISA. It's very unfortunate, isn't it ?

Gräf. (*crossing over to* Isadora).   My poor child !
(Isadora *dabs at her eyes.*)
(*Enter* Viktoria, *dressed in Italian peasant
costume.*)

Vik.   I'm so sorry to be late.   All these necklaces
took such a time to fasten.   Hullo, where did Kurt
spring from ?
(*Kurt rises.*)

Gräf.   He has brought some bad news.

Vik.   Oh, how dreadful.   Anything very bad ?
It won't prevent us from going to the ball, will it ?
It's going to be a particularly gay affair.
(*A faint sound of a tolling bell is heard.*)

Kurt.   I don't fancy there will be a ball to-night.
The news has come as quickly as I have.   The bells
are tolling already.

Bar. (*dramatically*).   The scandal is complete !

Gräf.   I shall never forgive you, Kurt.

Vik.   But what has happened ?

Kurt.   I should like to say a few words to Isadora.
Perhaps you will give us till nine o'clock to talk
things over.

Gräf.   I suppose it's the proper thing to do under
the circumstances.   Oh, why should I be afflicted
with such a stupid son !

(*Exit the* Gräfin, *followed by the* Baron, *who
waves his arms about dramatically, and by* Philip
and Viktoria.   Philip *is explaining matters
in whispers to the bewildered* Viktoria *as they
go out.*)

Isa. (*stupidly*).   This is very unfortunate, isn't it ?

Kurt (*leaning across table with sudden animation
as the door closes on the others*).   Isadora, I have come
to ask you to do something for me.   The search

party will arrive to arrest me at nine o'clock and I have given my word that they shall not find me alive. I've got less than twenty minutes left. You *must* promise to do what I ask you.

Isa. What is it?

Kurt. I suppose it's a strange thing to ask of a woman I'm betrothed to, but there's really no one else who can do it for me. I want you to take a message to the woman I love.

Isa. Kurt!

Kurt. Of course it's not very conventional, but I knew her and loved her long before I met you, ever since I was eighteen. That's only three years ago, but it seems the greater part of my life. It was a lonely and unhappy life, I remember, till she befriended me, and then it was like the magic of some old fairy-tale.

Isa. Do I know who she is?

Kurt. You must have guessed that long ago. Your aunt will easily be able to get you an opportunity for speaking to her, and you must mention no name, give no token. Just say " I have a message for you." She will know who it comes from.

Isa. I shall be dreadfully frightened. What is the message?

Kurt. Just one word : " Good-bye."

Isa. It's a very short message, isn't it?

Kurt. It's the longest message one heart ever sent to another. Other messages may fade away in the memory, but Time will keep on repeating that message as long as memory lasts. Every sunset and every night-fall will say good-bye for me.

(*The door swings open, and then slowly closes of its own accord.* Kurt *represses a shiver.*)

Isa. (*in a startled voice*). What was that? Who opened the door?

Kurt. Oh, it's nothing. It does that sometimes when—when—under circumstances like the present. They say it's old Karl-Ludwig coming in.

Isa. I shall faint!

Kurt (*in an agonized voice*). Don't you do anything of the sort. We haven't time for that. You haven't given me your promise; oh, do make haste. Promise you'll give the message! (*He seizes both her hands.*)

Isa. I promise.

Kurt (*kissing her hands*). Thank you. (*With a change to a lighter tone.*) I say, you haven't got a loaded revolver on you, have you? I came away in such a hurry I forgot to bring one.

Isa. Of course I haven't. One doesn't take loaded revolvers to a masquerade ball.

Kurt. It must be Karl-Ludwig's window then. (*He unbuckles his sword and throws it into the armchair.*) Oh, I forgot. This miniature mustn't be found on me. Don't be scandalized if I do a little undressing. (*He picks up an illustrated paper from a stool near stove and gives it to* Isadora *to hold open in front of her.*) Here you are. (*He proceeds to unbutton his tunic at the neck and breast and removes a miniature which is hung round his neck. He gazes at it for a moment, kisses it, gazes again, then drops it on the floor and grinds it to pieces with his heel. Then he goes to window, opens it and looks down.*) I wish the night were darker; one can see right down to the flagstones of the courtyard. It looks awful, but it will look fifty times more horrible in eight minutes' time. (*He comes back to table and seats himself on its*

158

edge.) As I rode along on the way here it seemed such an easy thing to die, and now it's come so close I feel sick with fear. Fancy a Von Jagdstein turning coward. What a scandal, as my dear mother would say. (*He tries to pour out some brandy, but his hand shakes too much.*) Do you mind pouring me out some brandy? I can't steady my hand. (ISADORA *fills a glass for him.*) Thanks. No (*pushing it away*), I won't take it; if I can't have my own courage I won't have that kind. But I wish I hadn't looked down just now. Don't you know what it feels like to go down too quickly in a lift, as if one was racing one's inside and winning by a neck? That's what it will feel like for the first second, and then—— (*He hides his eyes a moment in his hands.* ISADORA *falls back in her chair in a faint.* KURT *looks up suddenly at clock.*)

KURT. Isadora! Say that the clock is a minute fast! (*He looks towards her.*) She's fainted. Just what she would do. She isn't a brilliant conversationalist, but she was some one to talk to. How beastly lonely it feels up here. Not a soul to say, " Buck up, Kurt, old boy! " Nothing but a fainting woman and Karl-Ludwig's ghost. I wonder if his ghost is watching me now. I wonder if I shall haunt this room. What a rum idea. (*Looks again at clock and gives a start.*) I *can't* die in three minutes' time. O God! I can't do it. It isn't the jump that I shrink from now—it's the ending of everything. It's too horrible to think of. To have no more life! Isadora and the Baron and millions of stupid people will go on living, every day will bring them something new, and I shall never have one morsel of life after these three minutes. I *can't* do it. (*Falls heavily into chair, left of table.*) I'll go away somewhere where no one knows me ; that will be as good as dying. I told them they should not find me here alive. Well, I can slip away before they come. (*He rises and moves towards door ; his foot grinds on a piece of the broken miniature. He stoops and picks it up, looks hard and long at it, then drops it through his fingers. He turns his head slowly towards the clock and stands watching it. He takes handkerchief from his sleeve and wipes his mouth, returns handkerchief to sleeve, still watching the clock. Some seconds pass in silence. . . . The clock strikes the first stroke of nine.* KURT *turns and walks to the window. He mounts the window-seat and stands with one foot on the sill, and looks out and down. He makes the sign of the Cross . . . throws up his arms and jumps into space.*)

(*The door opens and the* GRÄFIN *enters, followed by an* OFFICER. *They look at the swooning* ISADORA, *then round the room for* KURT.)

GRÄF. He is gone !

OFFICER. He gave me his word that I should find him here at nine o'clock, and that I should come too late to arrest him. It seems he has tricked me !

GRÄF. A Von Jagdstein always keeps his word.

(*She stares fixedly at the open window. The* OFFICER *follows the direction of her gaze, goes over to window, looks out and down. He turns back to the room, straightens himself and salutes.*)

CURTAIN.

THE WATCHED POT

"The Watched Pot" was written in collaboration with Mr. Charles Maude, who has sent me the following account concerning the play :

"The circumstances of our writing 'The Watched Pot' were : Mr. Frederick Harrison was very interested in your brother's original 'Watched Pot,' but found it unsuitable for the stage, and brought Saki and myself together in the hope that our joint efforts would make it suitable. My share was shortening it, giving it incident, and generally adapting it for stage purposes. Saki used to write more as a novelist than a playwright.

"He and I used to have many friendly quarrels, as he was so full of witty remarks that it was a cruel business discarding some of his *bons mots*. We always used to terminate such quarrels by agreeing to use his axed witticisms in our next play. . . . Shortly before the war Saki at last gave in on the question of plot, and we had practically completed an entirely new story, still retaining the characters which he loved so dearly and which were so typical of his brain."

The character of Hortensia Bavvel is from life, but the tyranny of her prototype was confined to her own family. She died many years ago.

E. M. M.

THE WATCHED POT

(Alternative Title)

THE MISTRESS OF BRIONY

Characters.

TREVOR BAVVEL.
HORTENSIA. *(Mrs. Bavvel, his mother.)*
LUDOVIC BAVVEL. *His uncle.*
RENÉ ST. GALL.
AGATHA CLIFFORD ⎫
CLARE HENESSEY ⎪
SYBIL BOMONT ⎬ *Guests at Briony.*
Mrs. PETER VULPY ⎪
STEPHEN SPARROWBY ⎭
Col. MUTSOME.
THE YOUNGEST DRUMMOND BOY.
WILLIAM. *Page-boy at Briony.*
JOHN. *Under Butler at Briony.*

ACT I. *Briony Manor Breakfast Room.*
ACT II. *Briony Manor Hall (the next evening).*
ACT III. *Briony Manor Breakfast Room (the next morning).*

ACT I

Breakfast Room at Briony Manor.

LUDOVIC *fidgeting with papers at escritoire*, L., *occasionally writing.* MRS. VULPY *seated in armchair,*

R., *with her back partially turned to him, glancing at illustrated papers.*

MRS. VULPY (*with would-be fashionable drawl*). So sweet of your dear cousin Agatha to bring me down here with her. Such a refreshing change from the dust and glare of Folkestone.

LUD. (*absently*). Yes, I suppose so.

MRS. V. And so unexpected. Her invitation took me quite by surprise.

LUD. Dear Agatha is always taking people by surprise. She was born taking people by surprise ; in Goodwood Week, I believe, with an Ambassador staying in the house who hated babies. So thoroughly like her. One feels certain that she'll die one of these days in some surprising and highly inconvenient manner ; probably from snake-bite on the Terrace of the House of Commons.

MRS. V. I'm afraid you don't like your cousin.

LUD. Oh dear yes. I make it a rule to like my relations. I remember only their good qualities and forget their birthdays. (*With increased animation, rising from his seat and approaching her.*) Excuse the question, Mrs. Vulpy, are you a widow ?

MRS. V. I really can't say with any certainty.

LUD. You can't say ?

MRS. V. With any certainty. According to latest mail advices from Johannesburg my husband, Mr. Peter Vulpy, was not expected by his medical attendants to last into the next week. On the other hand, a cablegram from the local mining organ to a City newspaper over here congratulates that genuine sportsman, Mr. P. Vulpy, on his recovery from his recent severe illness. There happens to be a Percival Vulpy in Johannesburg, so my present information is not very conclusive in either direction. Doctors and journalists are both so untrustworthy, aren't they?

LUD. Could your Mr. P. Vulpy be correctly described as a genuine sportsman?

MRS. V. There was nothing genuine about Peter. I've never heard of his hitting even a partridge in anger, but he used to wear a horse-shoe scarf-pin, and I've known him to watch football matches, so I suppose he might be described as a sportsman. For all I know to the contrary, he may by this time have joined the majority, who are powerless to resent these intrusions, but my private impression is that he's sitting up and taking light nourishment in increasing doses.

LUD. How extremely unsatisfactory.

MRS. V. Really, Mr. Bavvel, I think if anyone is to mourn Mr. Vulpy's continued existence I should be allowed that privilege. After all, he's my husband, you know. Perhaps you are one of those who don't believe that the marriage tie gives one any proprietary rights.

LUD. Oh, most certainly I do. I am a prospective candidate for Parliamentary honours, and I believe in all the usual things. My objection to Mr. Vulpy's inconvenient vitality is entirely impersonal. If you were in a state of widowhood there would be no obstacle to your marrying Trevor. (*Resumes seat at escritoire, but sits facing her.*)

MRS. V. Marrying Trevor! Really, this is interesting. And why, pray, should I be singled out for that destiny?

LUD. My dear Mrs. Vulpy, let me be absolutely frank with you. Honoured as we should be to welcome you into the family circle, I may at once confess that my solicitude is not so much to see you married to my nephew as to see him married to somebody ; happily and suitably married of course, but anyhow—married.

MRS. V. Indeed !

LUD. Briefly, the gist of the business is this. Like most gifted young men, Trevor has a mother.

MRS. V. Oh, I fancy I know *that* already.

LUD. One could scarcely be at Briony for half an hour without making that discovery.

MRS. V. Hortensia, Mrs. Bavvel, is not exactly one of those things that one can hide under a damask cheek, or whatever the saying is.

LUD. Hortensia is a very estimable woman. Most estimable women are apt to be a little trying. Without pretending to an exhaustive knowledge on the subject, I should say Hortensia was the most trying woman in Somersetshire. Probably without exaggeration one of the most trying women in the West of England. My late brother Edward, Hortensia's husband, who was not given to making original observations if he could find others ready-made to his hand, used to declare that marriage was a lottery. Like most popular sayings, that simile breaks down on application. In a lottery there are prizes and blanks ; no one who knew her would think of describing Hortensia as either a prize or a blank.

MRS. V. Well, no : she doesn't come comfortably under either heading.

LUD. My brother was distinguished for what is known as a retiring disposition. Hortensia, on the other hand, was dowered with a commanding personality. Needless to say she became a power in the household, in a very short time the only power—a sort of Governor-General and Mother Superior and

political Boss rolled into one.   A Catherine the Second
of Russia without any of Catherine's redeeming vices.

MRS. V.   An uncomfortable sort of person to live
with.

LUD.   Hortensia did everything that had to be
done in the management of a large estate—and a
great deal that might have been left undone : she
engaged and dismissed gardeners, decided which of
the under-gamekeepers might marry and how much
gooseberry jam should be made in a given year,
regulated the speed at which perambulators might
be driven through the village street and the number
of candles which might be lighted in church on dark
afternoons without suspicion of Popery.   Almost the
only periodical literature that she allowed in the house
was the *Spectator* and the *Exchange and Mart*, neither
of which showed any tendency to publish betting news.
Halma and chess were forbidden on Sundays for fear
of setting a bad example to the servants.

MRS. V.   If servants knew how often the fear of
leading them astray by bad example holds us back from
desperate wickedness, I'm sure they would ask for
double wages.   And what was poor Mr. Edward
doing all this time ?

LUD.   Edward was not of a complaining disposition, and for a while he endured Hortensia with a
certain philosophic calm.   Later, however, he gave
way to golf.

MRS. V.   And Hortensia went on bossing things ?

LUD.   From the lack of any organized opposition
her autocracy rapidly developed into a despotism.
Her gubernatorial energies overflowed the limits of
the estate and parish, and she became a sort of minor
power in the moral and political life of the county,

167

not to say the nation. Nothing seemed to escape her vigilance, whether it happened in the Established Church or the servants' hall or the Foreign Office. She quarrelled with the Macedonian policy of every successive Government, exposed the hitherto unsuspected Atheism of the nearest Dean and Chapter, and dismissed a page-boy for parting his hair in the middle. With equal readiness she prescribed rules for the better management of the Young Woman's Christian Association and the Devon and Somerset Staghounds. Briony used to be a favourite rendezvous for the scattered members of the family. Under the Hortensia *régime* we began to find the train service less convenient and our opportunities for making prolonged visits recurred at rare intervals.

MRS. V. Didn't her health wear out under all that strain of activity?

LUD. With the exception of an occasional full-dress headache, Hortensia enjoyed implacable good health. We resigned ourselves to the prospect of the good lady's rule at Briony for the rest of our natural lives. Then something happened which we had left out of our calculations. Edward caught a chill out otter-hunting and in less than a week Hortensia was a widow. We are what is known as a very united family, and poor dear Edward's death affected us acutely.

MRS. V. Naturally it would, coming so suddenly.

LUD. At the same time, there was a rainbow of consolation irradiating our grief. Edward's otherwise untimely decease seemed to promise the early dethronement of Hortensia. Trevor was twenty years of age and in the natural course of things he would soon be absolute master of Briony, and the relict of

Edward Bavvel would be denuded of her despotic terrors and become merely a tiresome old woman. As I have said, we were all much attached to poor Edward, but somehow his funeral was one of the most cheerful functions that had been celebrated at Briony for many years. Then came a discovery that cast a genuine gloom over the whole affair. Edward had left the management of the estate and the control of his entire and very considerable fortune to Hortensia until such time as Trevor should take unto himself a wife (*Rises from seat and takes short steps up and down.*) That was six long years ago and Trevor is still un-married, unengaged, not even markedly attracted towards any eligible female. Hortensia, on the other hand, has—well, ripened, without undergoing any process of mellowing ; rather the reverse.

Mrs. V. Aha ! I begin to spot the nigger in the timber-yard.

Lud. I beg your pardon ?

Mrs. V. I begin to twig. Deprived by Trevor's marriage of her control of the money-bags, Hortensia, as a domestic tyrant, would shrink down to bearable limits.

Lud. (*seating himself*). Hortensia under existing circumstances is like a permeating dust-storm, which you can't possibly get away from or pretend that it's not there. Living with a comparatively modest establishment at the dower-house, she would be merely like Town in August or the bite of a camel—a painful experience which may be avoided with a little ordinary prudence.

Mrs. V. I don't wonder that you're keen on the change.

Lud. Keen ! There is no one on the estate or

in the family who doesn't include it in his or her private litany of daily wants.

Mrs. V. And I suppose Mrs. Bavvel is not at all anxious to see herself put on the shelf and does her best to head Mr. Trevor off from any immediate matrimonial projects ?

Lud. Of course Hortensia recognizes the desirability of Trevor ultimately finding a suitable consort, if only for carrying on the family. I've no doubt that one day she'll produce some flabby little nonentity who will be flung into Trevor's arms with a maternal benediction.

Mrs. V. Meantime you haven't been able to get him to commit himself in any way. But perhaps his mother would break off any engagement she didn't approve of ?

Lud. Oh, no fear of that. With all his inertness, Trevor has a wholesome strain of obstinacy in his composition. If he once gets engaged to a girl, he'll marry her. The trouble is that his obstinacy takes the form of his refusing to be seriously attracted by any particular competitor. If patient, determined effort on the part of others would have availed he would have been married dozens of times, but a touch of real genius is required. That is why I appeal to you to help us.

Mrs. V. I suppose Agatha considers herself in the running ?

Lud. Poor Agatha has a perfect genius for supporting lost causes. I've no doubt she fancies she has an off chance of becoming Mrs. Trevor Bavvel. I've equally no doubt that she never will. Agatha is one of those unaccountable people who are impelled to keep up an inconsequent flow of conversation if they detect you trying to read a book or write a letter, and if you should be suffering from an acknowledged headache she invariably bangs out something particularly triumphant on the nearest piano by way of showing that she at least is not downhearted. Or if you want to think out some complicated problem she will come and sit by your side and read through an entire bulb catalogue to you, with explanatory comments of her own. No, we are all very fond of Agatha, but strictly as a cheerful inane sort of person to have about the house—some one else's house for preference.

MRS. V. And what about Miss Henessey?

LUD. Oh, Clare; she's a rattling good sort in her way, and at one time I used to hope that she and Trevor might hit it off. I think in his own sleepy way he was rather attracted to her. Unfortunately, she only pays rare visits here, and even that she has to keep dark. You see, she's the favourite grand-niece and prospective heiress of old Mrs. Packington —you've heard of Mrs. Packington?

MRS. V. No; who is she?

LUD. She lives near Bath, and she's fabulously old, and fabulously rich, and she's been fabulously ill for longer than any living human being can remember. I believe she caught a chill at Queen Victoria's coronation and never let it go again. The most human thing about her is her dislike for Hortensia, who, I believe, once advised her to take more exercise and less medicine. The old lady has ever since alluded to her as a rattlesnake in dove's plumage, and has more than once, with her dying breath, cautioned Clare against intercourse with Briony and its inhabitants. So, you see, there's not much to be hoped for in that direction.

MRS. V. Awfully provoking, isn't it? What about Sybil Bomont?

LUD. Ah, Sybil is the one ray of hope that I can see on the horizon. Personally, she's rather too prickly in her temperament to suit me. She has a fatal gift for detecting the weak spots in her fellow humans and sticking her spikes into them. Matrimony is not reputed to be an invariable bed of roses, but there is no reason why it should be a cactus-hedge. However, she is clever enough to keep that side of her character to the wall whenever Trevor is alongside.

MRS. V. And you think she's got a good sporting chance with him?

LUD. She isn't losing any opportunities that come along, and I'm naturally trying my best to drive the game up her way, but the daily round at Briony doesn't give us much help. We begin the day with solid breakfast businesses; then there are partridges to be tramped after, and Trevor takes his birds rather solemnly, as though it hurt him more than it does them, you know. In the evening a solid dinner, and then Bridge for such small stakes that even Agatha can't lose enough in a fortnight to convince her that she can't play. Then bed.

MRS. V. Well, that's not a very promising programme for anyone who's working a matrimonial movement. Couldn't we get up something that would supply a few more openings. Why not theatricals?

LUD. Theatricals? At Briony! You might as well suggest a massacre of Christian villagers. Hortensia looks on the stage and everything that pertains to it as a sort of early door to the infernal regions.

MRS. V. What about a gymkhana?

LUD. Infinitely worse. The mention of a gymkhana would suggest to Hortensia's mind the unchastened restlessness of the Anglo-Saxon grafted on to the traditional licentiousness of the purple East. The very word " gymkhana " reeks with an aroma of long drinks, sweepstakes, and betrayed husbands, and the usual things that are supposed to strew the social horizon east of Suez.

MRS. V. Well, I'm afraid it's hopeless. I give it up.

LUD. (*rising hastily from his seat*). Dear Mrs. Vulpy, on no account give it up. I rely so much on your tact and insight and experience. You *must* think of something. I'm not a wealthy man, but if you help me to pull this through I promise you my gratitude shall take concrete shape. A commemorative bracelet, for instance—have you any particular favourite stones?

MRS. V. I love all stones—except garnets or moonstones.

LUD. You think it unlucky to have moonstones?

MRS. V. Oh, distinctly, if you've the chance of getting something more valuable. I adore rubies; they're so sympathetic.

LUD. I'll make a note of it. (*Writes in pocketbook.*)

MRS. V. I gather that we're to concentrate on Sybil?

LUD. Sybil, certainly. And of course if there's anything I can do to back you up—— (*Enter* CLARE *and* SYBIL *by door* : Left *back*) . . . no, I don't know that part of Switzerland ; I once spent a winter at St. Moritz.

(CLARE *seats herself on couch,* R. SYBIL *takes chair in centre stage.*)

CLARE. You needn't pretend you're discussing Swiss health resorts, because you're not.

MRS. V. Oh, but we are, Miss Henessey. I was just saying Montreux was so——

CLARE. You were discussing Trevor and possible Mrs. Trevors. My dear Mrs. Vulpy, it's our one subject of discussion here.

SYBIL. It's a frightfully absorbing subject, especially for me.

CLARE. Why for you especially?

SYBIL. Oh, well, dear.

LUD. We did touch on the subject, I admit, and Mrs. Vulpy has very kindly offered to help matters along in that direction if she can find an opportunity.

SYBIL. Have you had bad news from South Africa?

MRS. V. Oh, dear, no. My offer is quite disinterested.

SYBIL. How noble of you. How do you propose to begin?

MRS. V. Well, I was just suggesting a little departure from the usual routine of life here, something that would give an opening for a clever girl to bring a man to the scratch. But it seems that Mrs. Bavvel is rather against any of the more promising forms of entertainment.

SYBIL. We've had the annual harvest thanksgiving, but Trevor was seedy and couldn't help with the decorations.

MRS. V. Harvest thanksgiving?

CLARE. Yes, it's one of our rural institutions. We get our corn and most of our fruit from abroad, but we always assemble the local farmers and tenantry to give thanks for the harvest. So broad-minded of us. It shows such a nice spirit for a Somersetshire farmer to be duly thankful for the ripening of the Carlsbad plum.

Mrs. V. Is Mrs. Bavvel never absent at dinner parties or anything of that sort ? A little impromptu frolic is sometimes a great success.

Lud. Now if you're going to plot anything illicit I must really leave you. Hortensia is not in very great demand as a dinner guest, but she is taking me to-morrow to a meeting at Panfold in connection with the opening of a Free Library there, and there will be a reception of some sort in the Town Hall afterwards. I entirely disapprove of anything of a festive nature taking place here behind her back, but —we shan't be home much before midnight. It's a fairly long drive. Understand, I entirely disapprove.

(*Gathers papers and Exits, door* Left *front.*)

Sybil. This threatens to be rather sporting. What have you got up your sleeve ?

Mrs. V. Oh, nothing, only why not beat up your men and girl friends at short notice and have a Cinderella ? There's a lovely floor in the morning room and a good piano, and you could have a scratch supper.

Clare. And how about the servants ? Are we to beg them all individually to hold their tongues about the affair ?

Mrs. V. Oh, of course Mrs. Bavvel would have to know about it next day.

Clare. It's very well for you to talk like that, you're a comparative stranger here, and I dare say you'd find a certain amount of amusement in the situation. Those of us who know what Hortensia is like when anything displeases her—well, it would simply be a case of Bradshaw at breakfast and a tea-basket at Yeovil.

Mrs. V. But then we're playing to win ; it's a sort of *coup d'état*. With the fun and excitement of the dancing and the music, and of course the sitting-out places, and, above all, the charming sense of doing something wrong, the betting is that Trevor will be engaged to one of you girls before the night's out. And then the morrow can be left to take care of itself.

Sybil. It sounds *lovely*. I'm horribly frightened of Hortensia, but I'm game to get up this dance.

Clare. A *coup d'état* is a wretchedly messy thing. It's as bad as cooking with a chafing-dish ; it takes such ages to clean things up afterwards.

(*Enter* Agatha *door* Right *back, with two large baskets piled with asters, dahlias, etc., and long trails of ivy and brambles.*)

Agatha. Hullo, you idle people. I'm just going to arrange the flowers. (*Puts baskets down on escritoire.*)

Sybil. Are you ? Why ?

Agatha. Oh, I always do when I'm here. (*Begins slopping flowers and leaves about in inconvenient places.*)

Mrs. V. We're plotting to have a little impromptu dance here to-morrow night.

Agatha (*spilling a lot of dahlias over* Mrs. Vulpy). Oh, you dear things, how delightful ! But whatever will Hortensia say ?

Sybil. Hortensia is opening an Ear Hospital or Free Library or some such horror at Panfold, and won't know about it till it's all over, and then it will be too late to say much.

CLARE. I fancy you'll find that Hortensia's motto will be " better late than never."

AGATHA. Oh, I fancy she'll be rather furious. But what fun, all the same. But who will we get to come ?

SYBIL. Oh, we can get nine couples easily. There's all the Abingdon house party, they'll be dead nuts on it. And Evelyn Bray plays dance music like a professional.

AGATHA. What a lovely joke. I say—let's make it a fancy dress affair while we're about it.

SYBIL. Oh, let's have fireworks on the lawn and and Salome dances and a looping-the-loop performance.

AGATHA. That's talking nonsense. But fancy dress is so easily managed. I went to a ball in North Devon three years ago as Summer, and it was all done at a moment's notice. Just a dress of some soft creamy material with roses in my hair and a few sprays of flowers round the skirt. I've got the dress with me somewhere, and it wouldn't need very much alteration.

SYBIL. It will only want letting out a bit at the waist, and you can call yourself " St. Martin's Summer."

AGATHA. How dare you say such things ! Really, you're the most spiteful tongued person I know. I should think you'd better go as an East Wind.

SYBIL. My dear Agatha, I'm not one of the Babes in the Wood, so I wish you'd stop covering me with leaves. And don't let us start quarrelling. Of course you're as jumpy as a grasshopper at the idea of this dance, and I suppose you flatter yourself that you're going to pull it off with Trevor. Because a man has refused you twice there's no particular reason for supposing that he'll accept you at the third bidding. It's merely a superstition.

AGATHA (*furiously*). You utterly odious fable-monger ! I suppose it's considered clever to say ill-natured, untrue things about people you happen to be jealous of.

MRS. V. My dear girls, don't waste time in a sparring match. There's no sense in quarrelling when we want to get our little scheme started.

SYBIL. *I* don't want to quarrel ; I'm only too ready to be accommodating all round. If I *do* chance to land a certain eligible individual in my net I'm quite willing to turn my second-best prospect over to anyone that applies for him ; quite a darling, with a decent rent roll, and a perfect martyr to asthma ; ever so many climates that he can't live in, and you'll have to keep him on a gravel soil. Awfully good arrangement. A husband with asthma has all the advantages of a captive golf-ball ; you always know pretty well where to put your hand on him when you want him.

AGATHA. But if I had a really nice man for a husband I should want him to be able to come with me wherever I went.

SYBIL. A woman who takes her husband about with her everywhere is like a cat that goes on playing with a mouse long after she's killed it.

MRS. V. First catch your mouse. Which brings us back to the subject of the dance. I think we agree that fancy dress is out of the question ?

CLARE. There wouldn't be time.

MRS. V. Well, why not make it a sheet-and-pillow-case dance ? (*They all stare at her.*) Quite simple, every one drapes themselves in sheets, with a folded pillow-case arranged as a head-dress, and a little linen mask completes the domino effect. No trouble, only takes ten minutes to arrange, and at a given time every one sheds their masks and headgear, and the sheets make a most effective sort of Greek costume. Lulu Duchess of Dulverton gave quite a smart sheet-and-pillow-case at Bovery the other day.

AGATHA. Was it respectable ?

MRS. V. Absolutely. Oh, do take your blessed bramble-bush somewhere else. (AGATHA, *who has impaled* MRS. VULPY'S *skirt on a trail of briars, makes violent efforts to disentangle her.*) No, please leave my skirt where it is. I only want the brambles removed.

AGATHA. That's the worst of briars, they do catch on to one's clothes so.

MRS. V. That is one of the reasons why I never sit down in a bramble patch for choice. Of course, if one has a tame hedge following one about the house, one can't help it.

AGATHA (*gathering up remains of her foliage*). Well, I shall go and do the dining-room vases now and leave you irritable things to work out the dance programme. I'll think out a list of people we can invite.

[*Exit, door* Left *front.*

CLARE. Agatha would be almost tolerable in the Arctic regions where the vegetation is too restricted to be used as house decoration.

SYBIL. Look here, I'll bike over to the Abingdons' and get things in marching order there. I've just time before lunch. You're going to help us, I suppose, Clare ?

CLARE.   Oh, if you are all bent on having a domestic earthquake, I'll stand in with you.   I'll send notes over to Evelyn and the Drummond boys.   But I know the whole thing will be a horrid fizzle.

SYBIL.   You dear old thing.   You always turn up trumps when it comes to the pinch.

CLARE.   If you dare to call me a dear old thing I'll allude to you in public as a brave little woman. So there.

MRS. V.   Well, if you two are going to start sparring, I shall go and write letters.

[*Exit* MRS. VULPY, *door R. back.*

CLARE.   There's something I don't like about that woman.   She looks at me sometimes in a way that's almost malicious.   What on earth did Agatha bring her down here for ?

SYBIL.   Mrs. Vulpy is somewhat of a rough diamond, no doubt.

CLARE.   So many people who are described as rough diamonds turn out to be merely rough paste.

SYBIL.   Even paste has its uses.

CLARE.   Oh, afflictions of most kinds have their uses, I suppose, but one needn't go out of one's way to import them.   (*Exit* SYBIL, R. *back ; Enter* TREVOR, L. *back ; he is about to sit on couch.*)   Be careful where you sit, Trevor.   Agatha has been shedding bits of bramble all over the room.   (*They both begin picking bits of leaf, etc., off the couch.*)   When that parable was being read at prayers this morning about going to the hedges and by-ways to fetch in the halt and the blind, I couldn't help thinking Agatha wouldn't have stopped at that : she'd have brought in the hedges as well.

TREVOR (*seating himself with caution on couch*).   I've

just had about a wheelbarrow-load of gorse prickles removed from the cosy corner in the smoking-room.

CLARE. Gorse prickles ? (*Seats herself on couch.*)

TREVOR. Agatha said it was a Japanese design. If it had been an accident I could have forgiven it. I say, Clare, do you know you have got rather beautiful eyes ?

CLARE. How should I know, you've never mentioned it before.

TREVOR. Oh, well, I noticed it long ago, but it takes me ages to put my thoughts into words.

CLARE. That's rather unfortunate where compliments are concerned. By the time it occurs to you to tell me that I've got a nice profile I shall probably have developed a double chin.

TREVOR. And that will be the time when you'll be best pleased at being told you've got a nice profile. So you see there's some sense in holding back a compliment.

CLARE. Well, don't be horrid and sensible, just when you were beginning to be interesting. It's not often one catches you in the mood for paying compliments. Please begin over again.

TREVOR. Item, a pair of beautiful eyes, one rather nice chin, with power to add to its number. Quite a lot of very pretty hair, standing in its own grounds—or is it semi-detached ?

CLARE. I don't think your compliments are a bit nice ; I don't mind how long you keep them back.

TREVOR. I haven't finished yet. (*Takes her hand.*) Do you know, Clare, you've got the most charming hand in the world, because it's a friendly hand. I think if you were once friends with a fellow you'd always be friends with him, even——

CLARE. Even—— ?

TREVOR. Even if you married him, and that's saying a great deal.

CLARE. I think if I liked a man well enough to marry him I should always be the best of friends with him.

(Enter LUDOVIC, bustles over to escritoire.)

LUD. *(as they let go each other's hands).* Hullo, has Trevor been telling you your fortune?

CLARE *(rising).* Nothing so romantic; he's been explaining the finger-print system of criminal investigation. If I ever strangle Agatha in a moment of justifiable irritation Trevor will be a most damaging witness.

(LUDOVIC rings bell and then seats himself at escritoire.)

TREVOR. Shall I be disturbing you if I smoke a cigarette here?

LUD. Not in the least. I like seeing people idle when I'm occupied. It gives me the impression that I'm working so much harder than I am.

CLARE. Don't be long over your cigarette, Trevor, you've got to be let into a conspiracy that Mr. Ludovic isn't supposed to know anything about. *[Exit CLARE.*

TREVOR. Are they plotting to give you a birthday present or something of that sort?

LUD. Nothing so laudable.

(Enter WILLIAM, R. front.)

WILL. Did you ring, sir?

LUD. Yes, just arrange the flowers.

WILL. Yes, sir. *(Gathers up flowers and foliage from various places where AGATHA has stacked and strewn them and proceeds to re-arrange them with considerable taste.)*

LUD. *(to TREVOR).* No, it's your despotic mother

182

who mustn't get wind of the plot. I am merely the innocent bystander.

TREVOR. I'm awfully fond of my mother of course, but I must admit things would be a little more comfortable if she wasn't quite so—so——

LUD. Exactly. But she always has been and she always will be. As regards household affairs, of course I've no right to express an opinion, but her constant supervision of the political affairs of the neighbourhood is extremely embarrassing to the Party. My prospective candidature down here is becoming more and more doubtful under the circumstances. Hortensia is not content with having her finger in the pie, she wants to put the whole dish into her pocket.

WILL. (*who is standing near doorway*). Mrs. Bavvel is crossing the hall, sir.

LUD. (*becomes violently busy at escritoire*). The factory system in East Prussia presents many interesting points of comparison—— (*Enter* HORTENSIA, R. LUDOVIC *rises.*) Ah, Hortensia.

HOR. William, what are you doing here?

WILL. Arranging the flowers, ma'am.

HOR. They don't want arranging every day. They were arranged only yesterday. (*Seats herself on chair in centre of stage.* LUDOVIC *resumes seat.*)

WILL. It was brought on prematurely, ma'am.

LUD. Agatha had been trying some new effects in autumnal foliage; I told William to put things straight a bit.

HOR. I see. And where is Adolphus?

WILL. The cockatoo, ma'am? She's drying in the pantry after her bath.

HOR. It's not his day for a bath. He always bathes on Thursday.

WILL. She seemed restless, as if she wanted it, ma'am.

HOR. In future, remember he bathes on Thursdays only. And, William——

WILL. Yes, ma'am.

HOR. I think I've spoken about it before. You always hear me allude to the cockatoo as he, or Adolphus, therefore you are not to speak of him in the feminine gender.

WILL. Yes, ma'am. [*Exit, L. front.*

HOR. A quiet-mannered boy and always behaves reverently at prayers, but I'm afraid he's inclined to be opinionated. What coverts are you shooting this afternoon, Trevor?

TREVOR. The other side of the long plantation.

HOR. I understand that you are employing one of the Brady boys as a beater. I do not approve of the selection. Kindly discontinue his services.

TREVOR. But, mother, the Bradys are dreadfully poor.

HOR. Not deservingly poor. Mrs. Brady is the most thriftless woman in the parish. Some people can't help being poor, but Mrs. Brady is poor as if she enjoyed it. I'm not going to have that sort of thing encouraged.

LUD. (*rising from seat*). There is another aspect of the matter which I think you are losing sight of, Hortensia. Mrs. Brady may be poor in this world's goods, but she is rich in relatives. She has a husband and one or two uncles, and at least three brothers, and they all have votes. The non-employment of the Brady boy may lose us all those votes at the next election.

HOR. My dear Ludovic, I am not inattentive to

local political needs. I supervise the issue of pamphlets dealing with the questions of the day to all electors, in monthly instalments. When the next election comes you may be sure it won't take me by surprise.

Lud. No, but the result may. (*Resumes his seat.*)

Hor. Trevor, oblige me by taking an amended list of beaters to the head-keeper, with the Brady boy left out. Go now, or you will forget.

Trevor (*rising unwillingly*). As you will, mother. He made a very good beater, you know.

Hor. But not a suitable one. (*Exit* Trevor. Ludovic *throws up his hands.*) Who is this Mrs. Vulpy that Agatha has brought down? I don't care for the look of her.

Lud. I believe Agatha met her at Folkestone.

Hor. That doesn't make it any better. Agatha says she's seen trouble, but she doesn't explain what sort of trouble. Some women see trouble with their eyes open.

Lud. I believe she has a husband in Johannesburg.

Hor. To have a husband in Johannesburg might be a source of anxiety or inconvenience, but it can hardly be called seeing trouble.

Lud. Agatha is so good-natured that she's very easily imposed on.

Hor. I wish her good nature would occasionally take the form of consulting other people's interests. I suppose this Mrs. Vulpy is married after a fashion. though we really know nothing about her. She may be merely a husband-hunting adventuress, and of course Trevor is sufficiently important as a matrimonial prize to attract that sort of woman. Agatha ought to be more careful.

LUD. Wouldn't it be as well, in view of such dangers, if Trevor were to bestir himself to find a suitable wife?

HOR. Nothing of the sort. I must ask you not to give him any advice of that sort. Trevor is far younger than his years, and there is no need to suggest marriage to him for a long while to come. If I thought he had any present intentions that way I should be far more particular what sort of girls I had staying down here. Sybil Bomont and Miss Henessey, for instance, I've no objections to them as guests, but I should require quite a different type of young woman for a daughter-in-law.

LUD. Trevor may have his own views on the subject.

HOR. Hitherto he has expressed none. I must go and write to the Bishop.

LUD. About Trevor?

HOR. (*rising*). *No.* About the Dean of Minehead.

LUD. What has the Dean been doing?

HOR. He has treated me with flippancy. I had written asking if he could give me any material for a lecture I am going to give next week on the Puritan movement in England. He replies on a post-card (*reads*): "The Puritan movement was a disease, wholesome though irritating, which was only malignant if its after effects were not guarded against." Things have come to a disgraceful pass when a Church dignitary can treat the Puritan movement in that spirit.

LUD. Perhaps the Dean was only exercising a little clerical humour.

HOR. I don't think the subject lends itself to jest, and I certainly don't intend that my lecture shall be regarded in a spirit of frivolity. I've something better to do than provide an outlet for Deanery humour. My letter to the Bishop will contain some pretty plain speaking.

LUD. My dear Hortensia, the Dean of Minehead is one of the few churchmen in these parts who give us political support. It would be rather unfortunate to fall out with him.

HOR. In my opinion, it would be still more unfortunate to tolerate post-card flippancies on serious subjects from men in his position. I shall ask the Bishop, among other things, whether it is not high time that certain clerical clowns ceased their unfair competition with the music-halls.

(*Exit* HORTENSIA, R. *back.* LUDOVIC *goes through pantomime of tragic disgust.*)

(*Enter* BUTLER, L. *back.*)

BUTLER. Mr. St. Gall to see you, sir.

LUD. René ! What on earth brings him down here ? Show him in.

(*Exit* BUTLER, L. *back. Enter* RENÉ, L. *back, crosses stage without shaking hands, looks at himself in mirror*, R.)

RENÉ. I've lost my mother.

LUD. (*wheeling round in chair*). Do I understand you to mean that your mother is dead ?

RENÉ (*who has carefully settled himself in armchair*, R.). Oh, nothing so hackneyed. I don't think my mother will ever die as long as she can get credit. She was a Whortleford, you know, and the Whortlefords never waste anything. No, she's simply disappeared and I was wired for. It was most inconvenient.

LUD. But can't she be found ?

THE WATCHED POT

RENÉ. The butler says she can't. Personally I
haven't tried. Only got down late last night. And
I've had to come away with simply nothing to wear
I've been in Town for the last three days having
some clothes made, and I was to have had two new
lounge suits tried on this morning for the first time.
Naturally I'm a bit upset.

LUD. But about your mother's disappearance—
aren't you doing anything?

RENÉ. Oh, everything that could be done at short
notice. We've notified the police and the family
solicitors and consulted a crystal-gazer, and we've told
the dairy to send half a pint less milk every day till
further notice. I can't think of anything else to do.
It's the first time I've lost a mother, you know.

LUD. But do you mean to say there's absolutely
no trace of her? Why, I saw her in church only last
Sunday.

RENÉ. I expect they've looked for her there;
the butler says they've searched everywhere. The
servants have been awfully kind and helpful about
it. They say they must put their trust in Christian
Science, and go on drawing their wages as if nothing
had happened. That's all very well, but no amount
of Christian Science will help me to be fitted on when
I'm here and my clothes are in Sackville Street,
will it?

LUD. I think you might show a little natural
anxiety and emotion.

RENÉ. But I am showing emotion in a hundred
little ways if you'd only notice them. To begin with,
I'm walking about practically naked. This suit I've
got on was paid for last month, so you may judge
how old it is. And that reminds me, I wish you'd

188

do something for me. Something awfully kind and pet-lamb in my hour of trouble. Lend me that emerald scarf-pin that you hardly ever wear. It would go so well with this tie and I should forget how shabbily I'm dressed.

Lud. It would go so well that it would forget to find its way back again. Things that are lent to you, René, are like a hopeless passion, they're never returned. In the light of past experience I absolutely refuse to lend you a thirty-guinea scarf-pin.

René. How true it is that when one weeps one weeps alone. Anyway, you might lend me your pearl and turquoise one ; the pearl is a very poor one, and it can't be worth anything like thirty guineas.

Lud. I don't see why I should be expected to make you a present of it, even if it only cost five.

René. Oh, well, after all, I've lost a mother. I make less fuss about that than you do at the prospect of separation from a five-guinea scarf-pin. You might show a little kindness to a poor grass orphan. And, Ludovic, now that you've practically given way on that matter, I want you to turn your attention to something that's been worrying me dreadfully of late.

Lud. Gracious, what have you been doing now ?

René. Oh, it isn't now, the mischief was done twenty-three years ago, and then it wasn't exactly my doing. It's just this, that I'm twenty-three years old. If my mother had only held me over for a matter of four years I should be nineteen now, which is the only age worth being. Women always rush things so. I shouldn't mind so much being twenty-three if I had the money to carry it off well. The mater does the best she can for me ; she can't afford me an allowance, but she borrows money whenever she can from friends and acquaintances, and sends me haphazard cheques. It's quite exciting getting a letter from home. Of course that sort of thing can't go on indefinitely, and now that my only source of income has disappeared without leaving a postal address things have nearly come to a crisis. One can't treat life indefinitely as a prolonged Saturday-to-Monday. There are always the Tuesdays to be reckoned with.

Lud. I don't like to suggest anything so unbecoming as an occupation, but can't you manage to get entangled with a salary of some sort?

René. It's not so beastly easy. I've tried designing posters, and for three weeks I was assistant editor of a paper devoted to fancy mice. The devotion was all on one side. Now, Ludovic, if you'd only do what you sometimes half promised to do, and make me your personal private secretary, and let me do Parliamentary correspondence for you, and tell female deputations that they can't see you because you're in your bath, and all that sort of thing that a busy man can't do for himself——

Lud. My dear boy, I'm not at the present moment a member of Parliament, I'm not even standing as a candidate.

René. But, Ludo, why aren't you? You know you've had a hankering that way for a long time, and you can easily afford it. And it isn't a difficult job. All one has to do is to boil with indignation at discreet intervals over something—the Jews in Russia or impurity in beer or lawlessness in the Church of England. It doesn't matter particularly what, as long as you really boil. The public likes a touch of the samovar about its representatives. And, then, if you want to be a Parliamentary wit, *that* isn't difficult

nowadays. If the Government is making a mess of
Persian affairs just mew like a Persian kitten whenever
a Minister gets up to speak. It isn't anything really
hard I'm asking of you.

LUD. Thanks very much for coaching me. But
an indispensable preliminary to all this brilliance is
that I should be elected.

RENÉ. You could easily get a seat down here if
you wanted to. They've always wanted one of the
Bavvels to stand, and old Spindleham is not likely to
last another session, so the ball is practically at your
feet.

LUD. My dear René, under present circumstances
Briony would be an impossible headquarters from
which to conduct an election campaign. Have you
considered that Hortensia would have her finger in
the pie all the time ? She would speak at my meetings
and pledge me to the most appalling social and political
doctrines. She would get down the most unfortunate
specimens of the party to support me—in fact, by the
time election day came round I should feel inclined
to vote against myself. I should very probably be
defeated, and if I got in Hortensia would look on me
as her nominee, sent to Westminster to represent her
views on every subject under the sun. I shouldn't
have half an hour's peace. No, as long as Hortensia
remains in the foreground I shan't contest a seat in this
part of the country. That's absolutely certain.

RENÉ. Ludovic, this Hortensia business is getting
to be absurd. Everything you want to do down here
you run up against Hortensia, Mrs. Bavvel. When
are you going to get Trevor married and the old
woman dethroned ?

LUD. My dear René, as if we hadn't tried ! Talk

about bringing a horse to the water, we've brought water to the horse, gallons of it, and put it right under his nose. We've advertised eligible young women as if they had been breakfast foods.

RENÉ. And here am I, twenty-three years old, expected to wait indefinitely for my secretaryship and my daily bread until Trevor chooses to suit himself with a wife. It's really ridiculous. That's the worst of you middle-aged folks, if I may say so without offence. You're so jolly well content to wait for things to happen. It's only the old and the quite young who really know the value of hurry.

LUD. But, bless my soul, we can't compel Trevor to marry.

RENÉ. It's absurd of him to persist in celibacy that he isn't qualified for. He's decent enough in his way, but he hasn't got the strength of character to fit him for the graver responsibilities of bachelorhood. Can't be he rushed into marrying somebody?

LUD. Rushing Trevor is not exactly a hopeful operation. It's rather suggestive of stampeding a tortoise ; at the same time, I may tell you in confidence that something desperate of that nature is going to be tried to-morrow night in the absence of Hortensia and myself at Panfold.

RENÉ. Oh, Ludovic ! What ?

LUD. You must ask Sybil or some of the others for details. I know nothing about it and entirely disapprove, but the idea originated with me. Hush !

(*Enter* HORTENSIA, *door* R. *back.*)

(LUDOVIC *and* RENÉ *rise to their feet.*)

HOR. I want you to read my letter to the Bishop. Oh, Mr. St. Gall. I didn't know the neighbourhood was honoured with your presence. I needn't ask if

you're on a holiday ; that is a permanent condition
with you, I believe.

Lud. Mr. St. Gall has lost his mother—she's
disappeared.

Hor. Disappeared ! What an extraordinary thing
to do. Had she any reasons for disappearing ?

René. Oh, several, but my mother would never
do anything for a reason.

Hor. But was anything troubling her ? (*Sits
chair centre of stage.*)

René. Oh, nothing of that kind. She's one of
those people with a conscience silk-lined throughout.

Lud. Has she any relatives that she might have
gone to ?

René. Relatives ? None that she's on speaking
terms with. She was a Whortleford, you know, and
the Whortlefords don't speak. There is a cousin of
hers, a Canon, somewhere in the Midlands ; he's got
peculiar views—he believes in a future life, or else he
doesn't, I forget which. The mater and he used to
be rather chummy, but a hen came in between them.

Hor. A hen ?

René. Yes, a bronze Orpington or some such
exotic breed ; the mater sold it to him at a rather
exotic price. It turned out afterwards that the bird
was an abstainer from the egg habit, and the Canon
wanted his money back. I read some of the letters
that passed between them. I don't think the mater is
likely to have gone *there*.

Hor. But there is an alarming side to this disappearance which you don't seem to appreciate.
Something dreadful may have happened.

René. It has. I had been measured for two
lounge suits, one of them in a rather taking shade of

copper beech, and they were to have been tried on for the first time this morning——

Lud. (*hurriedly.*) As everything is naturally rather at sixes and sevens at the Oaks, I have asked St. Gall to stay to lunch. I suppose we can give him a bite of something ?

Hor. (*coldly*). I am always glad to show hospitality to your friends, Ludovic. I'll read you my letter to the Bishop at a more convenient moment. I'm just going to see Laura Gubbings ; she's going out to Afghanistan as a missionary, you know. That country has been scandalously neglected in the way of missionary effort.

Lud. There are considerable political and geographical difficulties in the way.

Hor. Not insuperable, however.

Lud. Perhaps not, but extremely likely to expand. We usually set out on these affairs with the intention of devoting a certain amount of patient effort in making the natives reasonably glad at the introduction of mission work ; then we find ourselves involved in a much bigger effort to make them reasonably sorry for having killed the missionaries.

Hor. Really, Ludovic, your reasoning is preposterous. I should be the first to oppose anything in the shape of armed aggression in Central Asia.

Lud. If you would oppose Miss Gubbings' missionary designs on that region I should feel more comfortable.

René. I say, can't she take me with her ?

Hor. I don't really see in what capacity you could be included in a mission party.

René. I could give my famous imitation of a nautch-girl. That would fetch the Afghans in shoals, and then Miss Gubbings could hold overflow meetings and convert them.

HOR. A nautch-girl ?

RENÉ. Yes, I did it for some friends at St. Petersburg and they just loved it. They said I got as far East as anyone could be expected to go. If I wasn't suffering under a domestic bereavement I'd do it for you now.

HOR. Not at Briony, thank you ! St. Petersburg may applaud such performances if it pleases. From the things I've heard from there——

RENÉ. Oh, for the matter of that, the things one hears about the Afghans—there is a proverb in that country——

LUD. (*hurriedly*). In any case Miss Gubbings is hardly likely to accept your collaboration in her labours.

HOR. Miss Gubbings is going out with a religious mission, not with a *café chantant*. From your description of your performance and from what I can guess of its nature, I don't think it would be likely to enhance either our moral or national reputation in the eyes of the Ameer's subjects. (*Rises from chair.*) A boy masquerading as a nautch-girl !

[*Exit* HORTENSIA, *door L. front.*

RENÉ. Another avenue of employment closed to me. By the way, where is Trevor ? I want to ask him to lend me some sleeve-links. These ones won't go at all with the scarf-pin you're lending me.

LUD. You'll probably find him at the head-keeper's lodge. Lunch is at one sharp.

[*Exit* RENÉ, *door L. back.*

Now perhaps I can have a few moments to myself and the Prussian Factory Acts.

(*Enter* SPARROWBY, R. *back.*)

195

SPAR. (*seating himself astride of chair, centre*). I say, I wish you'd do something to help me.

LUD. (*looks over shoulder and then back to pamphlet*). If it's anything in the way of sleeve-links or scarf-pins you're too late.

SPAR. Oh, nothing of that sort——

LUD. Or are you looking for a strayed relative? I can get you the address of a crystal-gazer.

SPAR. Oh, no, I haven't lost anyone; quite the reverse, dear old chap, I've *found* her.

LUD. (*half turning round*). Not Mrs. St. Gall?

SPAR. Mrs. St. Gall! Dear, no. I've found the one woman I could ever want to make my wife, and I want you to help me to pull it off.

LUD. (*returning to the perusal of his pamphlet*). Oh, I see. Delighted to be of any use to you. I don't quite know how you pull these things off, and I'm rather occupied these days, but on Wednesday next, in the early part of the afternoon, I can spare you an hour or two. (*Cuts page of pamphlet and continues reading.*)

SPAR. Oh, but one can't fix a precise time for that sort of thing. The trouble I'm in is that she won't be serious about it. She——

LUD. What does " Bewegungslosigkeit " mean in English?

SPAR. Oh, I don't know, it's a German word, isn't it? I don't know any German. (LUDOVIC *consults dictionary.*) She treats it as a sort of temporary infatuation on my part. She won't realize how hopelessly I'm in love with her.

LUD. (*yawning*). I thought it was the hopelessness of your suit that she did realize. Who is the lady?

SPAR. Sybil Bomont.

LUD. (*leaping round in his seat and letting dictionary*

196

fall). Impossible ! Out of the question. You mustn't think of marrying Sybil Bomont.

SPAR. But I can think of nothing else. Why mustn't I marry her ?

LUD. You must dismiss the matter completely from your mind. Go fishing in Norway or fall in love with a chorus girl. There are heaps of chorus girls who are willing to marry commoners if you set the right way about it. But you mustn't think of Sybil Bomont.

SPAR. But what is the objection ? Surely there's no madness in her family ?

LUD. (*contemplatively*). Madness, no. Oh, no. At least not that one knows of. Certainly her father lives at West Kensington, but he is sane on most other subjects.

SPAR. Then what is this mysterious obstacle ? There is nothing against me, I suppose ? I am fairly well off as far as income is concerned.

LUD. Ah ! And to what sort of environment are you proposing to take this young girl, who has been carefully brought up and kept shielded from the coarser realities of life ?

SPAR. Well, I live very quietly in the country and farm a few acres of my own.

LUD. Precisely : I had heard stories to that effect. Now, my dear Sparrowby, the moral atmosphere of a farm, however amateur and non-paying the farm may be, is most unsuitable for a young woman who has been brought up in the seclusion of a town life. Farming involves cows, and I consider that cows carry the maternal instinct to indelicate excess. They seem to regard the universe in general as an imperfectly weaned calf. And then poultry—you must admit that the

197

private life of the domestic barn-door fowl—well, there's remarkably little privacy about it.

SPAR. But, my dear Bavvel——

LUD. And are you quite sure that you are free to pay court to Miss Bomont—that you have no other entanglements ?

SPAR. Entanglements ? Why, certainly not.

LUD. Think a moment. What about Miss Clifford ?

SPAR. Agatha Clifford ! You must be dreaming. I haven't the ghost of an entanglement with her.

LUD. I thought I saw you both on rather intimate terms at breakfast this morning.

SPAR. (*indignantly*). She upset a sardine on to my knees.

LUD. I suppose you encouraged her to.

SPAR. Encouraged her ! Why, it ruined a pair of flannel trousers.

LUD. Well, I expect her sardine was just as irrevocably damaged. Anyway, you condoned her action ; I heard you tell her that it didn't matter.

SPAR. Oh, I had to say that. What else could one say ?

LUD. If anyone upset a sardine on to my lap I should find no difficulty in keeping the conversation from flagging. The difficulty would be to avoid saying too much. In your case I think you were rather too eloquently silent. The spilling of a sardine on to your lap may seem a small thing to you, but you must remember that women attach more importance to these trifles than we do. Believe me, I have watched your perhaps unconscious attentions to Miss Clifford with interest, and if anything I can do——

SPAR. But I assure you——

(*Enter* AGATHA *and* SYBIL, *door* L. *back.*)

AGATHA. Everything's going splendidly. Every one whom we've asked is coming, and Cook has been given a dark hint to have some fruit salads and mayonnaise and that sort of thing accidentally on hand—— Oh, I forgot you weren't to know anything about it. Promise that you'll forget that you heard anything.

LUD. I assure you I heard nothing. I was struggling with some technicalities in a German pamphlet. Dear Miss Bomont, do show me where I can find a better dictionary than this one.

SYBIL. Come along. There's one somewhere in the library.

LUD. And Agatha—Mr. Sparrowby wants you to help him to dig up some ferns for a rockery he's making at home.

(LUDOVIC *holds door*, L. *front*, *open for* SYBIL, *both Exit.*)

SPAR. I say——

AGATHA (*cheerfully*). By all means ; let's come now. I love rooting up ferns. Here are some baskets. (*Fishes three large garden baskets out of chest.*)

SPAR. But it's nearly lunch-time, and I don't really——

AGATHA. Never mind lunch. There's sure to be something cold that we can peck at if we're late. Come on ; the trowels are out in the tool-shed. I know a lovely damp wood where we can grub about for hours.

SPAR. But I've got rheumatism.

AGATHA. So have I. Come on.

(*Gives him two baskets to carry and leads the way off by door*, R. *back.*)

CURTAIN.

199

ACT II

The Hall. Briony Manor.

(CLARE *and* TREVOR *seated on couch, centre of stage. Enter* AGATHA, *door* L., *passes behind them. All three dressed in sheet costume, with hood thrown back, no masks.*)

AGATHA. I say, Trevor, it's going splendidly !

[*Exit* AGATHA, *door* R. *back.*

CLARE. If you ask me, it's going as flat as can be. No one seems to want to dance, and Cook is scared to death and has only sent us up half the amount of supper that we asked for.

TREVOR. There's enough to drink, anyhow ; I saw to that. I went down to the cellar myself.

CLARE. Yes, and the result will be that just when we want to be hurrying every one off the premises they'll be getting festive and reckless, and your august and awful mother will run up against half of them on the doorstep, or meet them in the drive. (*Enter door,* R. *back, veiled figure, who glides up to them.*) Hallo, who's this ? (SYBIL *unmasks and throws back hood.*) Oh, Sybil, I might have guessed.

SYBIL (*seating herself armchair centre of stage*). I fled away from that tiresome Sparrowby person who keeps on pestering me to sit out with him. Clare dear, do go and relieve Evelyn, she's played about six dances running.

CLARE. Oh, Evelyn would play all night without feeling tired. (*Rises.*) But one excuse is as good as another, I suppose. (*Walks towards door,* R.)

SYBIL. I don't know what you mean. (*Exit* CLARE, *door* R. *back.*) It's going awfully flat.

TREVOR (*lighting cigarette*). Oh, a frightful fizzle.

I think every one is a bit scared at what they're doing.

SYBIL. I know I am. There'll be fine fireworks to-morrow when Her Majesty gets to hear of it.

TREVOR. Fireworks ! There'll be a full-sized earthquake. I think I shall go cub-hunting if there's a meet within reasonable distance.

SYBIL. You won't find many of us here when you return. We shall be cleared out in a batch, like Chinese coolies. Trevor, why on earth don't you marry and get rid of this one-woman rule at Briony ? With all due respect, your mother is no joke. She's perfectly awful.

TREVOR. Oh, I suppose I shall marry somebody some day, but it's the choosing business that is so beastly complicated. Think of the millions and millions of nice women there are in the world, and then of the fact that one can only marry one of them —it makes marrying an awfully ticklish matter. It's like choosing which puppies you're going to keep out of a large litter ; you can never be sure that you haven't drowned the wrong ones.

SYBIL. Oh, but if you go on those lines you'll never marry anyone. You should just have a look round at the girls you personally know and like and make your choice from one of them. You'd soon find out whether she responded or not. I believe in grasping one's nettle.

TREVOR. But supposing there are half a dozen nettles and you don't know which to grasp ?

SYBIL. Oh, come, we're getting on. Half a dozen is better than millions and millions. And there must always be some one whom you prefer out of the half-dozen. There's Agatha, for instance. Of course she is your cousin, but that doesn't really matter. And in her way she's not a bad sort.

TREVOR. She passed through the hall just before you came in. If I'm to ask her to marry me I'd better go and do it now before I forget it.

SYBIL (*alarmed*). Oh, don't go and propose to her just because I suggested it. You'd make me feel an awful matchmaker, and I should never forgive myself if it turned out wrong. Besides, I doubt very much if she'd make the sort of mistress you'd want for Briony. One has to think of so many things, hasn't one ?

TREVOR. Precisely my standpoint. And if Agatha turned out a disappointment I couldn't give her away to the gardener's boy, like an unsatisfactory puppy. You see, it isn't so easy to grasp the nettle when you really come to do it.

SYBIL. Oh, well, Agatha doesn't exhaust the list. There's Clare, for instance, she's got some good points, don't you think ?

TREVOR. You don't say so with much conviction.

SYBIL. I'm awfully good pals with Clare, but that doesn't prevent me from recognizing that she's got rather a queer temper at times ; the things that she says sometimes are simply hateful, and she's not a bit straightforward. I could tell you of little things she's done—— (*Enter from door centre veiled figure.*) Who on earth is this ?

(SPARROWBY *throws off hood and mask and seats himself on small chair facing* SYBIL.)

SPAR. I've been following all sorts of figures about, thinking they were you. But I knew all the time they couldn't be you, because I didn't feel a thrill when I was near them. I always feel a thrill when I'm near you.

SYBIL (*viciously*). I wish you never felt thrills, then.

SPAR. You're dreadfully unkind, Sybil, but I know you don't mean what you say.

SYBIL. Sorry you find my conversation meaningless.

SPAR. Oh, I didn't mean that !

SYBIL. We seem equally unfortunate in our meanings.

SPAR. I say, Sybil, I wish you'd take me a little more seriously.

SYBIL. One would think you were an attack of measles.

(*Enter* MRS. VULPY *with* DRUMMOND, *door* L., *both unhooded. She catches sight of trio and rushes up.*)

MRS. V. (*to* DRUMMOND). Excuse me one moment. (*To* SPAR.) Naughty man, you know you promised me the kitchen lancers. Come along. Hurry.

SPAR. (*rising unwillingly*). But they're playing a waltz now.

MRS. V. They're getting ready for the lancers. Come on.

[*Exeunt* MRS. VULPY, SPARROWBY *and* DRUMMOND, *door* R. *back.*

SYBIL. The Vulpy woman is rather a brick at times. I say, *Trevor.*

(*During* SPARROWBY *duologue* TREVOR *has fallen asleep. Wakes hurriedly.*)

TREVOR. I nearly went off to sleep. Please excuse my manners. I was up awfully early this morning.

SYBIL. Well, do keep awake now. We're in the middle of a most interesting conversation.

TREVOR. Let's see, you were recommending me to marry Clare Henessey.

SYBIL. Oh, well—I don't think I went as far as that. Clare and I are first-rate pals, and I should awfully like to see her make a good marriage ; but I'd be rather sorry for her husband all the same. If anything rubs her the wrong way her temper goes queer at once, like milk in thunder-time, and she simply says the most ill-natured things.

TREVOR. That's another ungraspable nettle, then. I told you it wasn't so jolly easy.

SYBIL. But, Trevor, there are surely others, only you're too lazy to think of them.

TREVOR. As to thinking of them, I am not too lazy to do that ; it's the further stages I'm deficient in.

SYBIL. Of course I sympathize with your difficulty. I wish I could find you some one really nice, some one who would enter into all your pursuits and share your ambitions and be a genuine companion to you.

TREVOR. I hate that sort.

SYBIL. Do you ? How funny. At least, I don't know, I rather think I agree with you. Some women make dreadful nuisances of themselves that way. Well, you don't give me much help in choosing you a wife.

TREVOR. What do you think of Mrs. Vulpy ?

SYBIL. What ! That woman with nasturtium-coloured hair and barmaid manners. Surely you're not attracted by her.

TREVOR. I didn't say I was. I asked you what you thought of her.

SYBIL. Oh, as to that ; not a bad sort in her way, I suppose. Some people call her a rough diamond. If it was my declaration I should call her a defensive spade. But anyhow she's married, so she doesn't come into our discussion.

TREVOR. I want to tell you something, something that concerns you alone.

SYBIL. What is it?

TREVOR. Your hair's coming down behind.

SYBIL. Oh, bother! It's that horrid hood arrangement. I'll fly upstairs and put it right. (*Rises.*) I say, Trev, there's a much nicer sitting-out place on the landing, near that old carved press, where the tiresome Sparrowby person won't find me. Come up in two minutes' time, there's a dear.

TREVOR. Right-oh!

SYBIL. Now don't go to sleep.

[*Exit* SYBIL, *up staircase* L.
(*Enter* AGATHA, *door* R. *back, passes along back of stage.*)

AGATHA. Everything's going swimmingly; it's a huge success.

[*Exit* AGATHA, *door* L. *back.*
Enter RENÉ, *door centre, in evening dress with smoking jacket ; carrying bottle of wine, wine-glass, some grapes and peaches. Seats himself on arm-chair near small table.*)

RENÉ. Going rather flat, isn't it?

TREVOR. Frightful fizzle. I'm so sleepy myself that I can only just keep my eyes open. Was up at the farm awfully early this morning.

RENÉ. Some shorthorn or bantam was going to have young ones, I suppose. In the country animals are always having young ones ; passes the time away, I suppose. I know a lady in Warwickshire who runs a rabbit farm. She has musical boxes set up over the hutches.

TREVOR. Musical boxes ?

RENÉ. Yes, they play the wedding march from " Lohengrin " at decent intervals. I'm going to ask you an extremely personal question.

TREVOR. If it has anything to do with spare shirt-studs———

RENÉ (*who is delicately feeding himself while talking*). Don't be silly. It hasn't. I want to know—are you happy ?

TREVOR. Immensely.

RENÉ (*disappointedly*). Are you ? Why ?

TREVOR. One never has any definite reason for being happy. It's simply a temperamental accident in most cases. I've nothing to worry me, no money troubles, no responsibilities ; why should I be anything else but happy ?

RENÉ. You ought to marry.

TREVOR. You think that would improve matters ?

RENÉ. It would elevate you. Suffering is a great purifier.

TREVOR. You're not a very tempting advocate of matrimony.

RENÉ. I don't recommend it, except in desperate cases. Yours is distinctly a desperate case. You ought to marry if only for your mother's sake.

TREVOR. My mother ? I don't know that she is particularly anxious to see me mated just yet.

RENÉ. Your mother is one of those proud silent women who seldom indicate their wishes in actual words.

TREVOR. My dear René, my mother may be proud, but where her wishes are concerned she is not inclined to be silent.

RENÉ. At any rate, an unmarried son of marriageable age is always a great anxiety. There's never any knowing what impossible person he may fix his fancy on. As old Lady Cloutsham said to me the other day, *à propos* of her eldest son: " If Robert chooses a wife for himself, it's certain to be some demi-mondaine with the merest superficial resemblance to a lady ; whereas if I choose a wife for him I should select some one who at least would be a lady, with a merely superficial resemblance to a demi-mondaine."

TREVOR. Poor Lady Cloutsham, her children are rather a trial to her, I imagine. Her youngest boy had to leave the country rather hurriedly, hadn't he ?

RENÉ. Yes, poor dear. He's on a ranch somewhere in the wilds of Mexico. Conscience makes cowboys of us all. Unfortunately, it's other people's consciences that give all the trouble ; there ought to be a law compelling every one to keep his conscience under proper control, like chimneys that have to consume their own smoke. And then Gladys, who was the most hopeful member of the family, went and married a Colonial Bishop. That really finished Lady Cloutsham. As she said to me : " I always classed Colonial Bishops with folk-songs and peasant industries and all those things that one comes across at drawing-room meetings. I never expected to see them brought into one's family. This is what comes of letting young girls read Ibsen and Mrs. Humphry Ward."

(*An unearthly long-drawn-out howl is heard.*)
TREVOR (*sitting up*). What on *earth*—— ?
RENÉ. Only the idiotic Drummond boy, who pretends he's the Hound of the Baskervilles.

(*Enter* AGATHA, *door* L., *runs giggling across stage pursued by* DRUMMOND *in sheet with phantom-hound mask on head. Exeunt both, door R back.)*

TREVOR *(rising slowly)*. By Jove, forgot I'd promised to go upstairs. Sybil will be fuming her head off.

RENÉ. We can't get a rubber of Bridge presently, can we?

TREVOR. 'Fraid not. The women would be rather mad if we shirked dancing.

(Draws himself slowly together and lounges up staircase, L. Exit.)

(Enter SPARROWBY, door R. back.)

SPAR. Why aren't you rigged out like the rest of us, St. Gall?

(Takes Trevor's seat on couch.)

RENÉ. Well, for one thing I'm in platonic mourning, having partially lost a mother, so it would hardly be the thing. And another reason is that the hood arrangement would ruffle one's hair so.

SPAR. As if that mattered a bit. You're absurdly particular about your appearance and your clothes and how your tie is tied and about your hair. Look at me; it doesn't take me two minutes in the morning to do my hair.

RENÉ. So I should imagine. Isn't there a proverb, a fool and his hair are soon parted.

SPAR. I say, you're beastly rude!

RENÉ. I know I am. My mother was a Whortleford, and the Whortlefords have no manners. I'm sorry I called you a fool, though, because I want you to do something really kind for me. Trevor has suggested a game of Bridge and I don't want to back out of playing. The trouble is that I haven't a coin worth speaking about on me. If you'd be awfully pet-lamb and lend me something——

SPAR. I dislike lending on principle. It generally leads to unpleasantness.

RENÉ. Really this worship of Mammon is getting to be the curse of the age. People make more fuss about lending a few miserable guineas than the Sabine women did at being borrowed by the Romans. I know a lady of somewhat mature age who took rather a fancy to me last season and in a fit of sheer absence of mind she lent me ten pounds. She's got quite a comfortable income, but I declare she thinks more of that lost tenner than of the hundreds and hundreds that she's never lent me. It is become quite a monomania with her. It's her one subject of conversation whenever we meet.

SPAR. Don't you intend paying her back?

RENÉ. Certainly not. Her loss makes her beautiful. It brings an effective touch of tragedy into an otherwise empty life. I could no more think of her apart from her mourned-for loan than one could think of Suez without the canal or Leda without the swan.

SPAR. If that's your view of your obligations I certainly shan't lend you anything. By the way, where is Sybil Bomont? She's been sitting out about four dances with Trevor. It's about my turn now.

RENÉ (*with sudden energy*). Sybil has got a bad headache. She's lying down for a few minutes.

SPAR. Where? I particularly want to see her.

RENÉ. In the billiard-room, and she particularly doesn't want to see anyone.

SPAR. But I only want——

(*Enter* CLARE *and* AGATHA, *door* R. *back*.)

RENÉ. Agatha! Sparrowby is complaining that he's got no one to dance with.

AGATHA. Come along, they're just going to try that new Paris dance ; I can't pronounce it.

SPAR. But I can't dance it !

AGATHA. Neither can I. Come on.

SPAR. But I say——

[*Exit* AGATHA *dragging* SPARROWBY
off, door R. *back.*

RENÉ. Thank goodness, he's out of the way. People who make a principle of not lending money are social pests.

CLARE (*seating herself on couch*). This is going to be a dismal failure. By the way, have you seen Trevor anywhere ?

RENÉ. Yes, he turned rather giddy with the dancing, I suppose, so he's taking a turn or two out in the air.

CLARE. Is he alone ?

RENÉ. Oh, quite. So am I for the moment. Do stay and talk to me.

CLARE. You must be interesting, then. After sitting out successfully with Sparrowby and the two Drummond boys, I feel that there's nothing left in the way of dull and trivial conversation to listen to.

(*While she is talking* RENÉ *hands her half of the
remaining peach and resumes his seat.*)

RENÉ. Let's talk about ourselves ; that's always interesting.

CLARE. I suppose you mean, let's talk about yourself.

RENÉ. No, I'd much rather dissect your character ; I find some good points in it.

CLARE. Do tell me what they are.

RENÉ. You have a rich aunt who is childless.

CLARE. She's a great-aunt.

RENÉ. All the better. That sort of thing doesn't spoil by being kept in the family for a generation or two. The greater the aunt the greater the prospect.

CLARE. And what other good points do you find in me ?

RENÉ. I think I've nearly exhausted the list.

CLARE. I don't find you a bit interesting.

RENÉ. Well, be patient for a moment, I'm going to say something quite personal and interesting. Will you marry me ? The question is sudden, I admit, but these things are best done suddenly. I suppose it was the mention of your great-aunt that suggested it.

CLARE. The answer is equally sudden. It's " No."

RENÉ. Are you quite sure you mean that ?

CLARE. Convinced.

RENÉ. How thoroughly sensible of you. So many girls in your place would have said " Yes."

CLARE. I dare say. Our sex hasn't much reputation for discrimination. I didn't know that marrying was in your line.

RENÉ. It isn't. I dislike the idea of wives about a house : they accumulate dust. Besides, so few of the really nice women in my set could afford to marry me.

CLARE. From the point of view of reputation ?

RENÉ. Oh, I wasn't thinking of that. At twenty-three one is supposed to have conquered every earthly passion : of course it's the fashion in statesmanship nowadays to allow the conquered to have the upper hand.

CLARE. A convenient fashion and saves a lot of bother. Tell me, taking me apart from my great-aunt, are you pleased to consider that I should make a satisfactory wife ?

RENÉ. Satisfactory wives aren't made : they're invented. Chiefly by married men. But as things go I think we should have made what is called a well-assorted couple. I should have taught you in time to be as thoroughly selfish as myself, and then each would have looked after our own particular interests without having need to fear that the other was likely to suffer from any neglect.

CLARE. There is much to be said for that point of view. It's the imperfectly selfish souls that cause themselves and others so many heart-burnings. People who make half sacrifices for others always find that it's the unfinished half that's being looked at. Naturally they come to regard themselves as unappreciated martyrs.

RENÉ. By the way, I may as well tell you before you find out. Trevor isn't out of doors. He's sitting out with Sybil somewhere on the landing.

CLARE (*half rising from seat*). You beast ! Why did you tell me he'd gone out ?

RENÉ. Well, the fact of the matter is, I thought that if those two were left together undisturbed for half an hour or so, one or other of them might propose.

CLARE (*resuming seat*). Oh, that's the game, is it ? And has Sybil enlisted your services in this precious stalking movement ?

RENÉ. Oh, dear, no : I'm merely working in a good cause. Some one's got to marry Trevor, you know, and the sooner the better. Personally, I don't think it's very hopeful, but the whole motive of this otherwise idiotic dance is to head Trevor into a matrimonial ambush of some sort. He's so superbly sleepy that there's just a chance of it coming off, but I'm not sanguine.

CLARE. If he *is* to be rushed into marrying some one, I don't see why I shouldn't be in the running as well as anyone else.

RENÉ. Exactly what William was saying to me this morning.

CLARE. William ! The page-boy ?

RENÉ. Yes, he's rather keen on seeing you Mrs. Trevor Bavvel.

CLARE. That's very sweet of him, but I didn't know he took such an. intelligent interest in the matter.

RENÉ. It's not altogether disinterested. It seems they've got a half-crown sweepstake on the event, in the servants' hall, and he happened to draw you, so naturally he's in a bit of a flutter on your behalf.

CLARE. I didn't know we were the centre of so much speculation. Mercy on us, what would Hortensia say if she knew that she was nurturing a living sweepstake under her roof ! And is William good enough to consider that I have a fair sporting chance of pulling it off ?

RENÉ. I fancy he's rather despondent. He said you didn't seem to try as hard as some of the others were doing. He puts your chair as near Trevor's as possible at prayers, but that's all he's able to do personally.

CLARE. The little devil !

RENÉ. I believe that if the Vulpy woman wasn't handicapped with a preliminary husband, she'd carry Trevor off against all competitors. She's just got the bounce that appeals to a lazy, slow-witted bachelor.

CLARE. There's something I particularly object to in that woman. She always talks to me with just a suspicion of a furtive sneer in her voice that I

213

find extremely irritating. I don't know why Agatha inflicted her on us.

(*Enter* AGATHA, R. *back.*)

AGATHA. What's that you're saying about me?

CLARE. Only wondering what induced you to cart Mrs. Vulpy down here.

AGATHA. Oh, come, she's not a bad soul, you know, taking her all round. (*Seats herself on couch.*) We are all of us as God made us.

RENÉ. In Mrs. Vulpy's case some recognition is due to her maid as a collaborator.

AGATHA. You're all very ill-natured about her. Anyway, this dance was her idea.

CLARE. Yes, and a horrid mess it's going to land us all in. I daren't think of to-morrow. By the afternoon the news will have spread over the greater part of Somersetshire that a costume ball has been given at Briony in the temporary absence of Mrs. Bavvel.

AGATHA. I say, do you think she'll be very furious?

CLARE. If Hortensia is more intolerant on one question than on any other, it's on the subject of what she calls mixed dancing. I remember a county fête at Crowcoombe where she vetoed the project of a maypole dance by children of six and seven years old until absolutely assured that the sexes would dance apart. Some of the smaller children were rather ambiguously dressed and were too shy to tell us their names, and the curate and I had a long and delicate task in sorting the he's from the she's. One four-year-old baffled our most patient researches, and finally had to dance by itself round a maypole of its own.

AGATHA. I'm beginning to get dreadfully frightened about to-morrow. Can't we water it down a bit and pretend that we had games and Sir Roger de Coverley and that sort of thing ?

CLARE. We shall have to tone things down as much as possible, but Hortensia will hold an inquiry into the whole matter, and drag the truth out by inches. She'll probably dismiss half the servants and have the morning-room repapered ; as for us——

RENÉ. There's a very good up train at 3.15.

AGATHA. But I haven't made arrangements for going anywhere ; it will be most inconvenient.

CLARE. On the morrow of an unsuccessful *coup d'état* one generally travels first and makes one's arrangements afterwards.

(*A prolonged howl heard.*)

RENÉ. The idiotic Drummond boy again.

(*Enter* DRUMMOND, *door* R. *back.*)

DRUMMOND. I say, you make nice cheerful hosts, sitting there like a lot of moping owls. Do come and buck things up a bit ; there are only two couples dancing.

RENÉ (*tragically*). Yes, let us go and dance on the edge of our volcano.

AGATHA. Oh, don't, I feel quite creepy. It reminds me of that Duchess person's ball on the eve of Waterloo.

[*Exeunt* DRUMMOND, RENÉ,
AGATHA, *door* R. *back.*

(CLARE *remains seated. Enter* MRS. VULPY, *centre.*)

MRS. V. All alone, Miss Henessey ? By the way, where is that dear boy, Trevor ?

CLARE. I believe he's upstairs, and I don't think he wishes to be disturbed.

MRS. V. I suppose that means that you are waiting to catch him when he comes down, and that *you* don't want to be disturbed.

CLARE. Oh, please put that construction on it if it amuses you. I shouldn't like to think you weren't enjoying yourself.

MRS. V. Oh, I'm enjoying myself right enough, *Miss* Henessey, watching some of the little by-play that's goin' on. (*Seats herself.*) It is *Miss* Henessey, isn't it ? (*Gives a little laugh.*)

CLARE. What do you mean ?

MRS. V. Oh, well, only that we've met before, you know, at least I've seen you before, though you probably didn't see me. You were writing your name in the visitors' book at the Grand Anchor Hotel at Bristol, just about six weeks ago.

CLARE. I did stop there one night about six weeks ago. I don't remember seeing you there.

MRS. V. I remember not only seeing you, but the names you wrote in the book : Henessey wasn't one of them, nor Miss Anything either.

CLARE. How clever of you to remember. You seem to have a good head for business—other people's business.

MRS. V. Oh, well, I suppose it was the innocent vagueness of the names you had put down that arrested my attention. "Mr. and Mrs. Smith," London Your companion had gone upstairs with the luggage, so I didn't see Mr. Smith, and somehow at the time I had a feeling that I wasn't seeing Mrs. Smith—at least not the permanent Mrs. Smith.

CLARE. It sounds rather crude and compromising as you put it, I admit, but the explanation is not really very dreadful. Only——

MRS. V. Only you don't feel disposed to give an explanation at such short notice. You're quite right. Second thoughts are usually more convincing in such cases.

CLARE. Well, to be candid, I don't see that my travelling adventures are any particular concern of yours.

MRS. V. Perhaps you're right. I dare say they more immediately concern the lady whose guest you are. Shall I raise her curiosity on the subject ? As you've got such a satisfactory explanation ready, you can have no objection, I suppose.

CLARE. You know Mrs. Bavvel well enough to know that what might seem a harmless escapade to ordinary judges would not be regarded so leniently by her.

MRS. V. And Mr. Trevor ? He doesn't share his mother's prejudices. You won't mind if I let him into our little secret about the Smith *ménage* ?

CLARE (*rising from her seat*). Mrs. Vulpy, what particular gratification do you find in threatening to make mischief between me and my friends ? It shows you up in rather a bad light, and I don't really see what you expect to gain by it.

MRS. V. Simply, my dear girl, we happen to be interested in the same man.

CLARE. You mean Trevor ?

MRS. V. Of course. I know perfectly well that all you girls are hanging round here for a chance of snapping him up, and I'm clever enough to see which of you is likely to succeed. It won't be Sybil Bomont, whatever anyone may say.

CLARE. In any case, you can scarcely regard yourself as a competitor.

MRS. V. Because of being already married, you

mean ? Well, I don't mind telling you I've more definite news about my husband's condition than I've been pretending to have. He was past all chance of recovery when the last mail went out. I'm too honest to pretend to be anything but glad. If you knew the life we've had ! I've been a lonely woman since the day I married Peter, and now I don't intend being lonely any more. As soon as I set eyes on Trevor Bavvel I knew he was just the sort of man I wanted to begin life with over again.

CLARE. And do you suppose that you are so obviously *his* conception of the ideal life-mate that he'll throw himself at your feet as soon as he knows you are free to marry him ?

MRS. V. Oh, my dear, most things in life that are worth having have to be worked for. I've made a good beginning by enlisting his sympathy as a fellow-conspirator over this dance. The worse row we get into over it the better. Then, when my husband's estate has been straightened out, I shan't be badly off, and I shall come to this neighbourhood and do a little hunting and give Bridge parties and all that sort of thing. Provided nothing happens in the meantime, I fancy I stand a very fair chance of pulling it off.

CLARE. I see.

MRS. V. Ah, you do see, do you ? You understand now why I want your flirtation with Trevor to be nipped in the bud, and why I'm prepared to nip it myself if necessary with that little story of the Grand Anchor Hotel ?

CLARE. You are making one little miscalculation, Mrs. Vulpy. Trevor was a public-school boy, and in English public-school tradition the spy and the tale-bearer don't occupy a very exalted position.

MRS. V. Oh, you may call me hard names, but you can't wriggle away from me in that fashion. I've got you in my grip—so ! Either you leave the field clear for me or the story of your visit to the Grand Anchor Hotel with a gentleman, whom, for want of fuller information, we will call Mr. Smith, becomes public property.

CLARE. Some one is coming downstairs. Shall we go and see how the dancing is going on ? They're playing that Bulgarian March.

MRS. V. Oh, yes, let's go and hear it. I love Slav music, it takes one out of oneself so.

CLARE. Which is sometimes an advantage.

[*Exeunt* VULPY *and* CLARE.

(*Enter down staircase*, L., SYBIL *and* TREVOR.)

TREVOR. I say, it's getting nearly time to call this off.

SYBIL. Oh, nonsense, it's only just ten. They can't be back before eleven. Your mother is delivering an address, and she's not given to cutting her words short on these occasions, I believe.

TREVOR. Well, half an hour more, then. And let's make it go with a bit more fling for the wind-up.

SYBIL. Right-oh! (*Enter* SPARROWBY, L.) Lord, here's that pestering idiot again.

SPAR. Ah, at last I've found you ! Are you better ?

SYBIL. Better ?

SPAR. I was told you were lying down in the billiard-room with a bad headache.

SYBIL. Who on earth told you that ?

SPAR. St. Gall.

SYBIL. Oh, René ! Never believe a word he says. I'm in my usual health, but I'm frightfully hungry.

Trevor, do go and forage for something edible. I'll wait for you here. I was too excited to eat much at dinner, and I know I shan't dare to come down to breakfast to-morrow.

TREVOR. I'll go and parley with Cook.

[*Exit* TREVOR, *door centre.*

SPAR. What have you been doing all this time ?

SYBIL (*seating herself on couch*). Oh, don't ask me. Sitting upstairs with Trevor and trying to keep him from going to sleep. I assure you it wasn't amusing.

SPAR. I should never want to go to sleep if I were by your side.

SYBIL. What an inconvenient husband you would be.

SPAR. Oh, I wish you wouldn't be always fooling. (*Seats himself beside her.*) You don't know how much I love you !

SYBIL. Of course I don't ; I've only got your word for it that you care in the least bit for me. Now if you were to do something to prove it——

SPAR. I'd do anything.

SYBIL. Well, do something that would give you a name in the world. For instance, paint pictures and have them exhibited in the Royal Academy : it would be something to talk about when one went there.

SPAR. But I can't paint.

SYBIL. Oh, I don't think that matters as long as you exhibited. Of course, they wouldn't sell. Or why not found a religion, like Mahomet and Wesley and those sort of people did.

SPAR. But you can't found religions off-hand. You want inspiration and enthusiasm and disciples, and all manner of special conditions.

SYBIL. Well, then, you could invent a new system of scoring at county cricket, or breed a new variety of fox-terrier.

SPAR. But it would take years and years to produce a new variety.

SYBIL. I would wait—oh, so patiently.

SPAR. *Sybil*, if I was successful in breeding a new kind of fox-terrier, would you really marry me ?

SYBIL. I wouldn't exactly marry you, but I would buy some of the puppies from you. I've got an awfully jolly little fox-terrier at home. If you tell her " the Kaiser's coming," or " Roosevelt's coming," she lies quite still, but if you say, " King Edward's coming," she jumps up at once. Isn't it clever ? I taught her myself with gingerbread biscuits.

SPAR. Won't you realize that I'm asking you to be my wife ?

SYBIL. Of course I realize it ; you've asked me so often that I'm getting to expect nothing else. I wish you would vary it a little and ask me something different. Only don't ask me that dreadful thing about " this man's father was my father's only son," it nearly gives me brain fever.

SPAR. I wonder if you have a heart at all ?

SYBIL. Of course I've got the usual fittings. It's very rude of you to suggest that I'm jerry-built. But look here, joking apart, do do something to oblige me. Go and dance with poor Evelyn Bray ; she's been at the piano all the evening and hasn't had a scrap of dancing herself.

SPAR. If I do, will you give me a dance afterwards ?

SYBIL. I'll give you two.

SPAR. (*rising from his seat*). You angel. I wish you'd always be as kind.

[*Exit* SPARROWBY, *door R. back.*

SYBIL (*hearing some one coming*). Is that you, Trevor? I'm getting ravenous. (*Enter* AGATHA, *door centre.*) Oh, Lord!

AGATHA. Hullo, Sybil, have you seen Trevor?

SYBIL. No, I think he's dancing.

AGATHA. He hasn't been in the dancing room for about an hour; neither have you. (*Seats herself on chair right of couch.*)

SYBIL. I'm so hot, I'm sitting out here to get cool. I suppose it's the excitement. I say, do go and help Evelyn at the piano, she's getting quite fagged out, poor child.·

AGATHA (*acidly*). I've just played them a polka; Evelyn hasn't been near the piano for the last half-hour. If you hadn't been sticking to Trevor like a drowning leech you might have known that.

SYBIL (*furiously*). I haven't been sticking to him, and leeches don't drown, anyway.

AGATHA. Oh, I'm not up in their natural history. I only know they stick like mud. I'll say a floating leech if you like.

SYBIL. It so happens I've been listening to marriage proposals from that pestering Sparrowby all the evening.

AGATHA. I've had the infliction of dancing with him no fewer than four times, my dear, and he kept on complaining that he couldn't find you. Don't be disheartened: accidents will happen to the most accomplished fibbers.

SYBIL. Why is it that plain women are always so venomous?

AGATHA. Oh, if you're going to be introspective, my dear. (*Laughs.*)

(*Enter* TREVOR, *door centre.*)

TREVOR. All I could raise was some cold rice pudding and a bottle of pickled walnuts. If there's anything I detest in this world it's rice pudding.

AGATHA (*going over to table*). I loathe rice pudding, it's so wholesome. On the other hand, I simply adore pickled walnuts. (*Helps herself.*)

TREVOR. Won't you have some, Sybil ? (*Helps himself.*)

SYBIL (*rising from seat*). I'm not going to stay here to be insulted. I've been called a liar and a leech.

AGATHA. I said fibber, my dear, not liar.

[*Exit* SYBIL, *door R. back.*

TREVOR. Have you two been having a slanging match ?

AGATHA. Oh, no, only poor Sybil is so dreadfully short-tempered, she can't take anything in good part. She's a dear, sweet girl, one of the very best, but I should be awfully sorry for any fellow who married her. That reminds me, Trevor—you ought to marry.

(*Helps herself to another walnut.*)

TREVOR. There's a great deal to be said for that point of view : and as far as I can see there's no particular likelihood of its being left unsaid.

(*Helps himself to walnut.*)

AGATHA. I suppose the difficulty is to think of anyone you care for sufficiently.

TREVOR. Have you anything to say against Mrs. Vulpy ?

AGATHA. Good heavens ! Mrs. Vulpy ? That vulgar, over-dressed parrot, with the manners of a cockney sparrow. I should think she began life in a cheap-jack store. Surely you can't be thinking seriously of her ?

TREVOR. I asked you if you had anything to say against her. Considering the short notice you managed very well. Wasn't it you who brought her down here ?

AGATHA (*helping herself to walnut*). Well, yes, I suppose I did. Somehow in Folkestone she didn't seem such an awful rotter. Anyway, she's got a husband. No, the woman for you must be one with great similarity of tastes——

TREVOR. On the contrary, I avoid that kind. At the present moment I regard you with something bordering on aversion. (*Stirs frantically in jar.*)

AGATHA. Regard me with aversion ! My dear Trevor !

TREVOR. If it hadn't been for our duplicate passion for pickled walnuts this cruel tragedy wouldn't have happened. There's not one left.

AGATHA. Oh, Trevor, not one ? (*Stirs mournfully in jar.*)

TREVOR. No, the woman I marry must have an unbridled appetite for rice pudding.

AGATHA (*dubiously*). I dare say some rice pudding, nicely cooked, wouldn't be bad eating. (*Begins agitating spoon listlessly through rice pudding dish.*)

TREVOR. That is not the spirit in which my ideal woman must approach rice pudding. She must eat it with an avidity that will almost create scandal ; she must devour it secretly in dark corners, she must buy it in small quantities from chemists on the plea that she has neuralgia. Such a woman I could be happy with.

AGATHA. She might be odious in other respects. (*While talking is waving spoon in air.*)

TREVOR. One must not expect to find perfection.

AGATHA. I wish you would be serious when we are discussing a serious subject. I suppose matrimony is a more serious affair for us poor women than for you men.

TREVOR. How can I discuss anything seriously when you're covering me with fragments of rice pudding ?

AGATHA. Oh, you poor dear, I'm so sorry. Let me rub you down.

TREVOR. No, don't you ; I won't be massaged with rice pudding.

(*Enter* MRS. VULPY, *door centre.*)

MRS. V. What *are* you two people playing at ?

TREVOR. Only trying to find new uses for cold rice pudding. I was firmly convinced as a child that it couldn't be primarily intended as a food.

MRS. V. René is just going to do his nautch-girl dance. He wants you to go and play tom-tom music, Agatha.

AGATHA. Bother René. Why was I born good-natured ?

[*Exit* AGATHA, R.

TREVOR. Stay and talk to me, Mrs. Vulpy. I've seen the nautch-dance before.

MRS. V. You are such a sought-after young man that I feel I oughtn't to be taking you away from the others.

TREVOR. I'd rather sit and talk with you than with any of the others.

MRS. V. Dear me ! I thought you never worked up the energy to make pretty speeches.

TREVOR. I don't; it's my mere sheer laziness that makes me blurt out the truth on this occasion.

MRS. V. And am I really to suppose that it is the truth that you would rather sit with me than with any of the others?

TREVOR. You are the only woman of the lot that it is safe to sit out with. Perhaps you are not very securely married, but you're not exactly floating loose ready to take advantage of the artless innocence of a young bachelor.

MRS. V. And is that where my superior fascination begins and leaves off?

TREVOR. That's where it begins. I didn't say it left off there.

MRS. V. Now don't try to talk pretty. You know you're not capable of sustained effort in that direction. Nothing is more discouraging than to have a man say that you've ruined his life, and then to find that you haven't even given him after-dinner insomnia.

TREVOR. Oh, I promise to keep awake—only it's rather soothing and sedative to talk to a charming woman who has no intention of marrying one. You don't intend to marry me, do you?

MRS. V. My dear Trevor, I have intended marrying you ever since I first saw you.

TREVOR. They say the road to matrimony is paved with good intentions, don't they?

MRS. V. I have heard it put in a more roundabout manner.

TREVOR. In your case isn't there rather a big obstacle in the road?

MRS. V. You mean Peter?

TREVOR. I suppose he *is* a factor in the situation?

MRS. V. Of course he's my husband, and it's my duty to think of him before anyone else. But I am not going to be a hypocrite and waste sentiment in that direction. Our married life has been about as odious an experience as I wish to go through.

TREVOR. Still, I suppose even an unsatisfactory marriage has to be taken into account. There is no First Offender's clause in our marriage system. However uncongenial he may be, Peter remains your husband.

MRS. V. Well, that's the question. Peter was always selfish, but double pneumonia on the top of nervous breakdown may have overcome even his obstinate temperament. Why, at any moment I might get what I should be obliged to call in public "bad news." So you see I'm not so safe a person to sit and make pretty speeches to as you thought. And now I suppose my fascination has melted into thin air?

TREVOR. No, I shall merely have to label you "dangerous" along with the others.

MRS. V. Ah, Trevor, I'm much more dangerous than any of the others, if you only knew it.

TREVOR. Why so?

MRS. V. Because I really want you for your own self. The others are all after you for family reasons and general convenience and that sort of thing. I want you because—well, I've seen a bit of the world, and I know the worth of a man like you, who can't be flattered or humbugged or led by the nose——

TREVOR. Hush! Some one's coming. (*Enter* WILLIAM, *door* L.) Just clear these things away, William; I should like my mother to find the hall in its usual state. Now, Mrs. Vulpy, I must be going in to the dance. I've shirked my duty most horribly.

MRS. V. Well, let's have a dreamy waltz together, to set the seal on what we've been talking about. We are friends, aren't we?

(*Exeunt* TREVOR *and* MRS. VULPY, *door* R. WILLIAM *gathers up empty plates.* *Enter* RENÉ, *door centre.*)

RENÉ (*helping himself to wine*). William, can you find me any more peaches?

WILL. No, sir, I brought you the last.

RENÉ (*arranging himself comfortably on couch*). Well, try to discover a fig or banana somewhere, do; and if you remind me to-morrow I'll ask Mr. Ludovic to give you that yellow striped waistcoat that he hardly ever wears.

WILL. Thank you, sir. You don't know of no one wanting a page, do you, sir?

RENÉ. Why, are you thinking of leaving?

WILL. I expect I shall have to leave without having time to do any thinking about it, sir. When Mrs. Bavvel comes to hear about our goings on behind her back she'll behave like one of those cyclops that sweeps away whole villages.

RENÉ. Cyclone, William, not cyclops.

WILL. That's it, sir, cyclone, and I expect I shall be among the sweepings. I've no particular fancy to be going home out of a situation just now, sir. Home life is a different thing with you gentry, you're so comfortable and heathen.

RENÉ. When one comes to think of it, I suppose we are. It's a rather overcrowded profession all the same. (*While* WILLIAM *is talking* RENÉ *is helping himself to* TREVOR's *Russian cigarettes and filling his case.*)

228

WILL. Ah, sir, *you* haven't known what it was to be brought up by respectable parents.

RENÉ. Really, William !

WILL. My father is Plymouth Brethren, sir. Not that I've anything to say against Plymouth as a religion, but in a small cottage it takes up a lot of room. My father believed in smiting sin wherever he found it ; what I complained of was that he always seemed to find it in the same place. Plymouth narrows the prospective. Between gentry religion and cottage religion there's the same difference as between keeping ferrets and living in a hutch with one.

[Exit WILLIAM, *door centre.*

(*Enter the first four in couples by door* R. *back,* TREVOR *and* MRS. VULPY, DRUMMOND *and* CLARE *and* SYBIL, SPARROWBY *and* AGATHA, *prancing through hall and singing " Non je ne marcherai pas," which is heard being played on piano off.*)

AGATHA (*to* RENÉ). You slacker ! Come and join in.

(*They Exeunt in same order through door* L., *still singing.*)

RENÉ (*to himself*). I'm of far too tidy a disposition to leave half-emptied bottles lying about. Did I hear wheels ? (*Rises and listens.*) Stop your squalling, you people. I fancied I heard wheels. (*Listens again.*) My nerves are getting quite jumpy. (*Reseats himself.*)

(*Hall door* R. *thrown open. Enter* HORTENSIA, *who turns to some one in porch.*)

HOR. Ludovic, quick, catch the carriage ; I've left my pamphlets and notes in it. (*Catches sight of* RENÉ, *who is regarding her with helpless stare.*) Mr. St. Gall ! May I ask what you are doing here at this hour ?

RENÉ. Such a silly mistake. Old Colonel Nicholas asked me to go over to Bowerwood after dinner, as I was all alone. I distinctly told the groom Bowerwood, but he drove me here instead, and I didn't see where I was till he had driven off. So I've had to wait here till he comes to fetch me.

HOR. (*who has been staring fixedly at him and at the wine bottles and siphons on the table*). Will you repeat your story, please? I didn't quite follow.

RENÉ. Colonel Nicholas, thinking I might be lonely——

HOR. I hear music!

RENÉ. I've been thinking I heard harps in the air all the evening. I put it down to the state of my nerves. (SYBIL *with hood over head runs through laughing, from door L., and Exit door centre, without noticing* HORTENSIA.) Ah! Did you see *that!* Did you see *that!* (HORTENSIA *stares at doorway where figure vanished. Howl heard off. Enter* DRUMMOND *with phantom hound mask on, door L., runs through and Exit centre.*) Oh, say something or we shall .. both ... go ... mad! (*Sobs convulsively.*)

HOR. (*furiously*). Ludovic!

(*Enter* LUDOVIC, *hall door* R.)

LUD. What is happening?

(RENÉ *has collapsed in fit of pretended hysterics in armchair.*)

HOR. The boy is either drunk or mad! Something disgraceful is taking place in this house!

LUD. Something disgraceful here! René, what *is* all this?

RENÉ (*sitting rigid in chair and staring straight in front of him*). Only were-wolves chasing goblins to the sound of unearthly music. Will some one kindly see if my carriage has come ? I refuse to stay another moment in this house.

(*Enter* TREVOR, CLARE, MRS. VULPY, *from door L.* SYBIL *and* DRUMMOND, *door centre, all unhooded.*)

TREVOR. Oh, good God !

(RENÉ *pours out glass of wine and drains it, then lies back composedly in his chair. A prolonged pause, during which* HORTENSIA *surveys sheepish group of revellers.*)

SYBIL (*weakly*). We were having games.

MRS. V. Old English games.

DRUM. Charades.

CLARE. Historical charades.

SYBIL
TREVOR
MRS. V. } (*together*). Yes, historical charades.
DRUM.

(*Enter* AGATHA *and* SPARROWBY, *door R. back, prancing in together singing with fatuous exuberance* " *Non je ne marcherai pas.*" *They stop horror-stricken in centre of stage.*)

HOR. (*seating herself in high-backed chair, her voice trembling with rage*). May I ask who has organized this abominable and indecent orgy in my house ? Will somebody enlighten me ?

CLARE. It was something we got up on the spur of the moment ; there was nothing organized.

HOR. And what brought people in from outside ? I've heard a contemptibly ridiculous story about Mr. St. Gall's accidental arrival here ; how do you account for Mr. Drummond's presence ? Was he also trying to make his way to Bowerwood ?

DRUM. (*blunderingly*).   Yes.

RENÉ (*decisively*).   No. That's my story. I won't be plagiarized.

SYBIL.   He dropped in by chance.

DRUM.   Yes, quite by chance.

HOR.   Also on the spur of the moment ! A moment, be it observed, when I happened to be temporarily absent.   And knowing my strong objection to the questionable form of entertainment involved in promiscuous dancing you choose this moment for indulging in an aggravated and indecent kind of dance which I can only describe as a brawl.

MRS. V.   But, dear Mrs. Bavvel, I assure you there is nothing indecent in a sheet-and-pillow-case dance.   Lulu Duchess of Dulverton gave one at——

HOR.   Lulu Duchess of Dulverton is not a person whose behaviour or opinions will be taken as a pattern at Briony as long as I am mistress here.   While you are still under my roof, Mrs. Vulpy, I trust you will endeavour to remember that fact.   Whether, after this deplorable error of taste, you will see fit to prolong your visit, of course I don't know.   Apparently this monstrous misuse of the bed-linen which is intended for the sleeping accommodation of my guests was carried out at your suggestion.

MRS. V. (*bursting into tears*).   I think, considering the mental anxiety and strain through which I am passing, with a husband hovering between Johannesburg and Heaven, I'm being most unfairly treated.

[*Exit* MRS. VULPY, *door* L.

HOR.   I've refrained from complaining, Agatha, at the inconsiderate way in which you bring brambles and hedge weeds and garden refuse into the house, but I must protest against your introducing individuals of the type of Mrs. Vulpy as guests at Briony. Who is that playing the piano ?

SYBIL.   I think it's Evelyn Bray.

HOR.   Ah ! Who also dropped in accidentally, I suppose. Ludovic, will you kindly tell Miss Bray that we don't require any more music this evening. (*Exit* LUDOVIC, *door* R. *back.*) Had we not returned unexpectedly early, I presume this outrageous entertainment would have been kept from my knowledge. I may inform you that the mayor took upon himself to cancel the reception at the Town Hall, at which I was to have delivered a brief address, for the rather far-fetched reason of showing respect and sympathy at the sudden disappearance of Mrs. St. Gall.

RENÉ.   I say, that was rather pet-lamb of him.

HOR.   Mrs. St. Gall's son appears to treat the incident as of less serious importance.

RENÉ.   I came here for rest and sympathy, with the faint possibility of a little Bridge to distract my thoughts ; I wasn't to be expected to know that historical charades would be going on all round me. My nerves won't recover for weeks.

HOR.   I am a persistent advocate of the abolition of corporal punishment in the Navy and in Board Schools, but I must confess, Mr. St. Gall, that a good birching inflicted on you would cause me no displeasure.

RENÉ.   A most indelicate wind-up to a doubtful evening's amusement. I should insist on its being done *in camera.*

(*Enter* LUDOVIC, *door* R. *back.*)

SYBIL.   Really, Mrs. Bavvel, we must plead guilty to having planned this semi-impromptu affair just a little, but we thought it would be such a good occasion for making an announcement.

AGATHA. An announcement?

HOR. What announcement?

SYBIL (*looking at* TREVOR). An announcement that I'm provisionally—well, engaged——

SPAR. Oh, Sybil, you angel! Let me announce it! Sybil and I are engaged!

LUD. Engaged! You and Sybil? Impossible. I congratulate you, of course, but it's—most unexpected.

CLARE. You dear thing. Congratulations.

SYBIL (*furiously*). You misunderstand me. I'm not engaged! Do you hear?

SPAR. Oh, SYBIL, but you just said you were!

SYBIL. You fool! I was talking about something quite different.

[*Exit* SYBIL, *door* L.

HOR. There seems to be some confusion about this wonderful announcement.

LUD. I gathered that Miss Bomont was talking about something she's engaged on. Anyhow, she distinctly stated that she is not engaged to Mr. Sparrowby.

HOR. In any case this is hardly a fortunate moment in which to make announcements of secondary interest. (*Enter* WILLIAM, *door centre, carrying plate with banana. Stops horrified on seeing* MRS. BAVVEL, *who rises from chair.*) What are you carrying there, William?

WILL. (*miserably*). A banana, ma'am.

HOR. What are you doing with a banana at this time of night?

WILL. It's for her—him, the cockatoo, ma'am.

HOR. For Adolphus? At a quarter to eleven! He's never fed at this hour.

WILL. She—he seemed disturbed and restless as if he was asking for something, ma'am.

234

HOR. Disturbed ? I am not surprised. In the fourteen years that he has lived here he has never before experienced such an evening of disgraceful disorder. Trevor, perhaps you will see that your neighbours who dropped in so unexpectedly will leave with as little delay as possible. Those of you who are at present my guests will kindly retire to their sleeping apartments. William !

WILL. Yes, ma'am.

HOR. Tell Cook to send a cold supper for myself and Mr. Ludovic to the dining-room. Some beef and pickled walnuts and a few peaches.

WILL. (*weakly*). Yes, ma'am.

HOR. To-morrow I shall have a good deal to say on the subject of these deplorable proceedings. To-night I am too upset. I left Briony an orderly English home, I return to find it a casino.

(*Exit* HORTENSIA *up staircase L., followed by* LUDOVIC, *who holds up his hands in mock despair. The others stand blankly watching them disappear.* RENÉ *seizes banana which* WILLIAM *is holding on plate and exits R. eating it. He is followed by* DRUMMOND *and* AGATHA. WILLIAM *Exit, door L., leaving* CLARE *and* TREVOR *alone.*)

CURTAIN.

ACT III

Breakfast Room at Briony.

(LUDOVIC, *having just breakfasted, is still seated, chair pushed back from table, reading paper.* BUTLER *about to clear away breakfast things.*)

BUTLER. Shall I remove the breakfast things, sir ?

LUD. (*glancing at clock*). Is no one else coming down ? Where is Miss Clare ?

BUTLER. Miss Clare complained of a headache, sir, and had breakfast in her room.

LUD. And Mr. Trevor ?

BUTLER. Mr. Trevor breakfasted very early and went up to the farm. Miss Sybil breakfasted in her room.

LUD. Had she a headache also ?

BUTLER. She complained of a headache, sir. Mrs Vuply breakfasted in her room.

LUD. The same—complaint ?

BUTLER. No, sir, anxiety and nervous depression. She made a very big breakfast, sir. I don't know whether Miss Agatha has had her breakfast sent up. She wasn't awake half an hour ago.

LUD. By the way, do you know whether Mrs. Vulpy received any telegrams this morning ?

BUTLER. She received one, sir, that she seemed to be expecting.

LUD. Ah !

BUTLER. She held it for a long while looking at it, sir, theatrical like, and then said there was no answer.

LUD. Did she seem less depressed after she'd received it ?

BUTLER. She ordered some more kidneys and toast. I should say she was a lot more cheerful.

(*Enter* AGATHA *hastily, door* L.)

AGATHA. Hullo, Ludovic, only you here ? I meant to have breakfast upstairs, but I saw Hortensia go out to the rose garden, so I skipped down.

BUTLER. Shall I warm some of the breakfast dishes for you, miss ?

AGATHA. No, just make me some fresh tea, and leave the ham and sardines. (*While speaking has both arms on the table.*) I don't see any butter.

BUTLER. Your sleeve's in the butter, miss.

AGATHA. Oh, so it is. And you might bring in some more toast.

BUTLER. Yes, miss.

AGATHA. Isn't there any honey?

LUD. Your other sleeve is in the honey.

AGATHA. Oh, bother. (*Exit* BUTLER, *door centre.*) I say, did you breakfast with Hortensia? Was she very awful?

LUD. She told me she had lain awake most of the night boiling with indignation. She's now in the hard-boiled state of cold vindictiveness.

AGATHA. Mercy on us, whatever shall we do?

LUD. Personally I intend going for a few weeks on a visit to Ireland.

AGATHA. But we can't all go to Ireland.

LUD. One of the great advantages of Ireland as a place of residence is that a large number of excellent eople never go there.

AGATHA. You're disgustingly selfish; you don't think what is to become of the rest of us.

LUD. On the contrary, it's you that are selfish and inconsiderate. If one of you would only marry Trevor all this Hortensia discomfort and forced marching would be avoided.

AGATHA. But how absurd you are, Ludovic! One can't marry Trevor without his consent. No really nice girl would make advances to a man unless he showed himself attracted to her first; and, as regards Trevor, it wouldn't be the slightest good anyway; one might as well make advances to the

237

landscape. We poor women are so dreadfully handicapped. If I were only a man——

LUD. If you were a man you couldn't marry
Trevor, so that wouldn't help us. Your sleeve's in
the honey again.

(*Enter* BUTLER, *door centre, with tea and toast.*)

BUTLER. Is there anything else I can bring you,
miss ?

AGATHA. No, thank you. Oh, tell Cook, in case
I should be travelling later in the day, to cut me some
ham sandwiches. No mustard.

BUTLER. Yes, miss. Shall you want the dogcart
ordered ?

LUD. You had better say the waggonette and the
luggage cart ; there may be others leaving this afternoon.

BUTLER. The 3.20 up or the 4.15 down, miss ?

AGATHA. I'm not quite sure. I'll let you know
later.

BUTLER. Yes, miss.

[*Exit* BUTLER, *door centre.*

AGATHA. If Hortensia is in a never-darken-my-
doors-again kind of temper I shall go right off to
Town and on somewhere from there. On the other
hand, if it's the kind of outbreak that blows over in
a week or two, I shall merely go and stay with some
people I know at Exeter.

LUD. Nice people ?

AGATHA. Oh, dear, no. Quite uninteresting. I
met them somewhere in Switzerland ; they helped
to find some luggage that had gone astray. I always
lose luggage when I travel. They have porridge in
the mornings, but they live close to the station, so one
hasn't got to take a cab.

238

LUD. Perhaps it won't be convenient for them to have you at a moment's notice.

AGATHA. It's not at all convenient for me to go there, but at a time like this one can't stop to think of convenience. Especially other people's.

(*Enter* SPARROWBY *cautiously, door* L.)

SPAR. I've been afraid to come in before for fear of meeting Hortensia. I'm awfully hungry : I suppose everything's cold.

LUD. As a matter of public convenience I request you to be sparing with the ham ; it may be required later in the day for an emergency ration of sandwiches. Have you booked a seat in the waggonette ?

SPAR. I say, is it as bad as all that ? I hoped Mrs. Bavvel might have cooled down a bit.

LUD. She has. She has settled comfortably into a glacial epoch which will transform Briony into a sub-arctic zone in which I, for one, am not tempted to remain.

SPAR. (*seating himself at table and beginning to eat*). What an awful nuisance ; I don't at all want to leave Briony just now. I say, do you think I'm engaged to Sybil or not ? She certainly seemed to say that we were engaged last night.

LUD. I really haven't given it a thought. I don't think it matters particularly. The important question is, is Trevor engaged to anybody ?

SPAR. I think you're awfully unsympathetic.

LUD. It's absurd to expect sympathy at breakfasttime. Breakfast is the most unsympathetic meal of the day. One can't love one's neighbour with any sincerity when he's emptying the toast-rack and helping himself lavishly to the grilled mushrooms that one particularly adores. Even at lunch one is usually in rather a quarrelsome frame of mind ; you must have noticed that most family rows take place at lunch-time. At afternoon tea one begins to get polite, but one isn't really sympathetic till about the second course at dinner.

SPAR. But the whole future happiness of my life is wrapped up in Sybil's acceptance of my offer.

LUD. People who wrap up their whole future happiness in one event generally find it convenient to unwrap it later on.

(*Enter* CLARE, *door* L.)

CLARE. Morning, everybody. Have you brave things breakfasted with Hortensia ?

AGATHA. No, only Ludovic. He reports her as being pretty bad. It's a regular case of *sauve qui peut*.

CLARE. Such disgusting weather to travel in. Fancy being cooped up in a stuffy railway carriage all the afternoon. Anything in the papers, Ludovic ?

LUD. Very possibly there may be. Agatha and Sparrowby have kept me so pleasantly engaged in discussing their plans that I've scarcely been able to grapple with the wider events of the day.

AGATHA. Oh, I can always read and carry on a conversation at the same time. I suppose I've got a double brain.

CLARE. Why don't you economize and have one good one.

LUD. (*rising*). If you two are going to quarrel, I'm off. Other people's quarrels always make me feel amiable, and a prospective Parliamentary candidate can't afford to be amiable in private life. It's like talking shop out of hours. (LUDOVIC *walks towards door* L.)

Spar. (*jumping up and following him*). I say, Ludovic, I want to ask you—do you really think——
[*Exit* Ludovic *and* Sparrowby, *door* L.
(*Enter* Mrs. Vulpy, *door centre.*)

Mrs. V. Is the coast clear ? I'm scared to death of meeting that Gorgon again.

Agatha. Had breakfast ?

Mrs. V. Nothing worth speaking of. Oh, is there tea ? How adorable. (*Seats herself at table.*) Well, has anything happened ?

Agatha. The luggage cart has been requisitioned, and if you want anything in the way of sandwiches or luggage labels an early order will prevent disappointment.

Mrs. V. Gracious, what an earthquake. And all because of a little harmless dance. If any of you girls do succeed in marrying that young man, you'll have to break him of the farmyard habit. A husband who is always going to earth is rather a poor sort of investment.

Clare. As long as one marries him, what *does* it matter ? One can afford to be neglected by one's own husband ; it's when other people's husbands neglect one that one begins to talk of matrimonial disillusion.

Mrs. V. Other people's husbands are rather an overrated lot. I prefer unmarried men any day ; they've so much more experience.

Clare. I don't agree with you. Isn't there a proverb : " A relapsed husband makes the best rake " ?

Agatha. You're positively disgraceful, both of you. We used to be taught to be content with the Ten Commandments and one husband ; nowadays women get along with fewer commandments and want ten husbands.

MRS. V. It's no use scolding. It's the fault of the age we live in. The perfection of the motor-car has turned the country into a vast prairie of grass-widowhood. How can a woman be expected to cleave to some one who's at Lancaster Gate one minute and at North Berwick the next?

AGATHA. She can stay at home and lavish her affections on her babies.

CLARE. I hate babies. They're so human—they remind one of monkeys.

(*Enter* SYBIL, *door* L., *throws herself into chair* L. *centre of stage.*)

MRS. V. Well, it's no use taking a tragic view of yesterday's fiasco. There are thousands of as good men as Trevor in the world, waiting to be married.

SYBIL. That's just it; they don't seem to mind how long they wait. And when you come to have a closer look at the thousands there are very few of them that one could possibly marry.

AGATHA. Oh, nonsense; I don't see why one should be so dreadfully fastidious. After all, we're told all men are brothers.

SYBIL. Yes; unfortunately, so many of them are younger brothers.

AGATHA. Oh, well, money isn't everything.

SYBIL. It isn't everything, but it's a very effective substitute for most things.

MRS. V. By the way, tell me which is the nearest and cleanest way to the farm.

AGATHA (*who is about to leave room*). Through the white gates into the fir plantation, and past the potting sheds. You can't miss it. (*Suddenly turning back and sitting down abruptly.*) What do you want to go there for?

MRS. V. Merely to say my good-byes to Mr. Trevor, and while he is showing me round the farm buildings I dare say I'll find an opportunity to tell him how badly he's treated you all, and what an uncomfortable situation he's created, and generally work on his better feelings.

SYBIL. You might as well work on superior blotting-paper. (*Exit* MRS. VULPY.) I don't trust that woman a little atom.

CLARE. I believe she's had bad news from South Africa, and she's keeping it dark and going for Trevor on her own account.

SYBIL. He spoke very curiously about her to me last night, asked what I thought of her and all that.

AGATHA. Exactly what he did to me. I say, can't we stop her?

CLARE. Are you proposing to use violence? If so I think I'll watch from a distance; when you used to play hockey you were noted for hitting more people than you ever aimed at.

SYBIL (*jumping to her feet*). Hortensia's voice!

(CLARE *and* SYBIL *scurry out of the room by door* R. AGATHA *blunders into the arms of* HORTENSIA, *who enters by door* L.)

AGATHA (*trying to look at her ease*). Oh, good morning. Did it rain in the night?

HOR. I lay awake most of the night; I did not hear any rain. (*Rings bell.*)

AGATHA. Oh, I'm *so* sorry you didn't sleep well. Oak leaves soaked in salt water and put under the bed are an awfully good remedy. Let me get you some.

HOR. (*coldly*). Thank you, we don't want any more decaying vegetation brought into the house. My sleeplessness was not due to insomnia. Under normal circumstances I sleep excellently.

AGATHA. I feel that I ought to explain about last night.

HOR. You will have to explain. Every one will have to give an account of his or her share in the disgraceful affair, including the servants, who seem to have connived at it. I have ordered a gathering of the household for 4 o'clock in the library, which you will kindly attend. (*Enter* WILLIAM, *door centre.*) William, at this hour of the morning I expect the breakfast things to be cleared away.

[*Exit* HORTENSIA, R.

AGATHA. William, tell John that I shall have to leave here well before four to catch the 4.15. I've got lots of luggage to register at the station.

WILL. Yes, miss; the waggonette's ordered already.

AGATHA. I expect it will have to be the dogcart as well; there will probably be a lot of us wanting to catch trains this afternoon.

WILL. Yes, miss. What I envy about you, miss, is your play-going way of taking things.

AGATHA. Play-going way?

WILL. Yes, miss. You just sit and wait till things has been brought to a climax and then you put on your hat and gloves and walk outside. It's different for those who've got to go on living with the climax.

AGATHA. I hadn't thought of that; I suppose it is rather horrid.

[*Exit* WILLIAM *by door centre, carrying off*
breakfast things on tray.
[*Exit* AGATHA, *door* L.
(*Enter* LUDOVIC, *door* R. *He takes newspaper*
packet off table L., *opens wrapper, throws himself*
into a chair and begins reading.)
(*Enter* RENÉ, *door* R.)

RENÉ. Ludovic ! Aren't you all feeling like a
lot of drowned kittens ?

LUD. I don't know what a lot of drowned kittens
feel like. I hope I'm not looking like a lot of drowned
kittens.

RENÉ. Oh, don't talk about looks. (*Looks himself*
carefully over in the mirror.) I felt so jumpy last night
that I scarcely dared put the light out. I had a hot-
water bottle in my bed.

LUD. A hot-water bottle ? Surely it's too warm
for that.

RENÉ. Oh, there was no hot water in it, it was
merely to give a sense of protection. I suppose
there's a general stampede ? (*Seats himself, chair*
centre stage.)

LUD. The house resounds with the cutting of
sandwiches and the writing of luggage labels.

RENÉ. And what does *he* say to it all ?

LUD. Who ? Trevor ? He made a strategic
move to the farm at an early hour.

RENÉ. I believe he was so sleepy last night that
he doesn't really know whether he proposed to Sybil
or not.

LUD. Sybil did her best, but that miserable Sparrowby ruined whatever chance she had.

RENÉ. I've no use for that person ; he's just the
kind of idiot who comes up to you in a Turkish bath

245

and says, " Isn't it hot ? " Meanwhile, what are you going to do ?

LUD. I shall pay a long-projected visit to an old chum who lives in Kildare.

RENÉ. Nonsense, Ludo, you can't. Nobody really lives in Kildare ; I don't believe there are such places. And old Spindleham is really at the last gasp. The *Western Morning News* says he can't live out the week.

LUD. Under present circumstances, René, I've no intention of standing.

RENÉ. Oh, don't be so provoking. Go and see Trevor and tell him he must marry Sybil. Explain the circumstances to him. A wife is a sort of thing that can happen any day. But a Parliamentary vacancy is a different matter. There's your career to think of.

LUD. He will naturally retort that his whole future happiness has got to be thought of.

RENÉ. Oh, damn ! what about my whole future income ?

LUD. My dear René, the question is, whether we have not hunted Trevor into the wrong net. I have just met that Vulpy woman in full cry up to the farm, and something in her manner tells me that she's running a trail of her own.

RENÉ. But her husband——

LUD. I asked her if she had had any news of him. She was careful to tell me that she hadn't received any letters this morning. She was equally careful *not* to inform me that she did get a telegram. I fancy that telegram announced her promotion to the rank of widowhood.

RENÉ. But you surely don't think that Trevor would——

246

LUD. That's exactly what I do think. We've tried to badger and harry him into a matrimonial entanglement with all sorts of eligible and likely young women, and it's quite in the nature of things that he'll turn round and perversely commit himself to this wholly impossible person. You must remember that Trevor is a fellow who has seen comparatively little of the world, and what he's seen has been more or less of one pattern. Now that he's suddenly confronted with a creature of quite another type, with whom he isn't expected to interest himself, naturally he at once becomes interested.

RENÉ. Well, if this stumbling-block of a husband of hers has really been good-natured enough to migrate to another world, everything is plain sailing. Trevor can go ahead and marry the lady—after a decent interval, of course.

LUD. Absolutely out of the question. I should never forgive myself if such a thing happened.

RENÉ. But why—haven't we been moving heaven and earth to get him married ?

LUD. Married, yes, but not to Mrs. Vulpy. After all, Trevor is my only brother's only son, and if I can help it I'm not going to sit still and let him tie himself to that bundle of scheming vulgarity. Besides, a woman like that installed as mistress of Briony would only mean a prolongation of Hortensia's influence. Trevor would be driven to consult his mother in everything, from the sheer impossibility of putting confidence in his wife.

RENÉ. I think we're being absurdly fastidious about Trevor's wife. We've given him heaps of opportunities for marrying decent nonentities, so I don't see why we should reproach ourselves if he accidentally swallows a clumsier bait. Anyhow, I don't see how you're going to stop it if there's really anything in it.

Lud. That's just what's worrying me. To speak to him about it would be to clinch matters. With rare exceptions the Bavvels are devilishly obstinate.

René. Well, it would be rather a delicate subject to broach to her. She would scarcely relish being told that she's impossible.

Lud. I should put it more tactfully. I should tell her she wouldn't harmonize with local surroundings, that she has too much dash and go, and——help me out with some tactful attribute.

René. Too flamboyant.

Lud. I asked you for tact, not truth.

René. Too much individuality. I don't know what that means. But it sounds well.

Lud. Thank you, that will do nicely. A woman always respects a word that she can't spell.

René. You'd better jot it all down on your cuff. You'll forget it in a sudden panic when you're talking to her.

(*Enter* Butler, R.)

Butler. Colonel Mutsome

(*Enter* Col. Mutsome, R.)

[*Exit* Butler, *same door.*

Col. How do you do? (*Shakes hands with* Ludovic, *bows to* René.) What unpleasant weather. Quite damp. I hope dear Hortensia is well. I've a great admiration for Hortensia. I always say she's the first lady in Somersetshire.

René. Everything must have a beginning.

Col. I hear our member is not expected to live. (*Seats himself in chair*, R.)

248

LUD. I saw something to that effect in the local papers.

COL. I suppose we shall be having an election in a few weeks' time. Is it true that you are the prospective Party candidate ?

LUD. I saw it suggested in the local papers. There has always been some idea of getting a Bavvel to stand.

COL. I suppose you would accept !

LUD. That will depend very largely on family considerations.

RENÉ. Of course Ludovic means to stand. I caught him yesterday being ostentatiously sympathetic to the local chemist, a man with a hare-lip and personal reminiscences and a vote. No one listens to the personal reminiscences of a man with a hare-lip unless they've got some imperative motive ; when the man also has a vote the motive is unmistakable.

LUD. René, as a private secretary, you would have to be very private.

COL. I suppose you subscribe to all the principal items of the Party programme ?

LUD. Oh, I believe so—and to most of the local charities. That is the really important thing. It is generally understood that a rich man has some difficulty in entering the Kingdom of Heaven ; the House of Commons is not so exclusive. Our electoral system, however, takes good care that the rich man entering Parliament shall not remain rich. It is simply astonishing the number of institutions supported by involuntary contributions that a candidate discovers in his prospective constituency. At least he doesn't discover them—they discover him. For instance, I don't keep bees, I don't know how to, and don't want to

know how to. I don't eat honey. I never go near
a hive except at an agricultural show when I am
perfectly certain there are no bees in it. Yet I have
already consented to be vice-president and annual
subscriber to the local bee-keepers' association. On
consulting a memorandum book I find I am vice-
president of seven bell-ringers' guilds and about twenty
village football clubs. I cannot remember having
been so enthusiastic about football when I was at
school. I am a subscribing member of a botanical
ramble club. Can you imagine me doing botanical
rambles ? Of course you quite understand that there's
no bribery in all this.

COL. Oh, of course not. Bribery is not tolerated
nowadays.

LUD. At any rate, one gives it another name.
Let us call it altruism in compartments ; very intense
and comprehensive where it exists, but strictly confined
within the bound of one's constituency.

COL. I suppose you're sound on religious questions ? There is no truth in the story that you have
leanings towards agnosticism ?

LUD. My dear Colonel, no one can be Agnostic
nowadays. The Christian Apologists have left one
nothing to disbelieve.

RENÉ. Personally I am a pagan. Christians waste
too much time in professing to be miserable sinners,
which generally results in their being merely miserable
and leaving some of the best sins undone ; whereas
the pagan gets cheerfully to work and commits his sins
and doesn't brag so much about them.

COL. I trust you are only talking in theory.

RENÉ. In theory, of course. In practice, every
one is pagan according to his lights.

LUD. René, as a private secretary, I'm afraid you would become a public scandal. I shouldn't dare to leave you alone with an unprotected deputation.

(*Enter* TREVOR, *door* L.)

TREVOR. Morning, Ludovic. Hullo, Colonel, I didn't know you were here. (*Shakes hands with* COLONEL MUTSOME.) Morning, René. I distinctly heard you all talking politics. (TREVOR *seats himself in chair, centre stage.*)

COL. Politics are rather in the air. It seems we are threatened with a Parliamentary vacancy.

LUD. By way of meeting trouble half-way, Colonel Mutsome has come to ascertain whether there is any probability of my standing.

COL. I should have expressed it differently.

LUD. Things do not point at present to the probability of my becoming a candidate, but the Colonel has taken things betimes and has been doing a little preliminary heckling.

COL. Not heckling, exactly. My position as Vice-Chairman of the local Party Association gives me some opportunity for gauging opinion down here. Collectively the Government has, perhaps, lost some of its prestige, but individually I think Ministers are popular.

LUD. Including the irrepressible Bumpingford.

COL. Oh, certainly. Rather an assertive personality, perhaps, but of undeniable ability. He comes into the category of those who are born to command.

LUD. Possibly. His trouble so far is that he hasn't been able to find anyone who was born to obey him. So you think Ministers are in general popular?

Col. Compared with the leaders of the Opposition——

Lud. One should be careful not to say disparaging things of Opposition leaders.

Col. Because they may one day be at the head of affairs?

Lud. No, because they may one day lead the Opposition. One never knows.

Col. There is the question of Votes for Women.

Lud. Personally I see no reason why women shouldn't have votes. They're quite unfit to have votes, but that's no argument against their having them. If we were to restrict the right of voting to those of the male sex who were fitted for it we should have to enlarge Hyde Park to accommodate the protesting hordes of non-voters. Government by democracy means government of the mentally unfit by the mentally mediocre tempered by the saving grace of snobbery.

Col. You will be very unpopular if you say that sort of thing down here.

Lud. I have no intention of saying it. Some poet has remarked, " To think is to be full of sorrow." To think aloud is a luxury of sorrow which few politicians can afford to indulge in.

Col. (*suddenly*). By the way—was there some dancing at Briony last night?

Lud. (*in nervous haste*). Oh, no, just some Shakespeare readings and a little music. I wonder you haven't asked me about land values.

Col. I was coming to that.

Trevor (*eagerly*). It's rather an important question, particularly down here.

Lud. Most important.

RENÉ (*same eagerness*). It's quite one of the questions of the immediate future. An aunt of a Cabinet Minister was speaking to me about it only last week. She said it kept her awake at nights.

COL. Really—I quite understood that there was a Cinderella dance——

LUD. Oh, no, dear no, nothing of that kind. Some Shakespeare reading, in costume.

COL. In costume—but how very interesting. What scenes did you give?

RENÉ. The Ghost scenes from what-do-you-call-it.

COL. The Ghost scene from "Hamlet"? That must have needed a lot of rehearsal.

RENÉ. No, we had a lot of ghosts, so that if one forgot his lines another could go on with them.

COL. What an odd idea. What a very odd idea. But they couldn't all have been in costume.

RENÉ. They were, rows of them. All in white sheets.

COL. How very extraordinary. It couldn't have been a bit like Shakespeare.

RENÉ. It wasn't, but it was very like Maeterlinck. Whoever really wrote "Hamlet," there can be no doubt that Maeterlinck and Maxim Gorki ought to have written it, in collaboration.

COL. But how could they? They weren't born at that time.

RENÉ. That's the bother of it. Ideas get used up so quickly. If the Almighty hadn't created the world at the beginning of things Edison would probably have done it by this time on quite different lines, and then some one would have come along to prove that the Chinese had done it centuries ago.

COL. (*acidly, to* TREVOR, *turning his back on* RENÉ). How is your cold, Mr. Trevor ? You had a cold before we went to Worcestershire.

TREVOR. That one went long ago. I've got another one now, which is better, thank you.

COL. We had such a lot of asparagus in Worcestershire.

TREVOR. Yes ?

COL. We got our earliest asparagus in London, then we got more down here, and then we had a late edition in Worcestershire, so we've had quite a lot this year.

RENÉ. The charm of that story is that it could be told in any drawing-room.

COL. (*rising from seat*). I think I saw Hortensia pass the window. If you don't mind I'll go and meet her.

LUD. Let me escort you.

[*Exeunt* LUDOVIC *and* COLONEL MUTSOME, *door* R.

RENÉ (*lighting cigarette*). You've heard the story that's going about ?

TREVOR. That we held unholy revels here last night.

RENÉ. Well, *à propos* of that ; people are saying that you and Sparrowby proposed to the same girl and that Sparrowby threatened to break your neck if you didn't give way to him ; and that you gave way rather than have any unpleasantness.

TREVOR. What an infernal invention. I am damned if I let that go about.

RENÉ. I don't see what you can do to stop it.

TREVOR. I might break Sparrowby's neck.

RENÉ. No one could have any reasonable objection to that course ; Sparrowby is one of those people who would be enormously improved by death. Unfortunately, he is your guest, and on that account it wouldn't be quite the thing to do. He's sure to have a parent or aunt or some one who'd write letters to *The Times* about it : " Fatal ragging in country houses," and so on. No, your only prudent line of action would be to marry the girl, or any girl who came handy, just to knock the stuffing out of the story. Otherwise you'll have to take it recumbent, as the saying is.

TREVOR. I'm not fool enough to rush off and perpetrate matrimony with the first person I meet in order to put a stop to a ridiculous story.

RENÉ. My dear Trevor, I quite understand your situation.

TREVOR. You don't.

RENÉ. Of course I do. You don't want to interrupt an agreeable and moderately safe flirtation with a woman who has just got husband enough to give her the flavour of forbidden fruit. I'm not one of those who run the Vulpy down just because she's a trifle too flamboyant for the general taste. As a wife I dare say she'd be rather an experiment down here, but I've no doubt you'd be tolerably happy. She'd be more at her ease at a suburban race meeting than at a county garden party, but still—you could travel a good deal. And if you find her sympathetic it doesn't matter so very much whether she's intelligent or not. But all that is beside the point, because she's not available. Inconvenient husbands don't come to timely ends in real life like they do in fiction. If you seriously want to put your foot down on the gossip that is going about, and make an end of this uncomfortable domestic situation, your only course is to go straight ahead and propose to the first available girl that you run up against.   If it's the bother of the thing that you shirk let me open negotiations for you— my mission in life is to save other people trouble, on reasonable terms.   (RENÉ *becomes suddenly aware that* TREVOR *has gone to sleep, and rises angrily from his seat.*)   Of all the exasperating dolts !   I don't know how match-making mothers manage to grow fat on the business ;   a week of this would wear me to a shadow.

[*Exit* RENÉ *in a fury, door* R.
(*Enter* LUDOVIC, L.)

LUD.   Hullo, is René here ?

TREVOR.   He was, a minute or two ago.   I think I heard him leave the house.

LUD.   Has anything been heard of his mother ? So many distracting things have been happening that I clean forgot to ask about her.

TREVOR.   By Jove, so did I.   He'll think us rather remiss, but anyhow he seemed more concerned about finding me a suitable wife than about retrieving his lost parent.   Have you heard anything of the story that he says is going about ?

LUD.   (*seating himself*).   About last night, you mean ?

TREVOR.   Yes, that Sparrowby and I proposed to the same girl, and that Sparrowby bounced me into taking a back seat.

LUD.   Ah ! no—at least, probably what I heard had reference to that.   What an unpleasant scandal. Unfortunately, the fact that Sybil is leaving Briony in such a hurry will give colour to it.

TREVOR.   Was it Sybil, then ?

LUD.   I suppose so.   I think I heard her name mentioned.   What shall you do then ?

256

TREVOR. Do ? I don't know. What do you suggest ?

LUD. My suggestion would be so simple that you are not likely to accept it for a moment. If one shows people an intricate and risky way out of a difficulty they are becomingly grateful : if you point out a safe and obvious exit they regard you with resentment. In your case the resentment would probably take the form of going to sleep in the middle of my advice.

TREVOR. I wasn't going to sleep ! I was wondering which particular girl you were going to recommend to my notice. There seems to be a concentration on Sybil Bomont.

LUD. It's scarcely my place to fill in the details for you ; I suppose matrimony is an eventuality which begins to present itself rather prominently to you, and when you've settled that point the details soon fit themselves in. If the Bomont girl doesn't meet with your requirements there is your neighbour Evelyn Bray, whom you entangled in last night's entertainment—I shall never forget her face when I told her that Hortensia didn't require any more music —and there's Clare Henessey ; you used to get on famously with Clare.

TREVOR. Clare and Evelyn are very good sorts——

LUD. (*raising his hand*). Good sorts—— Oh, my dear Trevor, you are still in the schoolboy stage as regards women. The schoolboy divides womenkind broadly into two species, the decent sort and the holy horror, much as the naturalist, after a somewhat closer investigation of his subject, classifies snakes as either harmless or poisonous. The schoolboy is usually fairly well informed about things that he doesn't have to study, but as regards women he is altogether too specific. You can't really divide them in a hard-and-fast way.

TREVOR. At least there are superficial differences.

LUD. But nothing deeper. Woman is a belated survival from a primeval age of struggle and cunning and competition ; that is why, wherever you go the world over, you find all the superfluous dust and worry being made by the gentler sex. If you are on a crowded P. and O. steamer, who is it that wages an incessant warfare over the cabin accommodation ? Who is it that creates the little social feuds that divide benighted country parishes and lonely hill stations ? Who is it that raises objections to smoking in railway carriages, and who writes to house-masters to complain of the dear boys' breakfast fare ? Man has moved with the historic progression of the ages. But woman is a habit that has survived from the period when one had to dispute with cave bears and cave hyenas whether one ate one's supper or watched others eat it, whether one slept at home or on one's doorstep. The great religions of the world have all recognized this fact and kept womankind severely outside of their respective systems. That is why, however secular one's tendencies, one turns instinctively to religion in some form for respite and peace.

TREVOR. But one can't get along without women.

LUD. Precisely what I have been trying to impress upon you. Granted that woman is merely a bad habit, she is a habit that we have not grown out of. Under certain circumstances a bad habit is first-cousin to a virtue. In your case it seems to me that matrimony is not only a virtue but a convenience.

TREVOR. It's all very well for you to talk about

convenience. What may be convenient for other people may be highly inconvenient for me.

LUD. That means that you're involved in some blind-alley affair with a married woman. Precisely what I feared. Men like yourself of easy-going, unsuspecting temperament, invariably fall victims to the most rapacious type of cave woman, the woman who already has a husband and who merely kills for the sake of killing. You pick and choose and dally among your artificial categories of awfully good sorts and dear little women, and then some one of the Mrs. Vulpy type comes along and quietly annexes you.

TREVOR. I seem to have been annexed to Mrs. Vulpy by popular delimitation. Critically speaking, she isn't a bit my style, but I don't see anything so very dreadful about her. She's a trifle pronounced, perhaps—she tells me she had a Spanish grandfather.

LUD. Ancestors will happen in the best-intentioned families. Every social sin or failing is excused nowadays under the plea of an artistic temperament or a Sicilian grandmother. As poor Lady Cloutsham once told me, as soon as her children found out that a Hungarian lady of blameless moral character had married into the family somewhere in the reign of the Georges, they considered themselves absolved from any further attempt to distinguish between good and evil—except by way of expressing a general preference for the latter. When her youngest boy was at Winchester he made such unblushing use of the Hungarian strain in his blood that he was known as the Blue Danube. " That," said Lady Cloutsham, " is what comes of letting young children read Debrett and Darwin."

TREVOR. As regards Mrs. Vulpy's temperament, I don't fancy one need go very far afield.

LUD. Oh no, Greater London is quite capable of turning her out without having recourse to foreign blending.

TREVOR. Still, I don't see that she's anything worse than a flirt.

LUD. Oh, on her best behaviour, I've no doubt she's perfectly gentle and frolicsome ; for the matter of that, the cave hyenas probably had their after-dinner moments of comparative amiability. But, from the point of view of an extremely marriageable young bachelor, she simply isn't safe to play with. I don't want to run her down on the score of her rather common personality, but I wish to warn you that she is one of those people gifted with just the sort of pushing, scheming audacity—— (*Enter* MRS. VULPY, *door centre.*) Ah, good morning, Mrs. Vulpy (TREVOR *looks round and jumps to his feet*), just the sort of pushing, scheming audacity that makes them dangerous. Once we let them wriggle their way into the Persian Gulf they'll snap up all our commerce under our eyes.

MRS. V. You dreadful men, always talking politics.

LUD. Politics are rather in the air just now.

MRS. V. I feel as if we were all in the air after the dreadful explosion of last night. I am just wondering where I am going to come down.

TREVOR. It seems an awful shame, driving all you charming people away. My mother goes to absurd lengths about some things.

MRS. V. It's poor us who have to go the absurd lengths. I shan't feel safe till I have put two fair-sized counties between Mrs. Bavvel and myself. Oh, Mr. Trevor, before I leave you *must* show me the model dairy.

TREVOR. Right-o, I'll take you there now if you like.

MRS. V. Do, please. I just love dairies and cheese-making and all that sort of thing. I think it's so clever the way they make those little blue insertions in Gorgonzola cheese. I always say I ought to have been a farmer's wife. We'll leave Ludovic to his horrid politics.

LUD. Before I forget, Trevor, go and get me those trout flies you promised me, and I'll have them packed. Mrs. Vulpy won't mind, I dare say, waiting for you here for a few minutes.

TREVOR. Right you are. I won't be a second.

[*Exit* TREVOR.

LUD. I hope you don't despise me too much.

MRS. V. Despise you ! Oh, Mr. Ludovic, what ever should I despise you for ?

LUD. For being fool enough to put confidence in you as a fellow conspirator.

MRS. V. Why, I am sure I have been loyal enough to our compact. If the results haven't been brilliant, you can scarcely blame me for the break-down.

LUD. The compact was that you should help in an endeavour to get Trevor engaged to one of the girls of the house party. I don't think I'm mistaken in saying that the game you are playing is to secure him for yourself.

MRS. V. Never more mistaken in your life. Really, you seem to forget that I'm a married woman.

LUD. Your memory is even shorter. You seem

to forget that you received a telegram this morning to say that your husband is dead.

MRS. V. Whatever will you say next? You don't know what you're talking about.

LUD. Oh, it's correct enough ; I read it.

MRS. V. (*raising her voice*). How dare you intercept my correspondence. The telegram was marked plain enough, " Vulpy, c/o Bavvel." You're simply a common sneak.

LUD. I didn't read the intelligence in your telegram. I read it in your manner. You've just been obliging enough to confirm my deductions.

MRS. V. Oh, you're trying amateur detective business on me, are you ? (*With sudden change of manner.*) Now, look here, Mr. Ludovic, don't you set yourself against me. Why shouldn't I marry Trevor. You said yourself two days ago that it was a pity I wasn't a widow, so that I could be eligible for marrying him.

LUD. Of course, I spoke jestingly.

MRS. V. Well, it isn't a jest to me. I have had a wretched, miserable time with my late husband ; I can't tell you what a time I've had with him.

LUD. Because you have had a miserable time with the late Mr. Vulpy is precisely, my dear lady, the reason why I don't wish you to try the experiment of being miserable with my nephew. You are so utterly unsuited to him and his surroundings that you couldn't fail to be unhappy and to make him unhappy into the bargain.

MRS. V. I don't see why I should be unsuited to him. Trevor is a gentleman, and I am a lady, I suppose. Perhaps you wish to suggest that I am not.

LUD. You are, if you will permit me to say so, a very charming and agreeable lady, but you would not fit in with the accepted ideals of the neighbourhood. You have too much dash and go and—in—indefinable—characteristics. I don't know if you've noticed it, but in Somersetshire we don't dash.

MRS. V. Oh, don't fling your beastly county set and its prejudices in my face. I am as good as the lot of you and a bit better. I mix in far smarter circles than you've got here. Lulu Duchess of Dulverton and her set are a cut above the pack of you, and as for you, if you want my opinion, you're a meddling, interfering, middle-aged toad.

LUD. You asked me a moment ago why you shouldn't marry Trevor. You're supplying one of the reasons now. You're flying into something very like a rage. In Somersetshire we never fly into a rage. We walk into one, and when necessary we stay there for weeks, perhaps for years. But we never fly into one.

MRS. V. Oh, I've had enough of your sarcasms. You've had my opinion of you. You're a mass of self-seeking and intrigue. You're mistaken if you think I'm going to let a middle-aged toad stand in my path.

(*Enter* TREVOR.)

TREVOR. Here are all the flies I could find. Sorry to have kept you waiting, but I had to hunt for them.

LUD. Don't mention it ; we've been having such an interesting talk, about the age toads live to. Mrs. Vulpy is quite a naturalist.

MRS. V. I've got all my packing to do, so we'd better not lose any more time.

263

TREVOR. Right you are, we will go off at once.

[*Exit* TREVOR *and* MRS. VULPY, R.

(*Enter* AGATHA, L.)

(LUDOVIC *flings himself down savagely at writing table.*)

AGATHA. Have you seen Trevor anywhere?

LUD. He was here a minute ago. I believe he's now in the dairy.

AGATHA. The dairy! What's he doing in the dairy?

LUD. I don't know. What does one do in dairies?

AGATHA. One makes butter and that sort of thing. Trevor can't make butter.

LUD. I don't believe he can. We spend incredible sums on technical education, but the number of people who know how to make butter remains extremely limited.

AGATHA. Is he alone?

LUD. I fancy Mrs. Vulpy is with him.

AGATHA. That cat! Why is she with him?

LUD. I don't know. There's a proverb—isn't there?—about showing a cat the way to the dairy, but I forget what happens next.

AGATHA. I call it rather compromising.

LUD. It's a model dairy, you know.

AGATHA. I don't see that that makes it any better. Mrs. Vulpy is scarcely a model woman.

LUD. She's a married woman.

AGATHA. A South African husband is rather a doubtful security.

LUD. Then you can scarcely blame her for taking a provident interest in West of England bachelors.

AGATHA. It's simply indecent. She might wait

till one husband is definitely dead before trying to rope in another.

Lud. My dear Agatha, brevity is the soul of widowhood.

Agatha. I loathe her. She promised she would try to get Trevor to put an end to all this muddle and row by getting him engaged to—to Sybil or anyone else available.

Lud. How do you know she's not trying now?

Agatha. Oh, I say, do you think she is?

Lud. I think it's quite possible; also I think it's quite possible that Trevor is discoursing learnedly on the amount of milk a Jersey cow can be induced to yield under intelligent treatment. Frankly, I consider these milk and egg statistics that one is expected to talk about in the country border on the indelicate. If I were a cow or hen I should resent having my most private and personal actions treated as a sort of auction bridge. The country has no reticence.

(*Enter* Sybil, R.)

Sybil. Well, I've packed.

Agatha. Oh, dear, I haven't begun. I know I shall be late for the train; I'm always late for trains. I must go and dig up some foxglove roots in the plantation to take away with me.

Sybil. I refuse to let you bring more than five cubic feet of earth mould and stinging nettles into the carriage.

Agatha. Don't excite yourself, my dear. I'm going by a down train and you're going by an up, I presume.

Sybil. Don't be a pig. You must come with us to make a four for bridge; there'll be Clare and myself and you and the Vulpy. Otherwise we'll have to let that wearisome Sparrowby in, and I'd rather have a ton of decaying hedge and compressed caterpillar in the carriage than have Sparrowby inflicted on me for three mortal hours.

AGATHA. I'm not going to upset all my visiting plans just to suit your Bridge arrangements. Besides, you said the last time we played that I had no more notion of the game than an unborn parrot. I haven't got such a short memory, you see.

SYBIL. I wish you hadn't got such a short temper.

AGATHA. Me short-tempered! My good temper is proverbial.

SYBIL. Not to say legendary.

LUD. Please don't start quarrelling. You're making me feel amiable again.

(*Enter* MRS. VULPY, R., *trying not to look crestfallen.*)

MRS. V. I never knew a dairy could be so interesting. All the latest improvements. Such beautiful ventilation—and such plain dairymaids. What it is to have a careful mother.

LUD. You weren't very long in going over it.

MRS. V. Oh, I had to rush it, of course. I must go and superintend my packing. It doesn't do to leave everything to one's maid.

SYBIL. Hortensia! It's no use bolting, we're cornered.

(*Enter*, R., HORTENSIA *and* COLONEL MUT- SOME.)

MRS. V. Good morning, Mrs. Bavvel (*she bows to the* COLONEL.) (*Pause.*)

COL. Mrs. Bavvel has just been showing me the poultry yard. I've been admiring the black minorcas.

How many eggs did you say they've laid in the last six months, Hortensia ?

HOR.   I don't think Mrs. Vulpy is much interested in such matters.

MRS. V.   Oh, I adore poultry.   There's something so Omar Khayyám about them.   Lulu Duchess of Dulverton keeps white peacocks.   (*Pause.*)

COL.   Such a disappointment to us not to have had Mrs. Bavvel's lecture last night.   All on account of Mrs. St. Gall's extraordinary disappearance.   People are talking of a suicide.   Others say it's a question of eluding creditors.   Her debts, I believe, are simply enormous.

HOR.   One must be careful of echoing local gossip, but from the improvident way in which that household is managed one is justified in supposing that financial difficulties are not unknown there.

COL.   In any case, I feel convinced that we shan't see Mrs. St. Gall in these parts again.

(*Enter* RENÉ, *door* R., *followed by* TREVOR.)

RENÉ.   I've found my mother !

COL.   Mrs. St. Gall found ?   You've seen her ?

RENÉ.   No, but I've spoken to her.   She was having a bath when I got back, so we conversed through the bath-room door.   Touching scene of filial piety.   Return of the prodigal mother, son weeping over bath-room door-handle.   We don't run to a fatted calf, but I promised her she should have an egg with her tea.

COL.   But where had she been all this time ?

RENÉ.   Principally at Cardiff.

COL.   Cardiff !   Whatever did she want to go to Cardiff for ?

RENÉ.   She didn't want to go.   She was taken.

HOR. Taken !

RENÉ. She was doing a stroll on the Crowcoombe road when Freda Tewkesbury and her husband swooped down on her in their road car. They live at Warwick, at least they've got a house and some children there, but since they've gone mad on motoring they spend most of their time on the highway. The poor we have always in our midst, and nowadays the rich may crash into us at any moment.

COL. Your mother wasn't run over ?

RENÉ. Oh no, but Freda took her up for a spin and then insisted on her coming on just as she was for a day or two's visit to Monmouth and Cardiff. Freda is always picking up her friends in that impromptu way ; she keeps spare tooth-brushes and emergency night-things of various sizes on her car. Of course, you can't dress for dinner, but that doesn't matter very fundamentally in Cardiff.

LUD. But surely your mother might have telegraphed to say what had become of her.

RENÉ. She did, from Monmouth, with long directions about charcoal biscuits for the chows' suppers, and again from Cardiff to say when she was coming back. Freda gave the wires to her husband to send off, which accounts for their never having reached us. None of the Tewkesburys have any memories. Their father got a knock on the head at Inkermann and since then the family have never been able to remember anything. I love borrowing odd sums from Tewkesbury ; both of us are so absolutely certain to forget all about it.

HOR. And it was on account of this madcap freak that last night's function was postponed and my address cancelled.

COL. This promiscuous gadding about in motors is undermining all home life and sense of locality. One scarcely knows nowadays to which county people belong.

HOR. I trust that Mrs. St. Gall showed some appreciation of the anxiety and alarm caused by her disappearance.

RENÉ. I don't know. I wasn't in a position to see.

HOR. Altogether a most extraordinary episode— a fitting sequel to last night's Saturnalia.

COL. Saturnalia ! At Briony ?

HOR. Advantage was taken of my absence at Panfold last night to indulge in an entertainment which I describe as a Saturnalia for fear of giving it a worse name.

LUD. Perhaps we are judging it a little too seriously. A little dancing——

HOR. Dancing of a particularly objectionable character, in costumes improvised from bed-linen.

COL. Bed-linen !

HOR. To an accompaniment of French songs.

COL. *French* songs ! But how horrible. I was told that it was merely Shakespeare readings.

HOR. I regret to say that some of the servants appear to have lent themselves to the furtherance of this underhand proceeding. Among others it will be my unpleasant duty to ask Cook to find another place ; I shall give her a good character as a cook, but I shall be very restrained as to what I say about her trustworthiness.

TREVOR. But, mother, isn't that being rather extreme ? She's an awfully good cook.

HOR. I put conduct before cookery.

TREVOR. After all, she did nothing more than make two or three supper dishes for us ; she couldn't be expected to know that there would be French songs to follow.

HOR. It was her duty to consult me as to these highly unusual preparations. I had given my customary orders for the kitchen department and they did not include chicken mayonnaise or pêches melba. Had she informed me of these unauthorized instructions that she had received the mischief would have been detected and nipped in the bud.

TREVOR. I think it's scarcely fair that she should be punished for what we did. (TREVOR *rises and goes to window*, R. *centre.*)

LUD. I confess I think it's rather unfortunate that such an eminently satisfactory cook should be singled out for dismissal.

HOR. Scarcely singled out, Ludovic ; two or three of the other servants will also have to go.

COL. One must see that one's orders are respected, mustn't one ?

(*Enter* WILLIAM, L., *with card.*)

WILL. (*to* LUDOVIC). The reporter of the *Wessex Courier* would like to speak with you, sir.

LUD. Tell him I am unable to see any pressmen at present.

WILL. (*handing card to* LUDOVIC). He's written a question which he would feel obliged if you'd answer, sir.

HOR. What is the question ?

LUD. He wants to know if I intend standing in the event of a Parliamentary vacancy. (*To* WILLIAM.) You can tell him that I have not the remotest intention of standing.

(RENÉ *groans tragically.*)
WILL. Yes, sir.

[Exit WILLIAM, L.

HOR. Really, Ludovic, I think you are rather precipitate in your decisions. Differing though we do on more than one of the secondary questions of the day, I am nevertheless inclined to think that the Briony influence would be considerably augmented by having one of the family as Member for the division. Subject to certain modifications of your political views, I am distinctly anxious to see you representing this district in Parliament. I consider this impending vacancy to be a golden opportunity for you.

LUD. There are some people whose golden opportunities have a way of going prematurely grey. I am one of those.

COL. I must say we rather counted on having you for a candidate. I think I may voice a very general disappointment.

RENÉ. There are some disappointments that are too deep to be voiced.

(*Enter* WILLIAM, *door centre.*)

WILL. If you please, ma'am.

HOR. What is it?

WILL. Adolphus has laid an egg.

RENÉ. Oh, improper little bird.

HOR. An egg! How very extraordinary. In all the years that we've had that bird such a thing has never happened. I must admit that I'm rather astonished. See that she has everything she wants and is not disturbed.

WILL. Yes, ma'am.

[Exit WILLIAM, *centre.*
(*Enter* CLARE, R., *with telegram in hand.*)

CLARE. My great-aunt, Mrs. Packington, died at nine o'clock this morning.

(TREVOR *goes into fit of scarcely suppressed laughter.*)

COL. A great age, was she not ?

HOR. A great age and for longer than I can remember a great invalid. At any rate, a great consumer of medicines. I suppose her death must be regarded as coming in the natural order of things. At the same time, I scarcely think, Trevor, that it is a subject for unbridled amusement.

TREVOR. I'm awfully sorry, but I couldn't help it. It seemed too—too unexpected to be possible. Please excuse me. (*Goes to window and opens it. The others stare at him.*)

CLARE. The fact is, I was Mrs. Packington's favourite niece. There were things in her will which I couldn't afford to have altered. On the other hand, as I dare say you know, Mrs. Bavvel, she had a very special dislike for you.

HOR. I am aware of it. We had some differences of opinion during my husband's lifetime.

CLARE. It was a favourite observation of hers that you reminded her of a rattlesnake in dove's plumage.

COL. Oh, but what unjust imagery !

CLARE. She hated Briony and everything connected with it, and I had to keep my visits here a dark secret.

COL. How very embarrassing.

CLARE. Not at all. I like duplicity, when it's well done. But when Trevor asked me to marry him it did become embarrassing.

(*All the others start up from their seats. Enter* WILLIAM, *L., stands listening.*)

272

Hor. Trevor asked you—to marry him ?

Clare. Two months ago. Mrs. Packington wasn't expected to live for another fortnight, but she'd been in that precarious condition, off and on, for five years. At the same time, I couldn't risk letting Trevor slip ; he'd have forgotten everything and married some one else in sheer absence of mind.

Trevor. I don't altogether admit that, you know. A thing of that sort I should have remembered.

Clare. Anyhow, we married on the quiet.

Trevor. By special licence. It was rather fun, it felt so like doing wrong.

Lud. Do you mean to tell us that you are Mrs. Trevor Bavvel ?

Clare. Of Briony, in the County of Somerset, at your service.

René (shouts.) William !

Will. Yes, sir.

René. Has that journalist man gone ?

Will. A minute ago, sir.

René. Quick, send some one after him. Stop him. Tell him——

Lud. That in the event of a vacancy——

René. Mr. Ludovic Bavvel——

Lud. Will place himself at the disposal of the Party leaders.

René. Fly ! (Almost pushes William out of the door, L.)

Clare. And William—tell John to bring up some bottles of Heidsieck.

Will. Yes, miss, ma'am. [Exit.

Sybil. You dear old thing, you've taken all our breaths away ; I always said you and Trevor ought to make a match of it. (Kisses her.)

AGATHA. I shall put up evergreens all over the house. (*Kisses her.*)

HOR. On a subject of such primary importance as choosing a wife I should have preferred and certainly . expected to be consulted. As you have *chosen* this rather furtive method of doing things, I don't know that there is anything for me to do beyond offering my congratulations, which in the nature of things must be rather perfunctory. I congratulate you both. I trust that the new mistress of Briony will remember that certain traditions of conduct and *decorum* have reigned here for a generation. I think without making undue pretensions that Briony has set an example of decent domestic life to a very large neighbour-hood.

CLARE. My dear Hortensia, I think Briony showed last night what it could do in the way of outgrowing traditions. Trevor and I have had plenty of time during the last two months to think out the main features of the new *régime*. We shall keep up the model dairy and the model pigsties, but we've decided that we won't be a model couple.

(*Enter* JOHN *with four bottles of fizz.*)

JOHN (*to* CLARE). If you please, madam, will the waggonette and luggage cart be required as ordered ?

CLARE. No, I don't think anyone will be leaving to-day. I shall expect you all to prolong your visits in our honour. Oh, of course, I was forgetting Mrs. Vulpy has to go up to Tattersall's to see about some hunters. Just the dogcart then.

HOR. I shall require the carriage for the 4.15 down. There is a conference at Exeter which I think I ought to attend.

JOHN. Very well, madam.   [*Exit,* L.

[*Exeunt* HORTENSIA *and*
COLONEL MUTSOME, R.

AGATHA (*holding up glass*). You dear things, here's
your very good health, and may you have lots and
lots of——

RENÉ. Oh, hush !

AGATHA. I was going to say lots of happiness.

RENÉ. Oh, I was afraid you were going to lecture
against race suicide.

LUD.
SYBIL   (*speaking together*). " Mr. and Mrs.
MRS. V.   Trevor Bavvel." (*They drink.*)
RENÉ

TREVOR. Thank you all, and here's to the success
of the future Member for the Division——

CLARE. Coupled with that of his charming
secretary.

(LUDOVIC *and* RENÉ *bow.*)

(*Enter* WILLIAM, *centre, with enormous pile of
sandwiches.*)

WILL. Please, Cook thought that as the sandwiches wouldn't be wanted for this afternoon you
might like them now. Those with mustard on the
right, without on the left, sardine and egg in the
middle. And, please, I'm asked to express the general
rejoicing in the servants' hall, and Cook says that if
marriages are made in heaven the angels will be for
putting this one in the window as a specimen of their
best work.

CLARE. Thank Cook and all of you very much.
(*She whispers to* TREVOR.)

TREVOR. Of course, certainly.

CLARE. And tell John to open some Moselle in
the servants' hall for you all to drink our healths.

275

We're coming in presently to get your congratulations.

WILL. Yes, ma'am ; thank you, ma'am.

(WILLIAM *turns to go.*)

CLARE. And William——

WILL. (*turning back*). Yes, ma'am.

CLARE. How much did you win on the sweepstake ?

(WILLIAM *turns and flies in confusion.*)

CURTAIN.

www.ingramcontent.com/pod-product-compliance
Lightning Source LLC
Chambersburg PA
CBHW030648020726
47493CB00006B/1929